W9-AAZ-158

# Otto
### and the Bird Charmers

The Second Book of the Karmidee

# Otto

and the
Bird Charmers

CHARLOTTE
HAPTIE

Holiday House / New York

Library of Congress Cataloging-in-Publication Data
Haptie, Charlotte.
Otto and the bird charmers: the second book of the Karmidee /
by Charlotte Haptie.—1st ed.
p. cm.
Summary: Otto, son of the king of the magical Karmidee, tries to learn how thieves
known as the Bargain Hunters, several miniature people, and the City's inexplicably
cold weather are all strangely interconnected.
ISBN 0-8234-1883-9 (hardcover)
[1. Magic—Fiction. 2. Fantasy.] I.Title.

PZ7.H2113Or 2005
[Fic]—dc22
2004047461

for Jezzie

# Contents

THE City of Trees

CrabFac

TumbleMan

The Rainmaker

The Ice King

Key

1 SteepSide
2 HighNoon
3 WorkHouse
4 ClockTown
5 The Gardens
6 The Heights
7 The Whispering Park
8 Parry Street
9 BlueCat Wood

10 Skinker's Mint
11 Deux Visages
12 Cloudy Town
13 The Watchers
14 BirdTown

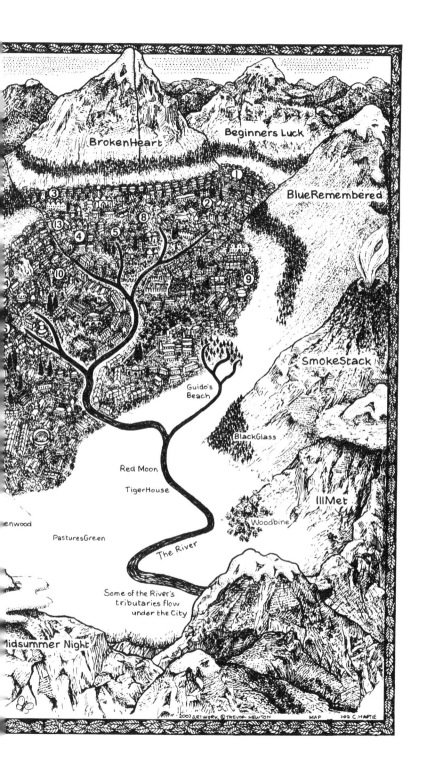

# Otto
### and the Bird Charmers

# The Secret City

Magic is real. There are magical people still, today, but they live in a secret City, ringed by mountains and far away.

They built the City themselves, long ago, as a place to hide from the world. It is called the City of Trees and they are the Karmidee.

Among them you will find the lamp-eyes, the dammerung, the artists, the mat-flyers, the widges and the multiples. And there are many others, more elusive even than these.

Normal humans discovered the City in the end. Explorers, invaders, tramping everywhere and taking everything for themselves. Even a magical and mysterious City that they could not understand.

The Karmidee were forced down to the mud flats by the river where they built themselves stilt houses.

Three hundred years ago Araminta, a Karmidee Queen, managed to seal the City again. No one else arrived from the Outside. The descendants of the invaders, the Citizens, are still there. They still control the City and they still consider that they are superior to the Karmidee. However they no longer remember exactly what life was like on the Outside. They believe that many Impossible and magical things are Respectable and Normal.

Otto Hush and his family live on Parry Street, many miles from the stilt houses, close to the elegant Boulevard. Otto's father, Albert, works in the Central Library. He is a quiet man, living among the Citizens. But he is also a King. The King of the Karmidee.

# The First Fog

Otto Hush, his mother Dolores and his sisters Hepzibah and Zeborah were walking down the Boulevard when the weather started to go wrong.

At least, Otto and Dolores were walking. The twins were wobbling along on roller skates. It was the first time that they had been out on them.

'So far so good,' murmured Dolores as they stopped to buy some balloons.

'Yes indeed, Citizen,' replied the balloon seller warmly. He thought that she was beautiful and was speaking to him about the balloon business or the preparations for the Spring Carnival or maybe even about his recent and just visible attempts to grow a beard.

In fact she was talking to Otto about the roller skates. Albert had made them and they were especially weighted to stop the twins flying about out of doors. Flying was not Respectable.

'Hepzie's trying to unbuckle hers,' said Otto.

Dolores was holding out the money to the balloon seller who wasn't in a hurry to take it. The balloons, which were not on strings, crowded and bobbed around his head, changing through the colours of the rainbow and back again.

'It's a dangerous job, you know. I have to watch out when the hat snatcher comes, that's a strong wind that is,' confided the balloon seller. 'I got stuck in a tree trying to coax them back down once, Fire Brigade, photographers, if it wasn't for the fact that I'm very fit . . .'

Otto was used to men trying to impress his mother. He stopped listening and looked back along the grand and teeming Boulevard towards the park. Something seemed to be happening down there. He screwed up his eyes against the sunlight.

'. . . interviewed on the news, giving autographs . . .' continued the balloon seller, reluctant, perhaps unable, to stop gazing into Dolores' eyes.

Hepzie and Zeb were jiggling about on the pavement. As an extra precaution they were on reins which Dolores was holding.

'There's some very weird-looking fog or something coming, Mum,' said Otto.

It was absolutely dazzling white and surging towards them, swirling around people, trees and trams and getting deeper as it travelled.

'Mum! Let's get out of the way. Now!'

'. . . invited to a party at Mayor Crumb's, this isn't my real job you know, I'm actually a lion tamer . . .'

Otto pulled at Dolores. Hepzie, skateless, drifted casually up into the air (she and Zebbie had been working on the buckles together). The balloon man stared at her open-mouthed. Then the fog was upon them all.

It was freezing and growing, full of horrible, eerie sounds, and it seemed to tug and push like a tide. People were running away from it, falling into each other and shouting. Someone crashed into Dolores. Dolores fell on to Otto and screamed, the reins were tangled round someone's leg, someone else stood on her hand. She was holding Zebbie but Hepzie had gone. Upwards. The reins trailing out of reach.

'Get her, Ottie!' screamed Dolores.

The fog was over Otto's head and he could see nothing in any direction.

'Get up there!' yelled Dolores somewhere.

He pulled his carpet out of his shoulder bag, unrolled it, scrambled on to it and yanked frantically at the fringe. Not the time to worry about doing Impossible things in public places. Up he went, raising one arm to shield his face, expecting to hit the branches of the nearest tree but bumping instead through the crowd of balloons.

On and up and then, yelling for Hepzie, he burst out of the roof of the fog into sparkling light.

All along the Boulevard the fog churned around the very tops of the trees. And there was Hepzie, sitting in the branches of the nearest one, just visible, about to be engulfed.

As he steered towards her she leapt away again and, to his horror, up she went, her first flight in the open air, whooping and giggling, higher and higher, waving to her brother who had come to join in.

Otto banked round. He saw her disappear over the edge of the Town Hall roof and he climbed steeply after her.

The fog was relentless behind him, filling the Boulevard, deeper and deeper. Below he could hear the scream of trams braking, people shouting, and among it all his mother's voice calling for Hepzibah.

The landscape of the Town Hall roof spread beneath him. An island in the glaring sea of fog. Great pointed gables, towers, gullies, gutters, gargoyles, roof gardens, something with a thatch, weather vanes. No time to look now. He could hear his own breath, in between shouts. The quick breath of fear.

'Hepzie! Hepzie!'

What if she didn't stop, if she just kept going up and up and up?

Time was passing. Here, with the roof stretching away in all directions, it was very quiet. She could be anywhere.

He circled a clock tower and gave a yell of horror.

There she was. She'd landed. She was on a little tiled flat bit deep down between steep slopes of slate and . . . WHAT? She was fighting with something. A bird.

He crashed part of the way and skidded the rest. 'Get off her! Get off her!'

It was a grey bird with a hooked beak and she had it by the leg and it was flapping its wings and seemed to be clawing at her hand.

'Git! Scram!' screamed Otto, swiping at the bird, which lifted away making a harsh sound, showing its bright eyes, all menace. Otto had an arm round Hepzie. He'd knocked a slate loose when he landed, he picked up a sizeable fragment and threw it. It hit the bird and the bird staggered backwards in the air, bleeding and lurching and then, with horrible cries from its throat, it struggled up and disappeared on the other side of a great jutting wall of slate.

'Nice bird!' screamed Hepzie, exploding into tears. 'Don't hit bird, don't hit bird!'

'Not a nice bird,' said Otto, his voice shaking, trying to hug her and getting hit himself.

She had something clutched in her hand. It was a thin gold chain.

'Where did you get this?'

'HEPZIE HELP BIRD!!'

'No. NO. Bird hurting Hepzie.'

'HEPZIE HELP BIRD OTTIE STUPID!!'

He was spreading out the mat. Ears scouring for a sound behind the barrage of her protests. Something was very wrong. He was sure they still weren't alone.

Then, when he'd bundled her on to his knee and been kicked again and they were finally in the air— he looked down and saw a man some way off, scrambling over a wall. There was a strange tower nearby with two doors on the front.

The man looked familiar. He wore a hat, tilted slightly forwards, and the sleeves of his coat looked a little too short on his long arms.

He seemed to be trying to climb towards the tower.

At that moment he turned and Otto saw his face.

'Dad!'

And at the same moment Hepzie, reaching up, covered Otto's mouth with her small strong hand.

He fought her off and the carpet tilted and he pulled it straight and looked again, expecting to see Albert give a slow curling wave, the one that he always gave when they spotted each other out somewhere, the one that was a joke between them.

But Albert didn't wave. He stayed very still where he had been climbing and stared.

The stare seemed to clamp on to Otto.

And now he clearly heard his mother, her voice full of panic, yelling from the Boulevard below.

He wrenched at the fringe of the mat.

Looked back as they turned to go down. Albert had gone.

# Walking Home

The fog had gone too. Only wisps and icy puddles and cold, cold air and people wandering about, a tram that seemed to have broken down and lots of shopping bags and things on the pavements. The balloons, winking their colours, making an escape towards the park.

Down where he'd left them Otto saw his mother with Zebbie on her hip, pacing about and scanning the sky. He landed quickly in an empty alleyway.

A moment later Dolores was crouching down, hugging both daughters tightly, rocking from side to side. She looked up at him, over their shoulders, through the dark red clouds of their hair and said softly, 'Thanks, Ottie.'

It was the first time he could remember her approving of him using his carpet.

They smiled at each other and then Otto shoved the mat into his bag.

Suddenly Hepzie sprang up into the air, far higher than was Possible, and although Dolores caught her quickly a man saw and stopped to stare.

'What's this?' said Dolores. The gold chain. Hepzie still wouldn't let it go.

'She was up on the roof, it's incredible up there, let's get out of here, Mum. I saw——'

'Ottie hurt bird!'

'Don't kick your brother, young lady. And never, never fly off like that again. Stay down here with Mummy. Is that clear?'

'Down here?' echoed Hepzie and Zeborah together in puzzled voices.

Upwards and downwards didn't seem to make much sense to them. 'Down here down here down down——'

'STAY WITH MUMMY,' said Dolores very sternly.

'Stay in the Muds with the other magicos and take this skinking weather with you more like,' said the Citizen who had stopped. He looked very cold and very wet and very interested in blaming someone. 'You look Normal but that fog wasn't and neither is that kid . . .'

He stood in their way, smirking nastily. A couple of other passers-by stopped too.

'Floated up just like a skinking bubble,' he told them, pointing at Hepzie.

Hepzie sneezed. Her hair all stood on end and then stayed like that, reaching wistfully into the air.

'Keep back, Citizen,' snapped Dolores. 'It's highly infectious. Haven't you seen it on the news? Ferenzi's Floating Sickness.'

Her accent, of course, was devastatingly Respectable.

The man hesitated long enough for them to go past. Fortunately he hadn't noticed that they were all standing outside Ferenzi's Shoe Repair Shop (We Restore Your Sole) which had been her inspiration.

'Horrible stinking bigot,' muttered Dolores. 'I'm so FED UP, Otto. I was really hoping this roller skate idea would work. And now look. We're never going to be able to take them out anywhere. They'll be trapped in the flat and me with them.'

A tram passed, very full of people, and slapped them with freezing spray from the puddles which filled the road.

Hepzie pulled miserably at her mother's hair.

'Ever since the summer it's been a nightmare,' continued Dolores. 'First the twins start bobbing about in the air when they're supposed to be starting to walk. Then I find out that your father, your FATHER, quiet hard-working Albert, the LIBRARIAN, was BORN and BROUGHT UP in a STILT HOUSE in one of the MUD TOWNS. In TIGERHOUSE, in fact. He pretends to be a Normal, Respectable Citizen so he can work in the library but he is secretly a MAGICO.'

'A Karmidee, Mum,' said Otto.

Another tram. Another arc of freezing water.

'Whatever. Then my own mother, the most Respectable, Normal woman you could imagine, and that extraordinary business, well, it wasn't even a *Respectable* animal like, like, well, like a *guinea pig* . . . And tells us that actually *SHE'S* been a magico all this time too. Living a lie! Living on the Heights! And your grandfather in the Golf Club and Secretary of the Big Fat Table Benevolent Fund!'

They trudged on. Otto's boots were making a squelching noise.

'Then of course I find out that your father is not only a magico, he's their King—'

'OUR King, Mum—'

'And all that terrible business happened and he had to try and save them—'

'You helped, Mum. And you were proud of him—'

'Yes, yes, I know. But here we are six months later and your father's all right, back at his beloved library, but what about the rest of us? Most of my friends heard the rumours and stopped speaking to me straight away. The ones I've got left can't understand why they never get to see the twins.'

Home to Parry Street and not a moment too soon. Past the newspaper seller who yelled, almost directly into Otto's ear, 'Bargain Hunters evade arrest! Biggest search in history of City is dead end! Read all about it!'

'Do you think Dad will have the paper today?' Otto asked Dolores.

'Sure to,' she said grimly. 'He's just as interested in those criminals as you are.'

# Herschell Buildings

Herschell Buildings at last and they went up in the lift as usual. Even here they couldn't let go of the twins. It was a cage of curly bars that creaked sedately from floor to floor while the staircase climbed around it. Anyone could see in.

Albert was already home. How had he got back from the Town Hall so quickly? No time to ask him now though, the twins were shivering and sneezing and everyone helped to undress them, talking about the sudden fog and the cold. Then Albert made hot drinks and he and Dolores had some sort of conversation in the kitchen while Otto dried his sisters after their bath.

Afterwards Albert came into the living room. Hepzie was sitting on Otto's knee with a picture book and Zebbie was discreetly adding to a large scribble she'd begun on the ceiling earlier in the day.

Otto watched his father from behind the book. Watched him spread a newspaper on the carpet, fetch brushes and tins and begin to clean his shoes in that careful, thoughtful way he had whenever he did anything, however small, however many times he'd done it before.

But tonight something was wrong. Albert stopped with the brush ready in his hand. And he seemed to be seeing something far away that made his quiet face quieter still.

Otto started to bite his nails. He guessed that his parents were in the middle of yet another of those strange jagged conversations that made him feel as if they were all walking nearer and nearer to the edge of a cliff and he was the only one who could see it.

Dolores burst in carrying lots of clean washing and dropping bits of it.

'Not only do I have to come to terms with the fact that you didn't tell me who you really are. And that you still won't talk about your family,' she paused for breath, 'I also have to cope with the fact that I talk like a Citizen, I live like a Citizen, but it turns out I'm really a Karmidee too. My mother is a widge and so am I. A *widge*. I can cast spells with the help of a cat. AND my son has an ability called heartsight and my daughters bob up into the air at every opportunity. I'm living with all these secrets all the time. My life used to be simple, Al. I didn't have any secrets at all.'

There was a pause.

When Albert spoke at last he sounded very tired.

'Then you were lucky indeed, Dolores,' he said.

And she looked at him, wordless, as if he had told her something new.


Later he came into Otto's room to say goodnight.

'Ah, that's where it got to,' he said.

Otto had the newspaper. 'They said they were sure they'd got them. They said they'd trapped them.'

'I know,' said Albert. 'In that warehouse in Skinkers Mint.'

'Well they haven't anyway. They've been searching Skinkers Mint for a month. It was all sealed off.'

'I know,' said Albert. They were both smiling.

'It says here the Art Police admit to being buffled—'

'Baffled—'

'Yes and . . . "the so-called Bargain Hunters are thought to have been responsible for the theft of numberious works of art and jewellery—" '

'That's probably numerous—'

' ". . . over a number of years from banks, galleries and museums. They claim these were originally made by the Karmidee and stolen from them many years ago. A spokeswoman from the Boulevard Public Gallery said tonight, 'We refoote and dispoote these ridiculous claims totally. These are artworks of the highest standard, totally Possible and Respectable, and could not have been done by the Karmidee who are, of course, primitive . . .' " It's true, isn't it, Dad? The pictures and things, they were all done by the Karmidee, a long time ago?'

'I'm sure of it. Pictures which flood out of boxes and fill rooms. Musical pictures. Pictures that have their own weather. They're not really Possible. Three-dimensional ones that fold up. It's all Karmidee stuff—'

'Hang on, there's a bit more . . . "The Bargain Hunters may well have sold many of the artworks to un-scroo-poo-lous collectors in the City. They are believed to have given the money to the Karmidee who consider these mysterious criminals to be heroes." '

'They've saved a lot of lives with the hospital they built in TigerHouse, and I think unscroopoolous is a much better way of saying it,' said Albert, who seemed to be laughing.

' "The Town Hall have offered a reward of 20,000 guilders for information leading to the capture of these criminals." '

'Hmm,' said Albert, serious now. 'That's not good news. Not good news at all.' He turned off the light.

Otto gave him the paper and settled down in his bed.

Albert walked over to the window. Then he stood there,

his hand on the long curtain, looking down into Parry Street.

'There's something I've been meaning to mention,' he said, after a moment. 'It's something you might hear one day somewhere and it's better that you hear it from me.'

Otto's eyes widened in the dark.

'I don't want to say very much about it,' continued Albert, slowly. 'The important thing to understand is that we have absolutely nothing to be ashamed about. No one's ever mentioned it to me, even last summer when, well, the Karmidee didn't have a very good opinion of me at one point. But just in case someone ever tries to, to insult you, it's better that you know.'

Otto swallowed.

'Our family, my father's grandfather, in TigerHouse, are descended from counterfeiters. Criminals. They made their living, I'm afraid, by using their particular Karmidee ability. The ability to counterfeit.

'They lived apart, not in the mud towns, in caves somewhere in the mountains, I don't know where, and they preyed upon their own people and upon the Citizens too. And they were despised by the Karmidee. In the end they were forced to renounce their ability. They swore never to use it again. And at some point, long before your grandfather was born, they moved into TigerHouse. Karmidee abilities can sometimes run in families, Otto. To an extent.'

'You mean they made fake coins and things, Dad? Copies of things?'

Silence from the window. Then Albert closed the curtains.

'Can you do it? Can Grandfather Cornelius do it?'

'No one has used the ability to counterfeit since that time, Otto. And I think it is better if you don't mention it to any of your friends.'

'But what exactly *was* it, Dad?'

The bedroom door opened.

'Al, can you come here a minute? Hepzie has poured blackcurrant juice everywhere and they keep licking the walls and fighting and going up to the ceiling and throwing things at each other. Plates and mugs and things.'

Crash. Sounds of shattering china. Whoops of triumph.

'Better go, Ottie,' said Albert, standing up.

'What were you doing on the roof?' asked Otto suddenly.

'What roof?'

'The Town Hall roof, Dad. I saw you when I was catching Hepzie, didn't you see me? I thought you did. Are you writing another architecture thing for the library?'

More crashes from the kitchen.

'Don't you dare let go of that now!' yelled Dolores' voice. Screams.

'No, I'm not writing anything about roofs,' said Albert. 'And I'm not paid to be that adventurous. I've never been up there. In fact, I didn't want to worry your mum, but we were always told as kids that the whole place was woven up with spells and energies. I'm not sure what it was all supposed to be about. Hidden treasure, something like that—'

'There was a bird,' continued Otto. 'Hepzie got into a bit of a situation.'

He sensed his father tense in the dark.

'What sort of bird?'

'I don't know. A falcon or something. Grey. With a speckly front.'

Albert stood up to go.

He seemed to hesitate and then went to the door.

'I was at work all afternoon,' he said again. 'All afternoon.'

'And what exactly did counterfeiters do?' asked Otto, sleepily, after a moment.

But by that time Albert was already in the kitchen, wearing a saucepan on his head for protection.

# Mattie Mook

Up in HighNoon in Mook's Famous Family Wool Shop, Mattie Mook was talking to her father too.

It wasn't really a conversation.

They stood awkward and apart. She was wringing her hands together and he was hunched like a vulture in his new suit.

'Don't pull such a face, Mattie. Your mother's fans expect her to start a tour at carnival time. She is, after all, one of the greatest Artistes in the City and it would be too much for her doing all the arrangements with the strain of performing as well. She is too delicate. She was exhausted when she got back last time. She stayed in bed for six weeks, remember? You had to cook all her meals and everything.'

Mattie remembered.

'I looked after this wretched place when I was younger than you are,' added Melchior firmly. 'I had to stand on a box to reach the till. Just like you do.'

They were standing next to the till at this moment. It was large and alarming and covered with brass levers, all sorts of keys and little bells. When the shop was open a golden sheep revolved solemnly on the top. Not now. Now it was dusk and the shop was closed. Hundreds of balls of wool glowed in the dim light like jewels.

Marlene Mook came cursing through from the storeroom, dragging her third costume bag. She looked fragile and frightening at the same time, like some sort of dangerous tropical insect.

'Stop moping, Lumpy,' she snapped at Mattie. 'You've got those ridiculous photographs for company. You talk to them enough. I've heard you.'

She gave the costume bag a nasty little kick. It had made the mistake of being heavy and cumbersome when full.

'The taxi will be here in a moment, dearest,' said Mr Mook. 'Six whole weeks away from this place. I can't wait, can you?'

'No, I can't,' said Marlene. 'And while we're away I'll send someone round to pump some of that special poison gas under the floor. Get rid of the vermin. I've marked it on the calendar, Lump. Don't forget.'

'Vermin?' said Melchior, raising his eyebrows.

'Rats, darling. Rats and other scuttling things that live in walls and floors and spread disease.'

'Wouldn't that be murder? What if the Police—'

'It isn't called murder when it's vermin, Melchior.' Marlene lowered her voice. The chill snake whisper all too familiar to Mattie.

'I've got a plan to get rid of this stupid place forever,' she hissed. 'Your shrivelled little ancestor isn't going to stop me just because it's legally still her shop. No one's seen her for years anyway. I expect she's died under the floor somewhere. And not a moment too soon. All I'm doing is making sure, that's all.'

'Gone to the great dolls' house in the sky,' said Melchior.

Between them, marooned and forgotten, Mattie said nothing.

A man with a camel arrived outside. The camel was draped in fringed blankets and wearing something very like a woolly hat.

It was the taxi.

The driver knocked on the glass panel in the door, opened it, saw Marlene and immediately and dramatically rolled himself into a ball, clapping his hands over his ears. Most people in the City did something like this if they recognized her. Even the camel, grunting in panic, managed to jam its head between its knees.

The taxi driver looked up anxiously from the cold cobblestones, still blocking his ears.

'Are you going to do it now?'

Marlene shook her head and smiled. Her long, long hair was bright sky-blue and her eyes matched it exactly.

'I can only perform on stage in a specially prepared environment with trained medical personnel on duty,' she said in a dainty, musical voice that Mattie never heard at home.

Mr Mook brought out the luggage and Marlene shocked Mattie by hugging her dramatically as if she cared about her.

'My kid sister,' she lied. 'Half-sister, that's why we look so different . . .' and she added in the snake whisper so that only Mattie could hear, 'pull yourself together, you big lump, haven't you got a handkerchief?'

Then, when all was ready, she tripped elegantly outside in her twinkling spiky boots and allowed herself to be assisted on to the taxi.

'Marlene the Scream,' said the driver, shyly marvelling. 'And on the back of my camel.'

That was her name, Marlene the Scream, High Frequency Voice Artiste. She could scream higher and longer and louder than anyone else in the history of the world. Entire audiences would faint on hearing her.

Spontaneous vomiting and rattling teeth had been reported. Windows, distant wineglasses and in some cases spectacles shattered. Animals and birds fled for miles.

The taxi clopped off away down the hill taking with it the sound of the Mooks chatting and laughing with the driver.

Mattie remained very still at the door of the shop for a long time.

Night came to the great and mysterious City of Trees.

The HighNoon Hotel opposite loomed towards her, sailing against the moon and clouds like a ship in the dark.

Behind her the empty rooms waited for her to face them alone.

At last she went back inside.

Mechanically, as if she were watching herself, she said goodnight to the Bandits locked in their dingy brown photographs on the wall behind the till.

There wasn't enough light now but she knew them so well she could see them in her mind. Roxanna Merryweather Mook and the Unknown Boy. The legendary and heroic WoolBandits. Children her own age from long ago, grim-faced, coats tied with string, big boots like moonstone miners.

Tonight they seemed far away indeed.

'Goodnight,' said Mattie softly. 'I wish you were here now.'

Then because she was weary and brokenhearted, she made a nest out of balls of wool under the counter and curled up in the middle of it.

Something was wedged there in the corner. Something curtained over with cobwebs.

Unaware that extraordinary things would soon be happening she reached up and pulled it free.

It was a book.

She stood up and took it to the window.

At that moment a tram came trundling up the hill and stopped right outside the Pearly Oak. Golden light fell into the Famous Family Wool Shop in diamonds and squares. She wiped the dust of the book with her sleeve and saw that someone had written on the cover.

## ROXIE MOOK PRIVAT BOOKE
## OPEN AT YOUR PERILL ON PAN OF DETH

With nothing to lose and her heart thumping like a drum Mattie Mook turned the first page.

# Otto on the Roof Garden

A week had passed. It was not long before dawn. A good time for mat flying.

Ever since the day of the fog it had grown colder and colder.

Otto crept out of the flat, closing the front door softly behind him.

He was wearing a great amount of clothing, including thick trousers, socks, serious boots, shirt, waistcoat, short coat, long coat (both lined), a scarf and a hat, and extra gloves. He had never flown his mat in such bitter weather and he was prepared for the worst.

He swayed along the creaking corridor and climbed the stairs unusually slowly. The lift would have been easier but it made so much noise.

At last he reached the top of the final staircase and opened the door on to the roof garden.

Up there, like everywhere else in the City, all was now strangely frosted and frozen.

He fumbled in his pockets, got in a mess with his mittens and nearly dropped his worm torch.

Finally he had the box. He opened it very carefully.

A moment passed and then a large green beetle climbed on to his hand. It looked as hard and bright as a polished stone.

He whispered to it and it launched itself clumsily into the air and set off into the icy dark, lurching, following the line of the buildings towards the end of Parry Street.

He put the box and the torch away.

Now it was a matter of waiting.

He leant his elbows on the parapet and retreated down into his layers of clothes.

Despite the cold he stayed very still.

Slowly the sky was drained of its darkness. The many streetlamps grew pale.

Far away across miles of rooftops the great mountains of the North and West were in sombre shadow as the sun rose. The savage peak of BrokenHeart. Beginners Luck, crouched and cragged. And the mysterious BlueRemembered, like a giant animal lying asleep.

Distant clocks chimed.

Perhaps she wouldn't come.

He pictured her superior smile in his mind. 'You wouldn't understand, Mr Otto. I was busy. Karmidee things. Complicated.'

Then, just as her imagined face was turning away he saw her, fast and swooping, bat black against the bleached sky.

Mab, his precious and painful friend.

# The Tower

They were flying towards the Town Hall. Otto still preferred to hunch right over on his mat or, even better, lie on his front.

Blue-grey chimney smoke lay across the rooftops of ClockTown and WorkHouse.

'You just have to stop thinking you could fall off,' said Mab, flying beside him, sitting up, casual as ever, and only holding the fringe with one hand. (The Karmidee call her the Little Moth.) 'Mind you, with your steering you *could* fall off, I suppose.'

Mab lives in TigerHouse, one of the mud towns by the river. A real Karmidee, as she likes to remind Otto. Not a Karmidee living in a flat on Parry Street and talking like a Citizen.

She pointed down at the park, skinny arm outstretched, perfectly balanced.

'Look at that, Mr Otto . . .'

The park had several different kinds of weather anyway. A snowy ice-rink at one end, tropical forest at the other. The Sunday Meadows in the middle, full of long grass and wild flowers, popular for picnics. They all stayed the same throughout the year and the Citizens thought it was totally Possible and Respectable.

Otto had to look directly down to see where Mab was pointing. Something he hated doing. Through narrowed eyes he saw the great sickening drop of empty air and then, below in the Meadows, every blade, it seemed, every petal, twinkling with ice.

The roof of the rainforest was blue-white and still. No parrots. No monkeys. Silence.

'It's never been known before,' said Mab. 'Never. People are talking about it at home.'

They were both getting very cold in the sky. She wiped her nose with the back of her hand and scraped her long pale hair away from her face.

They flew on, tracing the great sweep of the Boulevard, past the Karmidee Tower and on to the Town Hall. They landed near where Otto had found Hepzie and he was pleased to see that Mab was impressed. The Town Hall roof really was like a city itself.

Now he showed her the chain. He had found it on the bathroom floor.

Mab ran it through her fingers.

'Well?'

'I don't know. Isn't it a necklace? . . . Perhaps it's a bit long for a necklace . . . I don't know . . . Attacking birds, stealing jewellery . . .' She smiled. 'And I thought you were such a gentleman.'

'And look at that—'

There was the strange tower with the two doors, twinkling a little in the cold sun. The place where he'd seen Albert. Except of course Albert had been in the library all afternoon.

It was very hard to reach.

They scrambled and climbed and slid and, several times, fell. They found overgrown roof gardens, gullies choked with frozen leaves, all sorts of skylights and windows and carved animal gargoyles.

'You know this whole place is supposed to be a bit Impossible? I'm not sure you should have talked me into coming here—'

'See those weather vanes?' he gasped, clinging on to a chimney. 'They're next to it I think. I keep going towards them but they don't seem to get any nearer.'

Mab squinted at the weather vanes, glinting on a horizon of slate and stone.

'Maybe there's some energy here,' she said thoughtfully.

'You mean Karmidee energy?'

'Well why not? A spell of some sort. Something to stop us finding this place you saw. Finding it this way, I mean.'

A moment later they were back on their mats and flying slowly towards the weather vanes, keeping as low as they dared. The City was waking up. No point in being spotted on a carpet.

This time they reached the tower easily. Perhaps whoever had put the magic around it had no fear of visitors from the air.

It was very big, as high as five floors of Herschell Buildings, and it was shielded by gabled slopes of roof all around, making a sort of courtyard with the weather vanes at the four corners, like flags on battlements. Otto and Mab crept up through the air.

All around the Town Hall the vast City was stirring. Up here, in this mysterious place, it was very, very quiet.

They circled.

The two doors were side by side halfway up the tower. Side by side but still a long way apart.

A stone parapet linked them, like a path built on pillars, as if someone might come out of one door, walk straight ahead, then turn gently, parallel to the front of the tower, and finally, turn again and go in the other door.

There were more doors above these two. A large square one in the middle and other smaller ones, some very small, on each side.

At last, as silently as he could, Otto landed his mat in front of the tower.

Mab came down beside him, feather-light as always.

'So what do you think?'

'Ssh!'

'What's the matter?'

'Just keep your voice down, that's all.'

'But—'

'Sssh! Please whisper, Mab, please.'

He hadn't told her about seeing and not seeing his father here, the man with a stare like stone.

She sighed and rolled her eyes.

'Whatever's the matter with you, Otto? Haven't you noticed? Most of this stuff was painted once. Not just here, all over the place on this roof. Look at the doors. You can just see pictures on them but they're all faded. The gardens are overgrown, everything's clogged up with leaves . . .'

'So what?' hissed Otto. He was feeling worse and worse.

'So no one's been up here for a very long time. No one's taking care of it. This was obviously all built by the Karmidee, like just about everything else, and it's been well and truly forgotten, so just relax—'

Otto had his back to the tower with the doors.

Mab was facing it.

He heard a creak and a thud behind him. Saw her eyes widen.

He turned round and they jumped together.

The doors at each end of the parapet had sprung right open by themselves.

Inside all was dark.

Neither Otto nor Mab could even breathe.

Then there came a sound. Very faint, growing louder.

A whirring, like something winding up.

Otto heard Mab start to whisper something. She was reaching for her mat.

But there wasn't time. At that moment the whirring stopped abruptly with a clunk and tiny bells began to play inside the tower.

The music was slow. He'd heard it before somewhere. On the last beat, as the melody began again, a figure came gliding out of each of the two wooden doors on to the parapet.

Otto and Mab stayed absolutely still.

The figures were big, bigger than real people. They were wooden and, presumably, moving on rails.

They wore carved gowns which flowed to their feet and their long hair swirled and curled over their shoulders. They were smoothed by time and sun and rain. They were beautiful.

As they turned towards one another, for there was no doubt they were to meet, they both raised their arms, elbows bent, palms up. The start of a dance which Otto had seen many times, when he was watching the men and women in the streets at carnival time.

'Maybe it's some sort of show for kids,' whispered Mab. 'And we've set it off by landing here.'

Otto shook his head. He didn't take his eyes off the figures.

They rocked a little as they moved.

Now they must come face to face.

It didn't happen.

While the stately music continued as if all were well, the woman shuddered and stopped and went on gently shuddering.

'Well, she's stuck,' said Mab bluntly.

The man went a little way further and stopped too. He was halfway along the parapet. He reached his palms out. This was the moment when they should have met. He inclined his head stiffly. A courtly bow. He swung his arms a little way out to the side from the elbow, making circles with his palms. Then one hand by itself, then the other, turning his head slowly from side to side.

Half a dance.

The woman hadn't reached him. She didn't dance at all.

Then Otto and Mab both jumped again.

Behind the figures, higher up on the face of the tower, the square door had opened. There was a clock face inside, but instead of numbers there were pictures. Hard to make out from here. There were other dials too, clocks within a clock. All of them seemed to be moving. Hands going round, buzzing and clicking.

Some of the smaller doors around it opened part way.

The man bowed his head again. Then he held out one hand in a graceful farewell and glided backwards, his face turned towards the woman.

She, too, was going backwards now.

'Not stuck,' whispered Otto urgently, 'she just couldn't go forwards. And they couldn't meet. And now they're going away from each other again and it's all gone wrong.'

He felt as upset as if they were real people. As if their serene, dignified faces masked real flesh and blood despair. He felt as if he knew them.

It was horrible.

As the two figures disappeared and their doors closed behind them the other doors began to close too. Whatever it was, it was over.

And now large and lazy snowflakes began to fall.

'Perhaps it isn't a show for kids,' said Mab. 'Perhaps it's some sort of fancy clock. It just isn't working very well.' She rubbed her hands together. 'Let's go, I'm frozen.'

He had already unrolled his mat and was floating up to the parapet.

'What are you doing NOW, Otto? Let's just GO.'

He had been right, there were two narrow wooden rails. One for each foot, then.

'Hurry UP!' yelled Mab.

He guessed at the place where the woman had stopped. The rail on the left looked fine.

A piece of twine had been wound tightly round the one on the right. He picked at it and found the knot had been sealed over with glue.

The rails were set in grooves and there was a hint of metal, something bright, down underneath where the twine was tied.

He flew down again.

'Thank goodness, Detective Hush, now let's—'

But he hadn't finished yet. He leaned down from his mat, grabbed a twig from a choked gutter and went back up again.

Mab, cursing, followed him.

He scraped the end of the twig back and forth, loosening and then lifting whatever it was free.

It was a penknife. Untarnished. Recently lost. Gleaming with frost. He dropped it as if it burned him.

'Oh, for goodness' sake!' She grabbed it up.

'Nice,' she said thoughtfully. It was decorated with moonstones on one side and, on the other—

Otto snatched it away from her.

'What the SKINK'S got INTO you, Otto?'

'Let's look at it later, you're right, we should go, something might, someone might come or something,' he said. 'The person who dropped this.' He jammed the knife in his pocket.

She didn't argue.

They skimmed the roof, dodging round clocks and bell towers. Mab ahead, deft as a bird, and Otto, gritting his teeth, swerving and pitching behind.

The City spread beneath them, glittering in the cold. Many miles of rooftops, every shape of building. Parks and squares and covered markets. Far away in the south the river, now sluggish with ice, the wasteland. And the stilt houses of the Karmidee.

'I've got to go,' said Mab unexpectedly when they were safely landed on the roof garden of Herschell Buildings. 'I'm going up into the mountains. I'm leaving tonight.'

She brushed snow off her coat and mat. Not meeting his eye.

'Is everything OK?'

'Yes. Why shouldn't it be? I'm just going to see someone who lives up there, that's all. A caver—'

'A *caver*?'

'Yes. Why not?'

Her stare was even colder than the day.

'Well, you know, cavers . . .'

The cavers were ancient creatures, large and lizard-like, feared and respected by the Karmidee. Most of them lived in the warm caves in SmokeStack. They were almost never seen in the City.

'Well, it's a long way . . .' he finished lamely.

She nodded.

'Is your grandmother OK?'

She rolled her eyes.

'Don't fuss, Otto.'

'Well, honourable greetings to her, then.'

'And to your parents.'

Mab stayed for a moment as if perhaps she might say something more after all.

'Better get going,' said Otto. 'It's getting busy. No need to get seen.'

She nodded, hesitated, then took off abruptly. She waved down to him as she wheeled around and her face was pinched with cold and she looked lonely and small and for once, now when it wasn't needed, she was holding tightly to the fringe of her mat with both hands. He didn't notice these things properly at the time. Afterwards he remembered them.

# The New Hat

Downstairs in the flat Dolores had started making breakfast and Granny Culpepper had arrived to look after Hepzibah and Zeborah.

Her sleepy-eyed cat, Shinnabac, gave Otto one of his long, cool looks.

'I'm going to the markets, Ottie. And Mother is staying here with the twins,' shouted Dolores from the bedroom. 'And would you go up to Honeybun Nicely's for me, I've forgotten to get any Spring Biscuits.'

Granny Culpepper and Shinnabac started to amuse the twins by making the teaspoons and lumps of sugar dance round the room in the air. Granny Culpepper stared a spell hard at Shinnabac who emptied his head of thoughts so that the spell could amplify inside it. Only cats can empty their heads in this way. Then he stared the amplified spell at the spoons and sugar.

Dolores came hurrying into the kitchen. She was wearing a short, pale green coat with a fake fur hat and boots and muff. The green lit up the warmth of her amber skin. She looked lovely.

'Mother, I do think we should just do that sort of thing when we really need to, don't you? It gives the girls such a bad impression . . .'

Granny Culpepper pulled a face. The spoons were joined by the toaster, the kettle, and finally, alarmingly, by the entire kitchen table, cloth, jug of flowers and all.

Dolores sighed.

Everything drifted casually back to its usual place. Only the twins remained airborne.

'Would you like to see one of my spring cards?' asked Granny Culpepper cheerfully. 'I'm sending one of these to all of my regular customers.' She had recently opened a hat shop.

Otto examined a picture of a tree covered in blossom. The traditional symbol of the spring. On the back it said,

*The Compliments of the Season to all our Customers*
*Isabella Culpepper. Unforgettable Hat Ltd*
*Transform Disguise Delight Surprise*
*No ears too big*

'Very nice, Gran,' said Otto politely.

The twins were circling around his head. They were both wearing hats which she had presumably brought for them this morning. Hepzie's was lime green with stars on. Zeb's was black with gold flowers.

'I've got you a present, Otto,' said Granny Culpepper, handing him a hatbox. 'From me and your grandfather and Shinnabac.'

Oh no.

All eyes happily upon him, Otto opened the box.

Rustling of tissue paper.

It was a simple black City hat. Round like a stovepipe but not so tall. There was a single shell sewn on to the band. His Karmidee hat, of course, had shells sewn all the way round. A precious possession, but not always safe to wear in the City.

'Put on!' said Hepzie.

'Hat, mat, cat, spat, sh—' suggested Zeborah.

'CHIMNEY POT!' shouted Hepzie. They dived down excitedly.

'Thanks, Gran,' mumbled Otto.

His hair was in short locks. He'd only just grown it back. When they were on the run in the summer his mother had shaved most of it off.

The hat fitted perfectly.

'Now,' said Granny Culpepper, very businesslike.

And she reached over and gave three hard tugs on the front of the brim.

A gasp of surprise from Dolores.

The twins jolted to a halt. He saw their eyes widen and grow puzzled. Then afraid. They turned towards each other, touching their faces. Then they reeled away through the air.

'Remember, if you are ever in danger,' said Granny Culpepper quietly, 'three tugs on the front of the brim. It may give you time to escape.'

'Mother, please,' said Dolores.

Why couldn't she look at him? She had turned away and her voice was breaking.

'It's not right, Mother,' she said. 'Make it GO now, please . . .'

The twins, bobbing behind her, had begun to cry.

Otto ran out of the room and slammed into the bathroom.

He looked in the mirror and his eyes looked anxiously back at him, green in his light brown face. His white hair, his black freckles, everything, including the hat, looked the same.

He took off the hat. Put it on again.

Tugged three times at the brim.

Stared.

Took it off.

Went slowly back to the kitchen.

The twins sailed cautiously over to him, not coming too close.

He reached for Hepzie and she screamed and shot upwards for the ceiling.

'Can somebody tell me what the skink—'

'Listen,' said his grandmother. 'The greatest wisdom a person can have is to know themselves. The greatest wisdom and the hardest. For a Citizen to hate a Karmidee, just because they are a Karmidee, or the other way around, this is called prejudice.'

She looked at all of them. For once she was undoubtedly the oldest person in the room.

'And what is prejudice?' she demanded, making Otto jump. 'It is running away from that hard wisdom of knowing our own faults, our own weaknesses. It is looking at someone else instead of ourselves. Despising, ridiculing someone else.' She paused. 'Prejudice comforts the weak. It makes the small feel big. Prejudice is hard to give up, Otto. That is why our people are never truly safe.'

A silence followed.

'Keep it, Ottie,' said Dolores.

Otto turned the hat over awkwardly in his hands. It was lined with soft green material. Now he noticed a label inside.

'Granny,' he began, 'how—'

A new burst of ear-splitting crying from the twins.

Granny Culpepper collected them out of the air and bustled to the door.

Otto examined the label. It was embroidered.

In spiky gold writing it said:

# The Wedding Cake

The City was glistening and beautiful, decked out with snow and icicles and a sheen of frost.

Despite the midwinter weather, families were busy with their Spring Carnival shopping. All down the Boulevard they had piled on and off the tram, laughing, peering into parcels, steaming the windows with their breath.

Posters were everywhere.

## BIG REWARD FOR INFORMATION: BARGAIN HUNTERS MUST BE CAUGHT!

Otto seemed to be the only person on his own. Now he was walking up quieter streets and through a maze of lamplit arcades. The carnival decorations were already up. Children wearing traditional face paint wandered in groups, eating sticky things out of paper bags.

An older girl with a palette stepped into Otto's path.

'Two pieces for the Ice King,' she said, 'seven if you want the silver round your eyes.'

'No, thanks,' said Otto, gruffly.

He stayed away from Normal kids these days. It was too difficult waiting to hear what they thought of the Karmidee. In fact he had promised himself not to have another Normal friend. The problem was that he stayed away from the Karmidee too, except for Mab. They weren't unfriendly once they knew who he was, but they often weren't incredibly friendly either. He was too different, a Karmidee brought up as a Citizen.

He had decided he just wouldn't have any new friends at all for a while. It seemed easier. But lonely.

He left the arcades behind him. The buildings grew smaller and the streets narrower and now everything was on an incline. This part of the City was built on the lower slopes of Beginners Luck and it wasn't called SteepSide for nothing.

Steps where the pavements should be.

He rode the last mile in a cable car that went up between the houses and shops.

Honeybun Nicely's Amazing Cake Shop was on a little square, like a shelf, the only flat place for miles. She was in the window moving a giant wedding cake around. He opened the door and was blasted with wonderful hot air full of enticing smells.

'Otto, darling, how lovely to see you. Honourable greetings.'

'And to you, Madame,' said Otto, sweeping off his hat and knocking over a small pyramid of buns on the glass counter.

They hit the floor and bounced everywhere.

'Oh those wretched elasticated buns! They are so tiresome. Just leave them, Otto. I'm having trouble with some of my recipes at the moment.'

He jumped about trying to catch the buns. He tried to reach one that had rolled under the counter. The money Dolores had given him for the Spring Biscuits fell out of his pocket, followed by the penknife he'd found on the Town Hall roof.

Honeybun picked it up.

'What a beautiful knife, so unusual, such pretty stones . . .'

'It's my dad's,' said Otto. 'I gave it to him for his birthday. They put his initials on it for me.'

The moonstones were on one side. The initials AH were on the other, the side Mab hadn't seen.

He didn't take it from Honeybun, although she was holding it out to him. He just stood there, feeling very tired.

'He dropped it somewhere,' he added, 'and I found it.'

Honeybun looked thoughtful. Then she reached out and gently put the knife in the top pocket of his coat.

'Something is troubling you, Otto.'

He didn't speak.

'Parents,' she sighed, 'parents can be so very complicated.'

There was another small silence. Then she smiled her curvy smile.

'Some decorations have arrived for this cake this morning,' she said. 'Would you like to see them rehearse?'

She went through to the kitchen and came back with a wicker basket which she seemed to be carrying extremely carefully.

'Go in the back and help yourself to some warm blueberry reviver. I've just made a fresh pot,' she said. 'You look as if you need it. And you might like to try a muffin too. They're next to the Surprise Pies, fresh out of the oven.'

When he came back shortly afterwards, with his mouth full and crumbs already littered down the front of his coat, Otto saw that she had already put the decorations in place.

The wedding cake was a magnificent giant frosted castle, all white and gold rising from a moat of blue sugar waves.

Two figures stood on the top of the tallest tower. The bride and groom in their traditional striped and spotted wedding clothes. Beautifully made. The groom had slicked-back hair and a narrow black moustache. The muscles of his shoulders were almost too much for his blue and gold frock coat. The bride was black-skinned and her hair was wound up in a fantastic style, common on special occasions, but how had they found such tiny beads? And such perfect satin shoes? They looked so real, so incredibly life-like, except of course they were only ten centimetres tall.

Lower down, here and there on balconies and winding staircases, there were other figures. A wedding guest, presumably, and a bridesmaid who looked very like the bride and wore a bright scarlet dress. A man stood down by the castle gates, holding a horse with a scarlet and gold saddle. Waiting to take them for their honeymoon, perhaps.

'What do you think?' asked Honeybun.

'Fine,' said Otto, his voice muffled by muffin, 'really good.'

He didn't consider himself an expert on cake decoration.

'I'll start the music,' said Honeybun.

The cake and its moat were on a wooden stand with hearts carved on it and a small handle sticking out of the side. She reached down and turned it once. A musical box started to play.

The bride and groom began to dance. The music was a waltz. They began to circle the top of their tower in each other's arms.

'That's incredible,' whispered Otto, mouth empty at last. 'How do they do that?'

He moved as close as he could.

The others were dancing too now, on their balcony and staircase. The bridesmaid twirled her shimmering skirts.

Then, to his amazement, the bride and groom, hand in hand and very elegant, came down the staircase that wound around the outside of their tower and arrived at the castle gate.

The groom mounted the horse and the bride leapt up in front of him. The horse paced forward, rearing slightly, and all of them, except the horse, turned towards Otto and waved a grand wave of farewell.

The music stopped.

The cake decorations held their positions.

Then after a moment they relaxed.

The bride and groom dismounted and began the long climb back up to their tower. The horse nibbled briefly at the blue sugar moat.

Otto held his position for even longer. His mouth, regrettably, was open. His eyes were round.

The decorations were all gathering together. The groom broke off a chip of gilded icing. He nodded to Otto, who had not yet moved. The bride appeared to be dealing out tiny playing cards. The groom swung his arm with the light grace of an acrobat and threw the piece of icing in an arc that ended precisely on the tip of Otto's tongue.

Otto closed his mouth abruptly. 'They ARE real, aren't they . . .' he said at last.

The bridesmaid blew him a kiss.

'I mean, they're, they're little, they're little, they are actually little actually PEOPLE—' continued Otto fluently.

'Well they only come in one size,' said Honeybun thoughtfully. 'Do you think they're too small?'

He looked at her.

'It is Impossible, isn't it?'

'Well of course it is, darling, but the Normals love them. This cake is for Mr VeryDosh's sister's wedding party. At the end, when it's time to cut it, I collect all the decorations up and put them back in their special basket. They're staying with me for a week. They've got cakes booked every day. Come and see where they live when they're touring. I provide meals and fill up the water tank and things.'

'Are they a sort of Karmidee, like dammerung?'

'Well if they are, Otto, I've never heard of them. My theory is that they were once the same size as anybody else and have somehow been made little for some reason. But one doesn't like to ask.'

'Could a widge do that? Make people so little?'

'I don't think anyone would like to try, Otto. It's the

energy involved. To safely shrink a whole family, and all their furniture and their horse, and KEEP them small like this, day after day . . . And then getting them bigger again, all in proportion, all the size they were meant to be, you might get someone coming out of it with giant ears or something . . . and you've got all the internal organs to think about, too. Very hazardous.'

He followed her into the dark kitchen where the ovens were rumbling to themselves and the air seemed good enough to eat. Small round mirrors gleamed like moonlit windows.

She lifted the lid off a very large rectangular basket. There seemed to be several rooms inside with their own separate lids. All closed except one. It was carpeted and there were armchairs and a tray with a flask and mugs. The bale of straw was presumably for the horse. A cubicle in the corner no doubt concealed a tiny weeny toilet.

'It's incredibly expensive,' added Honeybun, 'but the VeryDosh family are so ridiculously rich—' She frowned. 'Do you know, darling, I've a dreadful feeling that I forgot to give Mr Softly's son the money this morning. You've heard of Max Softly, Otto, he's very, very Respectable. He must think they're Normal and Possible and all the rest. He's their agent. They live in a dolls' house at his office, apparently.'

Everyone had heard of Max Softly. Theatrical Agent. Businessman. Friend of the wealthy.

'The boy was in a terrible hurry. Oh, how boring of me. And I don't like to put all that cash in the post.'

Two customers came into the shop.

Honeybun was wearing an elegant black dress and a string of faultless moonstones. She looked as if she might be going to the Opera.

The customers looked around for somebody who might actually work in the shop. They both recoiled a little at the sight of Otto, covered in crumbs.

'Can I help you?' asked Honeybun in her low, sleepy voice. 'I am Honeybun Nicely.'

Otto peered round her at the wedding cake. The extremely small people were moving swiftly into their places, all playing cards out of sight.

'Oh yes, good morning,' began one customer.

'And spring greetings,' said the other warmly.

Citizens, much reassured by Madame Nicely's Respectable accent.

They began to look at the large display of iced cakes for special occasions. Pineapples. Trams. Nesting crate birds.

'We've been down on the Boulevard,' said one of them to Honeybun. 'The weather is very unpredictable, isn't it? There was a blizzard in the kitchen department in Banzee, Smith and Banzee—'

'Indoors?' said Honeybun pleasantly. She seemed to be trying to give Otto something.

'Yes, right downstairs and they had the heating on and everything but it went on for quite some time. Snow everywhere.'

'And then,' said the other customer, 'we were waiting for a tram and there was this shower of hailstones. Just there. Near to Happy Hardware, you know, Spanners to the Stars? The hailstones were really unusual. They were all shaped like little butterflies—'

'But made of ice,' said the first customer.

'Yes, little frozen butterflies. It didn't last long.'

'Remarkable,' said Honeybun. She had put a business card into Otto's hand. 'Go and phone the, er, supplier would you, darling, and ask him what I can do about my, er, oversight, while I attend to the lady and gentleman.'

'My nephew, such a charming, Respectable boy,' he heard her saying as he went through into the kitchen. 'Loves muffins.'

'You know,' said the second customer, 'some people are saying this business with the weather, well it might not be quite, well, not quite Possible, if you know what I mean.'

'It might be Impossible, magico work,' clarified the first.

The wedding cake music had started. Honeybun must have wound it up.

'Impossible? Oh no, I don't think so,' she said sweetly. 'I remember a rainbow once, when I was a girl, it landed in Costermonger Square. We were playing all afternoon, climbing up it, sliding down. It did stain our clothes a bit, mind you, red and yellow and pink—'

'Oh, that is reassuring,' said the woman. 'Look at the little decorations, dear, isn't it wonderful what they can do nowadays?'

# The Complete and Utter Encyclopedia

Otto had found the telephone in Madame Nicely's parlour.

'Can I have BlueCat Wood 916?' he asked the operator.

'Putting you through now, sir, spring greetings to you and your family, my name is Unterwhistle, thank you for using your telephone, we are here to help, you are never alone with a phone,' said the operator.

'Good afternoon,' said someone rather strange.

'Hello——' began Otto.

'You have reached the office of Max Softly, Theatrical Agent,' continued the voice savagely. 'Mr Softly cannot answer the telephone at present. If you have a complaint or think that you have been overcharged please replace the receiver now.'

There was a tiny pause.

'Mr Softly?' said Otto, much puzzled.

'If you would like to leave a message please speak after the short screech.'

There was a dreadful sound. Then a silence with some very faint scuffling noises.

Otto, dumbfounded, put the phone down. He waited for Honeybun to finish serving the latest customer. There are no answer phones in the City of Trees. They haven't been invented yet.

'Oh, of course,' she said, when he described what had happened. 'He must have got one of these new answer parrots working for him. Have you seen the posters? "Chatterbox Telephone Answering Service. You talk, we squawk." Did you leave a message? Apparently these parrots have very good memories and they're so dreadfully keen.'

The shop door was opening. More customers for Spring Biscuits and Surprise Pies.

'I'll take the money,' said Otto quickly. 'I'll deliver it today – now, if you like. I'm not doing anything else.'

'Really?' she smiled. 'That would be very kind of you. But it's an awfully long way. You know how far it is to BlueCat Wood—'

'I'd like to go. I might get to see their dolls' house and stuff.'

'Just let me see what these customers would like. I'll be back in a minute, help yourself to some more muffins.'

She picked up a small mirror and stared into it. Her golden hair, slightly disarrayed, coiled lazily and luxuriously back into place. (Madame Honeybun, although a widge, is allergic to cats and uses mirrors to amplify her spells.)

Otto ate two more muffins. Then, because only half a minute had passed, he looked around.

He was in a small parlour. The room was softly lit and uneven in shape, closer to a circle than a square. Gilt-framed mirrors among the bookshelves round the walls reflected one another. He sat down on the ruby-coloured sofa in a cosy pool of light.

There was a large and very old-looking book on the cushion beside him.

## THE CITIZENS' COMPLETE AND UTTER PROFESSIONAL ENCYCLOPEDIA OF CAKE DECORATION – UNABRIDGED

He could hear Honeybun selling something. There was a great rustling of paper bags. Not really thinking about anything, he opened the book somewhere in the middle and began to turn the pages.

There they were.

The people from the tower on the Town Hall roof. A

man and a woman. Made out of that stuff. What was it.
Marzipan.

They were standing on a cake all wound round with swirls
of blue sugar cloud and green icing leaves and things and they
were facing one another and holding up their hands, ready to
dance.

Underneath it said,

> Season: Spring Carnival.
> Difficulty level: very.
> Do not attempt unless experienced.
> Clouds tend to collapse.
> Origins of this ancient design unknown.
> Warning: May not be totally Respectable.

Honeybun had come into the room behind him.

'I like that one,' she said over his shoulder. 'But no one ever
asks for it.'

'Are they magical?' asked Otto, tracing over them with his
finger. 'Something to do with the Karmidee?'

'Definitely, darling, but how, in what way, I don't know.'

'Doesn't anyone know?'

She smoothed the thin page, yellowed with time.

'Some things the Karmidee managed to hold on to, Otto,
others they forgot.'

*　*　*

The shop doorbell rang again.

Honeybun took two large books from the shelves. There was a small door in the wall behind. The safe. She handed Otto a purse, which he put in the third inside pocket of his waistcoat.

'Hello?' called a customer.

'And the Spring Biscuits,' said Honeybun, pulling a face as the customer called again. 'Do tell Madame Dolores they're a bit strong. There's been some rather peculiar energy surges.'

'I don't think she likes being called Madame any more,' said Otto, without meaning to say anything at all. 'I think she wishes she wasn't a widge. She'd like to magic us all into Normal Citizens if she could, especially the twins.'

Honeybun looked extremely serious.

'But she can't, of course,' he added hurriedly, trying to cram his misery to the back of his mind again.

'Hello! ANYBODY HERE?' yelled several customers in unison. Honeybun didn't seem to hear them.

'Ever since the Outsiders came there have been people willing to persuade the Karmidee that their magical energy can be removed. That there is something called a Cure. That our people can take it and be made Normal,' she said gravely. 'But we are not ill, Otto, we are simply different. And we cannot be made Normal. Without our magical energy we are weak and lost. I have heard rumours that someone has been trying to make the Cure again. It is dangerous. Very, very dangerous.'

# The Tram Driver

It was mid-afternoon by the time Otto reached BlueCat Wood.

He took a cable car down out of SteepSide and then walked to the Boulevard and caught a tram and then another and finally one he'd never used before. Far away through places he didn't know.

BlueCat Wood was the end of the line.

It turned out to be full of curving streets. There were restaurants and galleries and offices with brass plates on the doors. Otto, at the back of the tram, waited for the other passengers to get out first.

Then he stopped on the pavement, consulting the map Madame Honeybun had given him.

'It's going to snow again grievously in a minute, Citizen,' the driver advised him loudly. 'Don't hang around too long.'

'I'm just here on a small matter,' said Otto.

'Never seen weather like it,' continued the driver. He was pouring himself a drink from a steaming flask. He glanced around, smacking his lips.

'You know what I think it is, Citizen, it's magico energy. Gone wrong. They do have it you know. Energy, that's what makes them magicos. It sort of leaks out through their skin—'

'Oh no, I don't think—'

'My personal view is that they are actually an inferior kind of human being.'

He pulled open his heavy black coat and put his flask in some inside pocket. His waistcoat was studded with carved bone buttons.

The tram, though stationary, was shaking and muttering all the time.

He pushed his stovepipe hat to the back of his head.

'I'm proud to be a Citizen,' he said. 'No doubt you are too. When I have a bad day I think to myself, Horatio, at least you're better than a skinking magico. Born better. Respectable. Normal. Superior.'

The automatic doors opened, slammed shut and opened halfway. All this was common, the trams were old.

'Wouldn't surprise me if they've got at these skinking trams too,' he grunted.

'I'm sure they've got nothing to do with the weather or anything else,' yelled Otto above the noise. 'And they're just different. You make the energy sound like a, a weapon, that's all wrong, it's not a weapon—'

'Why not? Why not a weapon, Citizen? If they put their primitive minds to it?'

'BUT IT ISN'T!' bellowed Otto. 'THEY'RE JUST DIFFERENT—'

The driver turned to face the juddering controls like a man about to wrestle a bull.

'*That's what I said, Citizen. Different. Inferior—*'

The doors crashed together for the last time and the tram lurched forward and carried him off and Otto heard the doors opening and slamming shut until it was round the corner and out of sight.

Everything was now very quiet.

Pinkish snowflakes shaped like hearts were drifting gently down, muffling the sounds and colours of the street.

# Max Softly's Office

The office was at the top of a steep flight of stairs.

There was an envelope lying on a mat at the bottom. It was addressed to Sween Softly, Max Softly's Theatrical Agency.

Otto, helpful, grabbed it on his way up.

At last. He'd arrived.

MAX SOFTLY, it said on the door, THEATRICAL AGENT. And underneath, on a card, in big clumsy letters, CLOSED AT THE MOMENT.

A huge poster on the wall beside it advertised the famous High Frequency Voice Artiste, Marlene the Scream and her forthcoming Lose Your Lunch Tour. Marlene herself took up most of the picture. She was balanced on very high shoes, her spider-thin arms flung back, her face shrunk to a crumpled frame around the scary darkness of her mouth. She was undoubtedly engaged in producing a legendary scream.

Otto had heard of Marlene, everyone had, and he remembered now that his old friend Dante had been to one of her concerts. It had been very extreme, Dante had said, although he himself had not been sick. It was all a question of will power, apparently, of which, of course, Dante had loads.

They didn't see each other any more. That had stopped when Dante had found out that Otto was a Karmidee.

Otto looked at the poster and then back at the hand-written notice. Beyond this closed door, he guessed, was the dolls' house he had come so far to see.

What did that mean, 'closed at the moment'? How long was the moment? Why should the office be closed? Surely the Spring holiday was a busy time.

He continued standing there, looking in. He had nowhere and nobody to rush off to visit. Skink it.

He turned to go at last. Then he heard something.

A mysterious and beautiful sound.

A lot of noise from the street, probably a glass wagon. And then, when it had passed by, there was the sound again. Music. Definitely. Not the radio, someone playing something.

Otto crouched down, took off his hat and pushed his ear against Max Softly's door. The music stopped and there was a sort of muffled sob and then a sniff. It didn't sound like an adult.

He stood up again and as he did so he lost his balance very slightly and fell against the door handle and the door swung open and whispered across dense and costly carpet. Otto travelled with it and sat down on this carpet with a soft thud.

No sign of any dolls' house here. This was a waiting room. There was a splendid sofa, bulging and buttoned, and a low table with magazines and another door, marked Office, standing partway open.

The music, someone playing the guitar, was now louder. The sound of crying was louder too.

Deciding that since the Agency was supposed to be closed, he should definitely not go any further and if someone was crying it was none of his business, Otto crept past the grand furniture and on into the Office.

A phone rang, making him jump. It was answered by a big grey parrot sitting on a perch on the desk.

'If you wish to leave a message,' it said sternly, 'please speak after this short screech.' And it screeched in a professional manner and then inclined its head to listen.

Otto looked around. No one else in here and no dolls' house either. The walls were covered in framed newspaper photographs of handsome Max Softly, smiling, dashing yet

Respectable, with his arm around various famous-looking people.

There was a poster on the desk with a picture of a boy holding a guitar. His name seemed to be Sween Softly the Child Prodigy. He had the same angles in his face as Max.

One more door to go, then. Half-open and called 'Agency Personnel Only'. Otto pushed it open a little further and went in.

This room was far less grand. There was a sink, a small stove and a kettle. A large dolls' house and two well-worn easy chairs. One was piled with bags of shopping. Mainly vegetables. There was also a sort of suitcase thing.

Sween Softly the Child Prodigy was sitting in the other, leaning forward with his eyes shut, picking out a tender tune on his guitar.

He was skinny and seemed to have a lot of joints.

Otto hesitated from one foot to the other. The floorboards creaked and Sween Softly opened his eyes and looked up.

He gave a yell of surprise, put the guitar on the floor, jumped to his feet and flung himself at Otto who, being also surprised, also yelled.

Otto backed fast into the door which slammed smartly shut behind him causing him to stumble backwards and downwards. Sween was slightly taller than he was and also seemed to have the advantage of growing larger by the second.

He looked desperate and mad. Otto seized at his legs, Sween fell with a crash and Otto rolled sideways, scrambled to his feet, leapt over a chair, didn't make it and landed on a lot of vegetables.

'I've come to see Mr Soft Agent the Maxical Theatrical!' he cried wildly, grabbing and throwing a number of turnips and things as fast as he could.

Sween ducked. Stood up and ducked again.

'Stop!' shouted Sween.

'I've come to see Sax Motley—'

'OK, OK, STOP!'

Otto, breathless, held on to the next turnip. He maintained a pose of menace.

'I'm sorry,' said Sween.

'I really have come to see—'

'I know. I believe you. Max Softly is my father. I'm afraid he's out at the moment. My name is Sween, Sween Softly.' He straightened his dark expensive clothes.

Like Max in the many photographs Sween had black hair in two long plaits.

Unlike Max, however, his face was blotched and his eyelids were swollen. He looked as if he had been crying for a long time.

'I'm sorry,' he added. 'I'm a bit tense. I thought I'd locked the door.'

Otto put down the turnip and climbed off the chair. There were quite a lot of vegetables on the floor.

'I'm Otto Hush,' he said. 'The door was open . . . well, sort of open, not locked . . . and I've brought this from Madame Nicely at the Amazing Cake Shop.' He handed Sween the purse, and the letter. 'And this was downstairs.'

Sween put the purse in his pocket. Then he just stood there, holding the envelope.

Finally, slowly, he picked up his guitar, put it in the suitcase thing, and led the way into the Office. Otto followed. He only had time to glance at the dolls' house.

The phone rang and the parrot sighed deeply and picked it up.

'Are you all right?' asked Otto.

'Of course,' said Sween, vaguely.

'She asked for a receipt,' said Otto after a moment.

But Sween didn't seem to hear him.

He went over to Max Softly's extravagantly large desk, picked up a ferocious paper knife and began trying to open the envelope.

His mind didn't seem to be on what he was doing.

After a moment Otto dared to take the knife and the envelope away from him. 'Are you in some sort of danger? Is someone after you?'

No reply. Otto now made a big mess of opening the

envelope himself, being unskilled in the use of office equipment. Then he spiked his finger with the edge of the knife.

The corner of a letter on thick cream paper was visible. Sween drew it out and Otto stood there, dabbing at his finger with the sleeve of his shirt.

It seemed to take a long time for Sween to read the letter and then he looked in the envelope, took out two photographs and looked at them too.

'Madame Honeybun asked me to ask you for a receipt,' said Otto.

Then everything changed.

Sween had clear violet blue eyes. He had thick eyelashes too. Girly, Dante might have said. Dante had a word for everyone. Stuck it on them like a badge.

Now, for the first time since they had met, Sween turned these clear eyes very definitely upon Otto. They were unexpectedly steady and cool in the blotched misery of his face.

'I know who you are, Otto Hush,' he said. 'And I need your help.'

Otto looked at him.

'You call Honeybun Nicely "Madame". Only a Karmidee would do that. A courteous way to address a widge. A lady widge anyway.'

'I'm not sure I know what you're talking about,' said Otto.

'And my father pointed out someone to me at the library. Your father. Also called Hush.'

'Your FATHER pointed him out?'

'Yes. The Quiet King. You look like him.'

'I do?'

'Yes, you look sort of, Quiet.'

Otto the Quiet couldn't think of a reply.

'You are the son of the King,' said Sween. 'I need your help.'

'But you're a—'

'I can trust you because of who you are.'

'But you're a—'

'A Citizen, yes. I had noticed that. But you'll understand in a minute. You've heard of the Bargain Hunters, have you?'

Otto nodded.

'Please read this.'

Otto took the letter.


Dear Sween,

I am addressing myself to you because I know that at present you are the only member of your family who is able to reply to me and carry out my requests. In short, I know that you are completely alone.

I have no wish to distress you. I would not

trouble you at all but unfortunately I have problems which only you can help me to solve.

You will find two photographs enclosed.

One shows a troupe of animated cake decorations performing recently in the window of the Amazing Cake Shop.

The other shows a number of persons engaged in stealing a picture from the City Art Gallery earlier this year. This daring theft took place in daylight and I think you will agree that the photograph is a good one. The sign of the Blue Hare, the trademark of the Bargain Hunters, was left at the scene.

These two pictures speak for themselves.

Clearly the Bargain Hunters have decided to evade arrest by the inspired and unusual means of shrinking themselves to an unexpectedly small size and gaining a less hazardous means of employment for a while.

I must tell you that by the time you receive this letter they will be in my care. I will be happy to return them to you, together with the negatives of these pictures, if you will give me the means, chemical or magical, by which this shrinkage was achieved.

I intend to use it to assist me in embarking on a new life. You can be sure you will hear no more from me.

I suggest that we meet on the first night of the Spring Carnival under the stage during the performance of Marlene the Scream. My costume will be The Rainmaker.

I would like you to bring a small animal. If you shrink it and restore it to normal size in front of me I will be satisfied as to the safety and efficacy of the process, whatever it may be.

If I do not see you there I will go to the police. There is a reward for the capture of the Bargain Hunters, which will be some compensation for my disappointment.

With kind regards
*Arkardy Firstborn*
Dealer in Fine Jewellery


'And here,' whispered Sween, 'are the photographs.'

One was a printed leaflet advertising Madame Honeybun's shop. There were the cake decorations. The bride and groom, the guest and the bridesmaid and the man with the horse.

The second photograph was of some people on the roof of

a building. Whoever took the picture seemed to have been hiding behind something, presumably close by on the same roof. Part of what looked like a statue blocked out the side of the picture.

However all the faces were clearly visible.

A man and a woman, tied together with a rope, were climbing out of a gable window carrying a large picture between them. Another, older man and a second woman were hauling on the other end of this rope which was tied round a chimney stack. A third man was near the edge of the picture and at that moment Sween had his thumb on this man's face.

Otto looked from one picture to the other.

One of the women did look very, very like the bride on the cake. The older man was the one who held the horse. The more he looked the clearer it became. The miniature cake decorations and the people stealing the picture really were the same.

Otto whistled through his teeth. He had recently learned to do this.

'So the Bargain Hunters, the real, actual Bargain Hunters, are sort of hiding by being little and being cake decorations.'

'Yes.'

'And this person, this Firstborn, who wrote this, he knows this and he's sort of threatening to go to the Art Police.'

'Yes.'

'But why? I mean why you?'

Sween was still holding tightly to the photograph. His thumb still hid the face of the man near the edge of the picture. He hesitated a moment longer. Then he simply handed the photograph to Otto.

'See for yourself.'

And there was handsome Max Softly. A giant edition of the miniature groom, without the miniature handlebar moustache and the short, slicked-back hair.

'MAX SOFTLY IS A BARGAIN HUNTER?'

'My family ARE the Bargain Hunters, Otto. The ones coming out of the window are my uncle and aunt, she's the bride on the cake. My grandfather and my cousin are pulling the rope.'

# The Red Kite

'YOUR FAMILY ARE THE BARGAIN HUNTERS!'

Otto clamped his hands on to the sides of his face as if his ears were going to fly off. 'Did you know?'

'Yes of course I knew. I've always known. He tells me everything . . .' Sween frowned.

'You mean all this time he's been so, so Respectable he's actually been a Bargain Hunter? Stealing pictures, breaking into places—'

'Yes, yes, yes. Although we prefer to call it reclaiming pictures . . .'

'And now he's little and wearing a disguise and living on a cake?'

'Well, not living. Working. He's always broke. He gives

all the money he makes to the hospital.'

Otto opened his mouth, left it open for a moment and then closed it again without using it.

Then suddenly he thought of something else and started waving the letter about.

'But what's this about "by the time you receive this they will be in my care"? What's that all about?'

'He's kidnapped them,' said Sween, his voice cracking a bit. 'Or maybe he hasn't done it yet. I've got to go there—'

'Let's warn her,' exclaimed Otto. 'Let's warn Madame Honeybun. Where's the phone—'

He rushed over to the parrot.

It jumped on to the telephone receiver with both feet and closed its claws around it. He reached out, ignoring a yell from Sween, and the parrot snapped at him and tore his sleeve.

'What the skink!'

The parrot stared and Otto and Sween stared back.

'Is it always like this?' whispered Otto.

'Well, it's only been here for a week. It sleeps in there . . .'

Sween pointed to a large painted box with a round hole for a door. Water and fruit were in a dish outside.

'I feed it and let it out for exercise and it tells me the messages at night. And I write them down. It takes the job very seriously. It hasn't let me use the phone since it arrived.' At that moment the phone began to ring again. The parrot stepped off it and immediately snatched it up with one foot. It began to talk, never taking its eyes off Otto and Sween.

'Forget the phone,' said Otto. 'I've got something else.'

He hustled Sween back into Agency Personnel Only, away from the parrot, who now seemed like a third and dangerous person in the room. Then he put something on the arm of the chair where Sween had been sitting.

A ball, about the size of an apple.

'Calling Madame Honeybun Nicely,' said Otto.

'What on earth—'

'Ssh! Calling Madame Honeybun Nicely, calling Madame . . .'

The inside of the ball flickered into life. It filled with pink light. There was a picture of a cake. Then a sign appeared.

*Improve your Mood with High Class Food*

'More than somewhat,' whispered Sween.

'It's called a crystal communicator,' said Otto, peering at the sign. 'They're usually bigger. This is a portable one.'

The sign faded. There seemed to be a cloud of steam and then, finally, Otto recognized Honeybun's parlour. She was sitting on her sofa and he judged that the communicator was some distance away, probably on the little table near the telephone. She had the cake decorations travelling basket on her knee.

'Madame Honeybun,' he gabbled, 'someone's going to try and kidnap the cake people.'

'Otto, it's you. I'm just closing . . . oh dear . . . can you give your communicator a shake, the picture is all breaking up—'

Hissing with frustration Otto picked up the glass ball and waved it about.

'That's better, darling. I've just got all the decorations back in their basket. Did you manage to deliver—'

'SOMEONE'S GOING TO TRY AND TAKE THEM AWAY,' shouted Otto, holding the communicator right up to his face.

'Please! Otto! I am NOT your dentist!'

He moved it away just in time to see that he was too late and then he saw the most horrible thing.

There was a crash in the parlour.

Something, something flying, came shooting down from somewhere AT Madame Honeybun. He heard her scream. She was fighting, it was all claws and wings. It had grabbed up the basket. There was a great flapping. The bird, because it *was* a bird, was dragging the basket upwards and she was clinging on, trying to pull it back down. The bird jabbed at her face, hooked beak like torn metal, she swung back her arm and hit it on the side of the head and it swerved, still in the air, but did not let go, and then, slashing at her, it was free and it suddenly lifted out of sight. Honeybun seized a mirror, staring a spell—

'Dad!' screamed Sween. He had been screaming all the time.

Honeybun rushed out of sight, there was more crashing.

Then silence.

A long red-brown feather floated down past the communicator, lifted slightly and then fell slowly spiralling, as if the sweet-smelling air in the little parlour had been spun by a typhoon.

Sween and Otto stared in horror.

Helpless.

Then Madame Honeybun returned.

The backs of her hands were bleeding and a long scratch ran down from her cheekbone on to her neck. Her lovely hair was slowly coiling itself back around her head.

'Otto, the most terrible thing—'

'I know, we saw, we—'

'We? Is Mr Softly *there*?'

'I'm his son,' said Sween shakily.

'I recognize you,' said Honeybun. 'You delivered them, dear. Excuse me, Otto—'

'On his behalf,' whispered Sween. 'I'm here on his behalf. What's happened, where's—'

'Please do excuse me, dear,' said Honeybun. 'Otto, may I speak with you alone?'

Otto nudged Sween, who walked out of view. Madame Honeybun dabbed at her cuts with a handkerchief. 'Completely alone please, darling,' she added without looking up.

Sween went into the Office.

'I have no reason to think that boy is one of us, Otto. You shouldn't let him see the communicator, really, communicators aren't all that Possible—'

'Yes, but Max Softly's—' Otto stopped and looked anxiously at Sween, or at least at his head, which had appeared round the door, bobbing like a puppet. Now he was waving his arms, shaking his head and mouthing, 'No.'

'There is a reason, Madame Honeybun, there really is, a very good one.'

He felt his face going hot.

She raised her perfect eyebrows very slightly.

'I will contact the police. I don't mean the Normal Police or any of the other ridiculous ones, I mean the useful, helpful ones who deal with burglaries and things. I will tell them that a large bird, a red kite, has kidnapped a team of professional cake decorations from my shop.'

She paused and seemed to be waiting, as if she expected to be interrupted.

'He doesn't, er, he doesn't want you to do that . . .' stammered Otto.

She nodded.

'I thought not. Otto, I must warn you. I suspect the work of a Bird Charmer. Mr Softly and his Agency may well be involved in something Impossible. Not only that, something dangerous. I must go now, darling. Tidy up. Do take every possible care. And your friend too.'

The communicator turned black.

'What is a Bird Charmer?' asked Sween. His voice was shaking.

'I don't know. I've never heard of one,' said Otto.

'And what does she mean, dangerous?'

They both stared at the crystal communicator.

'I don't know.'

'Is a Bird Charmer a sort of Karmidee?'

'I don't know,' said Otto.

'My dad,' whispered Sween.

'I'm sure your dad'll be all right,' added Otto quickly. 'That man who wrote the letter, that Mr Firstborn, needs all your relations to be all right because he needs to swap them for the shrinking mixture. You just have to meet him like he said. That concert is in about three days, isn't it?'

'Except I don't have any,' said Sween.

'You don't have any what?'

'I don't have any shrinking mixture, or whatever it's called. You think my family are skipping around on cakes for the fun of it? They're stuck like that. They're trapped tiny.'

# Sween's Plan

Sween began to talk a lot, waving his big-knuckled hands.

'Marlene's got it. Marlene the Scream. It must be hidden at her place. I'm sure of it. She runs the Mook Family Wool Shop in HighNoon. You'll have to go there. Case it. Find out as much as you can. Then we'll break in and steal it at night.'

'I'll do WHAT? And then we'll do WHAT?'

'You just have to go and have a good look around. Layout. Ways in. Try and find the safe. She's bound to have one. I'd go myself but if she's there and she sees me . . .'

Otto sat down heavily on one of the worn, comfortable chairs. He stood up again. Some turnips and things had got there first.

'Look. Marlene tricked them. She tricked my dad. She gave him this special liquid stuff. Said if they were ever in real danger they could shrink themselves to escape. Then it happened at Skinkers Mint. They used the stuff and they escaped down a drain. Now she won't give me the antidote. There's something she wants.' Sween paused. 'Something horrible.'

Otto looked over at the dolls' house. Furniture could be seen through the windows. Wires and pipes suggested electric light and a water supply.

'It's all up to me and she knows that,' said Sween.

'What's this horrible thing that she wants?' asked Otto, displacing vegetables and sitting down. The various words 'break' and 'in' and 'steal' and 'at night' were taking their toll on him.

'Their voices are too high for me to hear. My voice is too low for them,' continued Sween rapidly. 'We can't talk to each other.'

'What's this horrible thing she wants?' asked Otto.

'We all kept telling him he should wear a mask when they're doing a reclaiming. His face is so well-known. But he won't. He's just a big kid. Thinks he'll never get caught.'

'What's this horrible thing she wants?' asked Otto.

'And prison would finish him off, for sure,' said Sween.

Otto gave up for a minute. He took the bag of Spring Biscuits out of his pocket and Sween stopped pacing briefly to take one. There followed a tiny moment of unwrapping.

'Honestly,' muttered Sween. 'These things are so predictable. Listen to this, "A well-tended orchard will bear fruit". I mean, how useful is that?'

'I'm sure my dad would try to help you,' said Otto. 'He thinks the Bargain Hunters are magnificent, setting up that hospital and everything.'

'NO!' yelled Sween, causing Otto to spit out bits of biscuit. 'You mustn't tell anyone. No one. Not even him. It's very, very important.'

Otto peered down at his own message.

It said,

# THIS IS MADNESS

# A Visit from Mayor Crumb

When Otto finally arrived back at Herschell Buildings it was later than he had expected. The kitchen was full of steam. Pans of pasta and vegetables bubbled on the stove.

Dolores was worried. How could it take all day to go to the Amazing Cake Shop? Had he met up with some friends? He wasn't going down to the mud towns, was he?

Otto gave her the Spring Biscuits and told her he had delivered some money for Madame Honeybun.

'You see,' said Dolores to Albert, 'he's always on his own. He had quite a few friends, didn't you, Ottie, but he lost them all when they found out he's really a magico.'

The twins came floating happily into the room. Someone,

possibly Grandpa Culpepper, had wound white beads into the dark red clouds of their hair.

'Very pretty,' said Otto, as Zebbie stood on his head.

'His best friend was Dante. Do you remember him, Al? Very nice Respectable boy. You haven't seen him for months, have you, Ottie?'

'It's *all right*, Mum,' said Otto. Muffled by Hepzie hugging him round the neck.

'We're stuck in the middle,' said Dolores. 'We're not one thing or the other. He's got no friends at all that I know of. Unless you count that little wisp of a thing from TigerHouse and I don't want him going down *there*.'

The twins bounced into the air. Otto helped himself to some slices of tomato. Dolores clattered dishes out of the cupboard.

Only Albert was still. Standing by the sink, watching them all. His sadness reached his son like a gentle tide.

'I've got a friend, Mum,' said Otto, firmly. 'A Normal. His name's Sween Softly.'

'Not the Child Prodigy, the son of Mr Max Softly who paid for that statue of Mayor Crumb in Dealer's Square?'

'Yes, Mum.'

'But that's wonderful. What's he like?'

'Sort of intense, and Madame Honeybun said to tell you that some of the biscuits might be very strong. There was a surge of magical energy when she was baking them.'

'What? They're burnt? Can't she even make a few biscuits without relying on magic?'

'An energy surge would affect the messages inside. Not the biscuits,' said Albert mildly.

'The messages are burnt?'

'No.'

'Someone is coming to the door,' said Otto.

'What's wrong with them then?' Dolores, always on the edge of being angry these days and angry now, it seemed, despite the highly Respectable news about Otto's new friend.

'More accurate, I suppose,' said Albert. 'Not just health, wealth and happiness fortune messages. More personal perhaps.'

'Someone's coming to the door,' said Otto again.

'What do you mean?' snapped Dolores. 'Have you invited someone?'

The doorbell rang and everybody looked at each other.

'It's the message in my biscuit,' said Otto, 'that's what it says.' And he held up the fragile slip of paper and gave the last bit of biscuit to Hepzie.

'Don't let her eat upside down like that,' said Dolores. 'You know what happens.'

Albert went to the front door and they heard a murmur of voices as he took the visitor into the living room.

Dolores grabbed each twin by an ankle and whispered, 'I'll give them their bath.'

Otto looked round the door and saw Albert moving a number of toys, cushions and tiny shoes off the sofa.

The visitor was a big man wearing a big coat and a scarf and a hat which together almost completely hid his face. He removed the hat now. Then he removed the scarf.

Otto took a step back in surprise.

It was Mayor Crumb himself.

'This is an unexpected privilege, your Mayorfulness,' said Albert, taking the Mayor's coat and then sitting down himself on the edge of a chair already occupied by a large toy elephant with jammy ears.

Mayor Crumb hesitated. Despite the cold he twinkled a little with sweat.

'I would not have intruded without warning,' he said. 'But it is a delicate matter which I wanted to handle myself, Mr Hush.'

Albert nodded.

The Mayor ran his fingers through the short hedgehog stubble of his hair. A new style for him. Not entirely successful.

He looked thoughtfully around the room. The sofa and chairs were covered in dark, faded velvet. The curtains on the tall windows, also velvet, were drawn closed. A large, lamplit table was spread with newspaper and covered with bits of wire, plywood, pots of paint, sugar almonds, gold leaf, glue, polished pebbles, small springs and a number of feathers. Albert and Otto, as usual, had been working on a mobile.

The Mayor seemed to contemplate this table and the family life it implied rather wistfully. Then he turned to Albert.

'I am aware of the excellent work you do in our Central Library Archives Department,' he said. 'But it may surprise you to know that I am here to see you in your other, er, capacity.'

Albert nodded.

Otto, still watching at the door, felt his stomach contract with fear. Was his father going to be arrested? Were there some Normal Police waiting outside?

'Obviously I know who you are. I mean I know that you are the, er, King of the Karmidee. I believe they call you Albert the Quiet.'

'Otto,' said Albert the Quiet loudly, 'would you go and fetch a pot of coffee and a plate of biscuits please.'

Otto rushed to the kitchen. Now he wouldn't know what they were saying. He tipped some of the Spring Biscuits on to a dish, inflated some of the fashionable floral guest plates and wound up the kettle.

He could hear a bad-tempered bath in progress through the wall.

While the kettle was heating up he crept back to the living-room door.

'. . . those dark days in the summer, when even I, I'm ashamed to say, was misguided,' the Mayor was saying, '. . . of course, the Karmidee live a very different life from the Respectable Citizens here in the City.' He paused and then added, 'Not that of course I think you are, er, primitive, Mr Hush.'

'The Karmidee simply have a different sort of energy from Normal human beings.' said Albert. 'It doesn't remain in the limits of their bodies. It can manifest in many ways – coloured lights, temperature changes, especially at times of emotion. Then there are the widges—'

'And there are some who can turn into animals too, aren't there?' interrupted Mayor Crumb, sounding eager and sad at the same time. 'The ones they call the dammerung. Dammerung is from a word which means twilight, isn't it? The time between night and day. Not quite one thing or the other. A person might have the ability to turn into a tiger, for instance. And such a person, even when she was human, might still possess the beauty and mystery of the tiger.'

He had once loved a woman who was a dammerung, although he hadn't known her true nature at first. She was gone now.

'Yes,' said Albert. 'And there are many other abilities as

well. There are those we call lamp-eyes, they can see in the dark, and then there are those who—'

There was a terrible noise coming from the kitchen by now. A series of bangs like someone bursting balloons.

'Otto,' said Albert, clearly in no doubt about the location of his son, 'the new kettle would seem to have boiled.'

When Otto came back with the tray with everything crammed on it at angles Mayor Crumb was nodding vigorously, giving Albert all his attention.

'. . . very, very rare . . .' Albert was saying.

Otto poured the coffee. It came out slowly and made a peculiar gurgling noise, presumably Dolores had bought a different sort of bean.

'Thank you so much, young man,' said Mayor Crumb, taking a Spring Biscuit genteelly between square-tipped finger and thumb.

There was a polite pause with almost silent munching.

'Usually the Town Council are confident that nothing Impossible or magical goes on these days,' said Mayor Crumb eventually. 'Despite certain events in the summer they have continued to believe that our City is very much like the Outside and that everything here is absolutely Normal and Respectable and Possible.

'The Citizens, of course, take the same view. Some say the Karmidee were here before the Citizens built the City, some say they arrived afterwards to work as servants. I myself have recently formed a very different theory, Your Majesty.'

Otto saw Albert's face redden very slightly. His voice remained the same as ever.

'Karmidee Kings and Queens are not addressed as Your Majesty,' he said. 'Nor do we require our people to pay for us to live in palaces. Nor do we rule them. We are chosen only because we happen to be born with a certain birthmark in the shape of a butterfly. We must try and help our people if it is needed. It is a matter of honour.'

Mayor Crumb stirred his coffee. He had taken the message out of the Spring Biscuit. Unlike Otto, still at the door, he didn't seem to be desperate to know what it said. He had put it on the edge of his saucer unread.

'Yes, Your— er, Mr Hush. Forgive me.'

He took a sip from his cup, spluttered briefly and put it down.

'So,' he continued after a moment, 'you must be wondering why I am here. As you must have noticed I came incognito. It is a delicate matter. There is a great deal of concern throughout the City about the weather. It started with a number of small incidents . . .'

He pulled a piece of paper out of the pocket of his jacket and began to read out a list.

*Extremely small but very frightening thunderstorm in telephone box in Skinkers Mint.*

*Clouds shaped like trams collide over Pig Street Hill.*

*Small tornado-like winds reported in parks, on wasteland and in foyer of Museum of Musical Instruments.*

*Blizzards inside large shops.*

*Severe and sudden freezing fog containing wailing noises on the Boulevard.*

*Hailstones shaped like butterflies in localized areas.*

*Tropical monkeys growing white winter coats, also some camels and hamsters likewise. Never seen before.*

*Crate birds seeking veterinary assistance after attempting to put on leg warmers borrowed from washing lines.*

*Strange black and white birds thought to be called pingins observed in water meadows.*

He stopped. 'I was a little disconcerted, myself, when I turned on the tap last night and hailstones came out into the bath. It was rather noisy and startling. Unfortunately some Citizens are beginning to ask whether these things are strictly Possible.'

He smiled very slightly.

Albert took a mouthful of coffee, swallowed it with a look of alarm and then, like his visitor, immediately put down his cup.

'However,' continued Mayor Crumb, 'since these early events the situation has become much more serious. All areas of the City and the mountains are now frozen. This includes places like the vineyards, olive groves, cotton fields and coconut farms where it has never been cold before. The survival of the City could be threatened.'

The Mayor fumbled with his last bit of biscuit.

He dropped it on the floor.

For a moment it looked as if his hand was shaking.

'I have come to believe,' he continued in a great rush, 'that the Karmidee actually BUILT this City and that a great deal of what goes on here is EXTREMELY IMPOSSIBLE AND MAGICAL, INCLUDING THE WEATHER. I could tell them that the only reason the Karmidee do not explain all this to the Citizens, the Normals, whose ancestors came here so long ago and stole the City from them, the only reason that the Karmidee do NOT explain it all and prove it too, is that the Citizens, bless them, would also have to be told about the Outside, where everything is really Normal and Impossible things do not happen at all.'

He paused for breath, avoiding Albert's eye.

'And why must they never find out about the Outside? Why must they be tricked into thinking they can visit it at any time when in fact no Citizen has left the City for three hundred years?'

Albert cleared his throat, presumably working on a reply.

'BECAUSE,' exclaimed the Mayor triumphantly, 'BECAUSE the Karmidee would never be safe if the City was opened to the Outside. That is their greatest fear. Freak shows, laboratories, hospitals, prisons. They would never be safe again. This City, with all its injustice, is still their only hope of survival.'

Albert stared at the Mayor.

For a moment neither of them spoke.

'If the weather were to become more predictable, *and appropriate for the time of year*,' said the Mayor, in a much quieter voice, 'that would be very helpful. Also it is ESSENTIAL that the many special areas, where farming takes place, are restored to their *own particular* weather conditions as soon as possible.

'We have a new group on the Town Council now, they call themselves the Guardians of the Normal. They are an Ultra-Normalist Faction. Perhaps you have heard of them? I'm afraid they were at first considered to be something of a joke.'

'Do you mean the Gorms?' asked Albert.

'Yes. The Gorms. Perhaps some of them are well meaning. Although I consider them misguided. They keep talking about *curing* the Karmidee. They even seem to have laid their hands on some sort of *Cure Potion*. It is supposed to *remove* Karmidee energy. They have started to advertise it in the newspapers. If this disastrous weather continues and the Karmidee are blamed then the Gorms may well start to try and force people to take this Cure.'

Mayor Crumb paused. He seemed to be choosing words with great care.

'And then there is the problem of their leader. This man is only interested in money. He is only involved in politics to use his power and influence to get wealth for himself. There are two things you should know about him, Mr Hush. The first is that he has boasted, after drinking an excess of bloodberry juice at a formal dinner, that he knows a *person of influence* among the Karmidee who will help the Gorms to persuade the Karmidee to take the Cure.'

Albert gasped in horror.

'I am friendly with various leaders among the Karmidee,' continued Mayor Crumb. 'And I have no idea who this person of influence could be. And I do not need to ask if it is yourself.'

'Of course not,' whispered Albert.

'The second thing you should know is that the Leader of the Gorms has also been heard to refer to a private business deal he is negotiating in the mud towns, involving some rare kind of precious stone. I suspect that all these things are connected. At the moment I don't know how.'

Mayor Crumb had finished what he had come to say.

He fixed his eyes on Albert.

Otto felt his skin grow cold under his clothes.

He understood now what this extraordinary visit was all about. Mayor Crumb, of all people, had come in the dark all wrapped up in his incognitoes to warn Albert.

He was trying to help the Karmidee.

Both men stood up in silence.

Mayor Crumb picked up his scarf and began to wind it over his mouth and nose. Then he put on his hat and pulled it down. Then he held out a large hand and Albert shook it.

'Your visit and your words tonight will be remembered with honour,' said Albert.


A few minutes later Mayor Crumb was walking home, a solitary figure going back to his empty flat. The black sky above was vast and freezing.

On the Boulevard he came to a place where a number of water pipes had burst earlier in the day. Several miles of the road had been flooded. Now it was a river of ice.

Citizens on their way home from the fashionable restaurants were falling, and laughing, and pulling each other up and falling again.

The Mayor glided skilfully through them in his big boots. He was a large man, hampered tonight in bulky clothes, and frequently puzzled by many things. But he skated well. And with all the grace of his honest heart.

# Dolores

Back in the flat nothing very graceful was happening.

Everyone was in the living room. The twins were circling quietly, occasionally shaking their heads and sending drops of water on to Albert and Otto.

Dolores stood at the door, holding the towels and frowning.

'So you're sure you've no idea who this so-called person of influence might be, Al?'

'There are the Heads of the various Guilds, and the WaterPeople, of course, and the dammerung keep pretty much to themselves, they may have some sort of—'

'None of them would try and do this, Dad.'

'I agree that it seems unthinkable. I just can't think of anyone else who would be trusted enough to *have* any influence . . .' He trailed off and sighed. 'The Cure is a terrible thing, Dolores. It is an evil old recipe made from powdered minerals from inside the mountains. I am amazed that someone has got hold of it again. It does nothing but harm—'

'I don't see that it would be so terrible for people to become Normal, Al.'

Otto saw his father's eyes narrow. He looked at his wife and his look was loveless indeed.

'It is poison,' said Albert softly. 'It takes the being from us. Takes away ideas and hopes and dreams. We just *are*.'

Dolores, flustered, held out a towel and Zebbie drifted into it.

'And what's all this about the weather anyway,' she muttered. 'Are you saying it's being controlled somehow? It doesn't just happen?'

'Of course it doesn't just happen. We know the whole City was built by the Karmidee. It isn't really Possible to have weather like we have in the park, ice all the year round on the skating rink and so forth. And it's not just that, the vineyards always have the right amount of sun, then there's the rice fields and all the kitchen gardens, the orchards, the hot houses, Guido's Beach, PasturesGreen—'

'So it's all done by Impossible means, Dad?' asked Otto. 'And now it's going wrong?'

'Yes. And Mayor Crumb has worked that out. In fact he is

the first Citizen I've ever met who has worked out the truth about the City.'

'So how DOES it all work, AL? Does someone in the mud towns know? Can they fix it?'

Otto and Dolores looked at Albert.

Hepzie, very wet, came and sat on his lap.

'Well, I've read all the Karmidee documents in the Archives. And I've never come across anything about the weather. You have to appreciate, when we were driven out of our own City by the Outsiders and so many terrible things happened, a lot of very important knowledge was lost. It has been lost for hundreds of years.'

'Oh, marvellous,' said Dolores. 'The weather's going to go on like this. They're already blaming the magicos. Maybe they'll start going around arresting them. It's all going to happen again. And you, the King, Albert the Librarian, or whatever they call you now, you'll have to DO something. They trust *you*. They respect *you*. *You'll* have to try and fix it. And WE'LL all be running around like criminals. Just like last time. And there's the twins . . .'

There was a pause. Albert looked very grave.

'Dolores, it's a question of—'

'Honour! Honour! I KNOW THAT, AL. But what about US, your FAMILY? If they're blaming the Karmidee for the weather and they know you're, you're the King, or whatever, they could blame *you*. You were nearly arrested last time, remember? They could throw us out of the City, Al. *They could make us go and live in the mud towns.*'

Both twins began to wail.

'Do you want your son to end up like their grandfather Cornelius?' demanded Dolores, winding a towel around Hepzie. Pushing Albert away when he tried to help.

'Cornelius the Lion, they call him, you told me. Who knows what he might have done, what he might have become? But the doors are closed to the Karmidee, aren't they, Al? Unless you can hide your magical energy. Unless you are willing to change your accent and invent a surname for yourself, like *Hush*, for example. Unless you are lucky enough to be a bit of a scholar. Well, he couldn't hide his energy that easily, I gather. Or maybe he just didn't want to try and change himself so much. Or maybe he just couldn't. So he stayed there in the mud towns, didn't he, Al?'

At the sudden mention of his father Albert's face seemed to have frozen over.

'He's spent his life there,' continued Dolores. 'His whole life. And it hasn't agreed with him. Making those carvings, no money, no learning, blaming the Citizens, blaming his own people, full of bitterness—' She pointed at Otto. 'Well, HE isn't going to be like that. And NEITHER are the girls.'

'Please, Dolores—' said Albert, painfully.

'You can't deny it, Al. Karmidee are given the second part of their name when they are grown up, aren't they? A name that suits them. And you said that his name suits him perfectly. Cornelius the Lion. You said he's like a lion trapped in a cage. All the time you were growing up you were trapped in a cage with a bad-hearted, angry lion. People who are trapped can get that way, Al. But it's NOT going to happen to MY CHILDREN.'

She bundled up the twins.

Otto and Albert were left alone.

Otto read Mayor Crumb's neglected fortune message.

## ATTENTION ALL IDIOTS.
## VERY SMALL DIRTY SOCK JAMMED
## DOWN SPOUT OF COFFEEPOT.

'Who do you think this Karmidee person is who is willing to help the Gorms persuade people to take the Cure?' he asked. His mouth felt dry.

'The Karmidee have various leaders, as you know,' said Albert in a blank voice. 'Respected. None of them would betray our people.'

'I found your knife, Dad,' added Otto, trying to make his voice sound OK and actually feeling mad and dangerous. He brought the penknife out of his pocket. 'Guess where it was.'

'Wherever I lost it, I suppose,' said Albert, staring at the door. Slammed shut by Dolores.

As soon as he was in his room Otto set free the green beetle to call Mab.

Then he remembered that she had said she was going away to the mountains.

He sat at the window.

The moon was bright. The distant giants, BrokenHeart, Beginners Luck and BlueRemembered, lay harsh and remote under their cloaks of snow. It would be very cold up there by now. Only the hungry wolves, hunting on and on through the black trees. And the sound of the wind.

And he wondered again why Mab had set off on such a dangerous journey at all and whether she was safe.

He fell asleep at the window, wrapped in blankets, waiting for the beetle to come back without her. And he dreamed about a lion in a cage. Broken, eyes still burning, great paws rattling the bars.

When the first trams clanked past and woke him the beetle had still not returned.

# Night at the Wool Shop

Mattie Mook had finished her first week looking after the Wool Shop on her own.

It had been busy but she was used to serving the customers and unlike her parents she loved wool. She could recognize any of the six hundred different kinds available in the shop. She knew all about shades and mixtures and weights and knitting patterns. She knitted all her own clothes.

No knitting tonight though.

As soon as she had tidied up the shop and eaten her partially defrosted broccoli sandwich (kindly left for her by Marlene) she sat down under the till with a candle and looked at the Privat Booke.

Most of it had turned out to be writing and pictures cut

out of newspapers, stuck in with glue and some straighter than others. There was also a Wanted Poster, which had been folded up and kept between the pages. It was very old, of course, like the cuttings. She opened it out now to have another look although she had already stared at it for some time the night before.

It was the little girl in the photograph behind the till. She was wearing the same clothes but looked blurred. She was running and looking back over her shoulder. Her face, like Mattie's, was sort of round. She looked as if she was laughing. Someone else, very blurred, was running beside her.

Underneath it said:

### THIS CHILD MAY BE A WOOLBANDIT
*Height small. Hair black curly. Pale skin. Thought to be very good at combat knitting. Do not approach. Contact the Chief Excise Officer.*

By reading through the first of the cuttings Mattie had already learnt a lot.

### POOR SUFFER IN ANOTHER WOOLTAX WINTER
*The Town Hall announced today that there are no plans to reduce the wool tax which is leaving many of our Citizens short of good clothes and blankets.*

*Honorine Merryweather runs the Mook Family Wool Shop with her husband Peabody Mook.*

*'Only the better-off customers can afford to buy wool at these prices,' she told the* Evening Ponderer. *'These taxes are causing real suffering. If the Town Hall need to raise money so badly why don't they tax something like bananas? No one ever made a warm coat out of bananas.'*

*We asked the Town Hall for a comment but there was no one available to speak to us.*

There was a photograph of a family standing in the street somewhere dressed in very ragged clothes. They looked cold.

## SHEEP SPEAK OUT
## IN WOOL TAX ROW

*In an exclusive interview, through an interpreter, in a secret location, an anonymous spokessheep from one of the biggest of the sheep families told our reporter at dawn this morning:*

*'The Excise Officers have set up patrols all around the North side of PasturesGreen and at the dyeing and finishing houses in Scheiners Ginnel. It is impossible for us to bring any of our wool into the City without passing checkpoints where the sacks are weighed, stamped and recorded. We would like to tell the people that we deplore this tax, which we understand is needed to raise money to*

pay *for the Mayor's new Banqueting Hall and Opera House. As sheep we do not understand the need for banqueting halls. It is healthier to eat out of doors. Also we do not like singing. We prefer to hum in harmony very quietly.'*

*We asked the Town Hall for a comment but there was no one available.*

On the next page there was a hand-written entry. It looked like a child's writing, Mattie thought. The letters were formed very carefully and it all went down a slope to the right-hand side of the page. Mattie's writing did that too sometimes.

My bithday. Went to Park.
Caractacus got me litl silvr beare.

Tonight Mattie read one more cutting.

### *EXCISE OFFICERS*
### *OUTWITTED AGAIN*

*Shame-faced Excise Officers admitted last night that a considerable amount of wool seems to be entering the City ILLEGALLY. Sheep representatives INSIST that ALL wool is passing through the checkpoints at the edge of PasturesGreen. Nevertheless good quality wool is reaching some parts of the City where it can be bought at VERY AFFORDABLE prices. This wool has NOT BEEN TAXED.*

## Posing as Person

*Our undercover* Daily Determined *reporter, posing as a person in need of blankets, obtained an address where wool has been DELIVERED, by night, DESPITE the VIGILANCE of the Excise Officers who are now being supported in their investigations by the Police and the Special Reserve Town Hall Security Guards.*

Very sleepy now, Mattie turned the page. She found some more handwriting.

Who are you? Reading my booke.
Frend or foe? Why do you stare?
Wellcom frend. Foe bewar.

Mattie shivered.

She curled up under the till in her pile of wool.

She had been into the house as little as possible since her parents had left but on one daring raid she had gone up to her room in the attic and rescued a box from under her bed.

In it were the things she called her secret presents. Over the years, ever since she could remember, little objects had appeared, one at a time, on her pillow while she was asleep. Usually after a particularly nasty day with Marlene.

Among many small things there was a brooch made out of coloured glass in the shape of a flower, a parcel of gold-dust wrapped in a fragment of tartan cloth, a number of interesting buttons, one shaped like a crescent moon, and a tiny silver bear.

At first she had thought that her father might be leaving these things to try and cheer her up. It was, she thought, their secret. But in the end, when she had dared to mention something about it, he had been so short with her and clearly so surprised that she had decided it wasn't him after all.

Little treats of food had appeared too.

Mattie had started to pretend that the presents were left by the children in the photographs.

And once, on the floor, all spelt out in chocolate raisins it said,

## CURAGE MATTIE I LOVE YOU

Now she tucked the box under the edge of her nest and closed her fingers around the silver bear.

A strong wind had started to blow across the cluttered rooftops of HighNoon, brushing its shoulders against the mountains, carrying clouds.

One moment the shop was filled with white moonlight. Then a cloud would leave it in darkness again. Then, as the cloud sped on, the hushed light would return.

Mattie heard the rattle of claws on the polished floor. She looked across to the corner where she knew there was a hole in the wainscot.

A rat was sitting there in the moonlight.

Mattie was used to the HighNoon rats. They could smell out gold, some said. Long ago, when the gold prospectors lived their crazy lives and spent their money in the shadow of Beginners Luck they had kept rats to help them. Now the descendants of those rats moved from house to house under the floors, living where they chose. Mattie often heard them.

She stared at the rat and the rat stared back. Eyes like silver beads. Caring for no one.

Then all was in darkness again.

Mattie settled into her nest of wool. She had chosen all the colours for their comforting names. Teddy Bear Brown. Cosy Rose. Wanderer's Return. She thought she heard the sound of the clawed feet as the rat went away. Then, when she was very drowsy, another breath of moonlight filled the shop.

The rat hadn't gone after all.

The corner was much darker this time. She couldn't see very well.

But she was sure that something was there. Something with its own thoughts.

Watching her as she fell asleep.

# Arkardy Firstborn

It was early on the next day. The man known as Arkardy Firstborn was already sitting in the back of his exclusive jewellery shop. A small office on the top floor of an expensive building on the Boulevard. Necklaces, rings and belt-buckles sparkled discreetly in the cool light.

He was not there very often. Customers only visited by appointment.

So far no one had come in this morning.

Mr Firstborn didn't seem to mind. He was preoccupied with something else. He sat at his bureau, which was piled with textbooks and sheets of beautiful writing paper, and he tapped a pencil gently against his fingers. He was wearing very fine, grey cotton gloves.

One particular book lay open in front of him. It was hand-written and looked very old. In the middle of the page, almost faded away, the title was decorated with a great wave of curls and embellishments.

*The Ancient and Venerable Art*
*of Bird Charming*
*by*
*Daedalus WellBeloved*
*Master Bird Charmer*

Tap tap tap went the pencil.

The radiators in the shop gurgled.

Mr Firstborn continued to stare at something on top of his bureau.

It was a wooden perch. But Mr Firstborn was not a customer of the Chatterbox Telephone Answering Service.

The perch was empty. A broken piece of gold chain lay at its base, reflecting fragments of the morning sun.

Mr Firstborn put down his pencil and took off one of his gloves. He raised his pale hand.

The shadow of his long fingers flickered across the parchment page of the book. He reached through the sunlight and seemed to search with his fingertips. Then he touched the invisible air very gently and precisely, the way a musician might test the strings of a harp.

Outside the birds roosting in the trees stirred as if a sudden wind was blowing.

Mr Firstborn gazed through the window. His thoughtful eyes were as grey as the sky.

# Otto at the Wool Shop

The customer had already selected ten different shades of wool. A great deal of thought and discussion had taken place.

'And some green?' repeated the rosy girl at the till.

'Yes please, Mattie,' said the customer. Relaxed and gracious. Mattie was the rosy girl's name, apparently.

'We've got Spring, Pond, Marsh, Moss, Apple, Lettuce, Lime, Pine and Snot all on special offer,' said Mattie. Otto was finding the Wool Shop surprising. This continued to be the case. 'Of course, even on special offer, all our wool is guaranteed non-itch,' added Mattie. 'It meets the exacting Mook standards of delicious comfort.'

The woman looked around. It seemed likely that she didn't

need to concern herself with special offers. What would it be now, another half-hour? He gritted his teeth.

There was no space on the walls except behind the till. There was a big bay window and the rest of the shop was made up of eight walls, really, if you counted them, which Otto had found time to do.

They were each covered floor to ceiling with a honeycomb of open-ended boxes packed with balls of wool, roughly arranged clockwise in the order of the colours of the rainbow.

Every shade and mixture had its own name.

Some were obvious. Others, like Otto's favourite at present, Wanderer's Return, required thought. Wanderer's Return was a rusty red with a small amount of deep orange mixed in as well. He had realized, after about an hour, that this was probably a warm fireside. Here the Wanderer would sit and get cosy and have something nice to eat and not have to stand up and . . .

'I don't believe I've ever seen that green, that one right at the top in the corner,' said the customer.

The girl at the till picked up a long wooden pole with a hook on the end and whisked it through the air. The customer and Otto both ducked. They had done this several times already.

With impressive skill Mattie caught a ball of wool from one of the highest boxes and flicked it, putting the pole down beside her just as the wool landed neatly on the counter under the customer's nose.

'Ms VeryDosh, I must warn you that this wool may not be completely Possible,' she said, solemnly, blushing as she spoke.

Otto immediately moved to get a better view.

The wool was green but not just one green. It seemed to be more than one shade and it seemed to keep changing, like the light in a forest. Threads of gold were shot through it.

The customer prodded at the wool, diamonds flashing on her short smooth fingers. Even Otto knew that the VeryDosh family were extremely rich and had been for many generations.

'That is genuine gold thread,' said Mattie rather sternly.

Ms VeryDosh had picked the wool up and was brushing it against her cheek.

'I must warn you—' began Mattie again.

'Yes, yes, I know, dear, it's not totally Respectable. In what way is it not totally Respectable? Is it dangerous?'

'I don't think so, I'm sure we wouldn't sell it if it was actually dangerous,' said Mattie. 'The thing is nobody knows, it's just been passed down the family, the knowledge I mean, the knowledge that it isn't Respectable, and when I tell people that they always decide to leave it. Nobody's bought any for years.'

'How sweet,' said Ms VeryDosh. 'I'll take ten balls please, and that will be all for today.'

Mattie didn't move. The green and gold wool seemed almost to be glowing.

'The tradition is,' she said at last, her blush now reaching a heroic shade only a fraction lighter than Tomato Surprise, 'the tradition is that this particular wool is not sold by itself at this time of year. It is only sold with another one, excuse me—'

The customer and Otto ducked for their lives once more and another ball of wool landed by the first.

Otto breathed in sharply.

This wool was blue. The changing blue of a river under a deep blue sky perhaps. Many shades of blue. And running through it, twisting waves of silver thread.

'I don't quite understand,' said the customer.

'They are only sold together,' said Mattie simply.

'But I don't need any blue . . .' said the customer in a soft voice, stroking the blue wool cautiously, as if it were alive. 'It's extraordinary, I've never heard of such a thing.'

Then she returned to her firm, elegant manner.

'Please wrap up ten balls of each and charge it to our account. I would like the delivery by ten a.m. tomorrow.'

'Yes, Ms VeryDosh,' said Mattie.

The wool was out of sight and the customer at last turned to go. She nodded pleasantly to Otto as she passed. As if he hadn't been waiting there for days. Then she thought of yet another thing to say.

And at that moment he definitely saw something very unexpected. A small strange nose that reminded him of a tortoise but wasn't. And two dark eyes. Peeping, just for a moment, out of the top of her black velvety shoulder bag.

'Can you tell me the names of them?'

After all, every single shade and mixture had a name.

'I'm sorry, Ms VeryDosh,' said Mattie. 'The names have been forgotten too. A long time ago.'

'I'm sorry,' she said again, this time to Otto. 'But in a minute I really have to close for lunch.'

'But I've been standing here for—'

'I know, I'm sorry, but yesterday I tried going without lunch and it didn't agree with me. I fainted at four-fifteen.'

She frowned fiercely.

'It's very, very busy now because of this weather and there's no one here except me, you see, so there's no one to take over or clear up at the end or polish the floor and the counter and cash up and get all the orders done or set out the special offer signs in the morning. Except me. And some of the orders don't come in until midnight. If anything goes irregular, anything at all, my mum's going to send me to her cousin to work in boiling, skinning and scum removal. I am a great disappointment.'

Otto stared at her in dismay. Undoubtedly a burglary would be irregular.

'And she knows how I am. I love the wool. I need it.'

This was horrible. Don't say anything about shrinking. Go back and talk to Sween.

'I'd like some wool for my granny,' said Otto, randomly. Granny Culpepper couldn't knit.

'What colour?'

'Well, green. Greenish. Or maybe red. Sort of red with specks in.'

'You don't know anything about the history and geography of wool, do you, the science of it, the harmony and the counterpoint?'

'I suppose not really, no.'

'Most of these names are very old. We have a mixture here, look—'

He ducked as she waved the stick with the hook on. 'In the days of the wool tax, when only rich people could afford wool, this was called Autumn Leaves. It's dark orange and rust, you see, with threads of yellow. The WoolBandits managed to smuggle some into the City. They gave it another name. We still use that name today, to honour their memory.'

Otto squinted up at the label. It seemed to say something about What Have You Stood In.

'I'll have some Pine and some Moss, please, and, er, Wanderer's Return, two balls of each, please.'

'Certainly.'

She wrapped the wool in tissue paper and then put it in a paper bag with a picture of crossed knitting needles on the side. Then she pressed a button on the till.

There were a number of bings and rings and the drawer shot out with terrible force.

'Quite a till,' said Otto admiringly.

'Moody,' said Mattie. And for the first time she smiled.

'You seem to know a lot about wool.'

The smile was gone. 'Wool is my life,' she said, very serious. 'And I can rely on it, you see, and it's warm.'

He nodded. Then when she didn't smile or say any more he nodded again.

'Do you know anything about making people small?' he asked abruptly.

Her eyes widened.

'No. Nothing at all. I only know about wool.'

They stared at each other.

Then she held her hand over the counter, just about the height of the cake decorations, and lowered her voice. 'Do you mean small people about this high?'

'YES, YES! Just like that, yes.'

'No,' said Mattie. 'I don't know anything about that.'

He nodded yet again.

Mattie stayed patiently just across the counter.

Her clothes were distinctive, which is difficult to achieve in the City of Trees where many fashions can be seen at the same time. She wore a tall red hat, knitted of course, with a broad band and woollen flowers all around the brim. There was a small knitted bird at the front. At that very moment Otto thought he saw one of the flowers moving.

'Is there any other wool you would like?' asked Mattie.

For a splinter of a second Otto saw a face there. A little round grinning face in among the flowers. Then it was gone.

Mattie straightened her hat, it seemed to be tilting to one side.

Otto found his voice.

'Shrinking people,' he said. 'Making them really small. It can be done, you know.'

'No,' said Mattie.

'Like the one riding around on your hat at this very moment.'

Her black eyes became as round as buttons. She jumped off her box and he discovered that they were the same height.

She very carefully lifted her hat off her head and stood it up on the floor.

'As you can see,' she said, her voice unsteady, 'there is no really small person on my hat. Really small people do not exist.'

'Well there was,' said Otto, 'and they do. I've seen some before.'

They were both watching the hat very intently.

'Why are you staring at it like that if you don't believe me?' asked Otto.

He was alarmed to see her eyes fill with tears.

She wiped them away crossly and sniffed. Still fixed on the hat. The woollen flowers and the woollen bird. Two long black ribbons were now evident. They would have been hanging down her back of course.

Suddenly she gave a sort of yelp and rushed to the till and the box where she'd been standing. She snatched up the box. Nothing underneath but floor.

Then she looked across to the corner between the wall of orange and yellows and the wall of greens.

Then she began to cry properly and showed no further interest in trying to stop.

Otto floundered about.

He picked up the hat and put it carefully on the counter. He produced a handkerchief, which had only been used to wipe something off the twins. He stood next to her, helpless as she sat on the floor and hid her face in her hands. Finally he put his arm around her shoulders.

'What is it?' he said, in a whisper. 'What is it?'

'The ribbon,' she said, as far as he could tell. 'She must have climbed down the ribbon and, I don't know, jumped or something.'

'Who?'

'The person on my hat.'

'But you said there wasn't anyone on your hat.'

'But I want it to be true,' cried Mattie, with tears of terrible loneliness on her face. 'I WANTED IT TO BE HER.'

# The Girl in the Picture

'Who? WHO DID YOU WANT IT TO BE?'

'Go away now, please. You didn't see anything,' she said suddenly, as if she hated him.

'But you DO know about it, don't you? You do, I'm sure you do. I've got this friend, we're trying to help some people who are in trouble, we need to know about making people small and making them big again, anything you can tell us. Because we must help them.'

Neither of them moved.

'I've got a friend too,' said Mattie, as if he had said that she hadn't. 'I've got a friend and she helps people too.'

'I didn't mean—'

She walked back into the shop and he followed her.

'That's her,' said Mattie. 'She's the one.'

She was pointing at one of two faded photographs on the wall behind the till.

He looked. Saw a girl. Another version of Mattie herself. This one rock-faced against the world.

'That's her,' said Mattie.

At first he didn't understand what she meant. Then he did.

'You mean that's who was on your hat?'

She nodded. 'But little, with little footprints.'

'But that was taken a very long time ago, that's a very old picture,' he said carefully. 'And the person isn't small, she's standing next to a lamppost look, she's the same size as you and me.'

'But,' said Mattie, 'her footprints are small, so she must be small all over.'

She locked the door of the shop, thwarting several cold customers who were toiling up the hill. And she swore Otto to the frightening and binding Oath of the Mountain, which is understood by adults and children alike in the City of Trees.

Finally she showed him the Privat Booke.

It was open at the page where she had been reading the night before, just before she fell asleep.

'It was right beside me all night,' she explained, pointing to a pile of balls of wool crammed under the counter till.

Her bed, Otto realized.

133

There was a newspaper cutting stuck on the page.

## *WOOL SHOP UNDER SCRUTINY*

*Excise Officers have today interviewed Honorine Merryweather and Peabody Mook, owners of the Mook Family Wool Shop in HighNoon, in connection with the smuggling of cheap untaxed wool into the City. No charges have been brought.*

*A solicitor speaking on behalf of the family told reporters tonight, 'It has been suggested that our daughter Roxanna is one of the so-called WoolBandits. We deny this. It has also been suggested that she is skilled in Extreme Knitting, Dangerous Knitting and even the martial art of Combat Knitting. We insist that she is not a criminal.'*

## Unknown boy

The Ponderer *has learnt from a source close to the Customs Office that Officers believe that the WoolBandits are actually an unknown boy and girl who work together, possibly without any assistance. The Customs Office believes that they may soon know the identity of the boy who, they believe, comes from a well-respected family. Arrests are imminent.*

### Cleverer

*In a Council Meeting today there were renewed calls for the Chief of the Excise Department, Roland Carmichael, to resign. Here at* The Ponderer *we must ask who is running the wool trade, Mr Carmichael or two under-age persons, whoever they may be, who would seem to be cleverer than the combined might of Mr Carmichael and his Department and the entire City Police Force.*

### Hotly

*The Excise Officers have hotly denied that Chief Excise Officer Carmichael has resorted to seeking Impossible Assistance. They deny that he has visited the mud towns. They insist that he has not been seen in the Merchant Hill area talking to an unidentified person in a purple hat. They deny that he has been forced to reconsider his plans to stand for Mayor next year. They deny that the public thinks he is ridiculous. They deny that he may be going on sick leave, resigning to spend more time with this family or becoming a market gardener.*

'In the morning,' said Mattie, over Otto's shoulder, 'this was there too.'

MATTIE YOU ARE NOT A LONE
LOVE ROXIE

The pencil had almost cut through the paper in some places. It was as if it had been dragged up and down the page. And all around the words there were smudges. And one or two of these were more than smudges. They were very small footprints.

# Chief Bagsey

There was one more cutting to read. After that the pages were blank.

### DUEL IN HIGHNOON

*An extraordinary confrontation took place on Saturday between the Chief Excise Officer, Roland Carmichael, and two young persons believed to be the famous WoolBandits – Roxie 'Lightning Needles' Mook and an Unknown Boy. Witnesses say the adversaries met by chance outside the HighNoon Hotel.*

*A verbal altercation began. Mr Carmichael drew his pistol and threatened the boy. Undaunted, Miss Mook immediately threatened him in return with her pearly knitting needles and a large ball of wool (Vampire Red).*

*He refused to lower his weapon.*

*She raised her needles and witnesses describe how she then moved so fast that she became a blur and sparks and a cloud of smoke came from her flying needles. Within seconds Mr Carmichael was lying struggling on the pavement, knitted into a large drawstring bag with a raised floral motif.*

*Miss Mook and the unidentified boy then left the scene.*

*The Excise Office has today issued a statement strongly deploring the numerous unflattering names which have been used to refer to the Chief Excise Officer. These include Mr Wriggle and Chief Bagsey.*

'She's here now,' said Mattie, 'and she's small enough to fit through the rat hole in the wainscot. But if all you want to know is how she got like that, I don't know.'

A number of puzzled customers were walking about outside the shop in the snow. One or two had shamelessly pressed their noses against the sparkling clean windows, trying to see what was going on.

Mattie let them in.

Otto went and looked at the hole in the wainscot. The shop was so neat and orderly, it seemed strange that a hole should have been tolerated there at all. He crouched down to look closely.

The edge was very smooth. In fact it looked as if it had been deliberately carved out. It was more of an archway than a hole.

To the fascination of some of the customers he lay down and brought his face as close to it as he could. The shop was cosily warm, heated like almost all buildings in the City by a stove and large radiators, ancient but effective. Close to the hole in the wainscot Otto felt the chill touch of outside air.

He ran his fingers around the edge of the archway. Found something. Something old and rusty and broken that could only have been put there deliberately.

A tiny door hinge.

# Weather Report

It was the start of another freezing night.

Otto arrived home to the flat before either of his parents.

Grandpa Culpepper had put some music on the gramophone and was teaching Hepzie and Zeborah something called the sweetheart salsa. They floated anyway so the steps weren't so important.

'I don't think Mum really likes them putting food on the ceiling,' said Otto.

He was in the kitchen, getting himself a small sandwich of egg, pickle, jam, lettuce and peanut butter.

Sticky bits of cooked pasta, no longer quite sticky enough to hold on to the ceiling, were plopping around him like yet another weather condition.

'Your mother phoned to say that she would be later,' said Grandpa Culpepper. 'She is now one hour later than she said she would be when she said she was going to be late.'

'Where is she anyway?'

'I have no idea. She is my daughter and therefore tells me things afterwards rather than before. If at all.'

He was dancing as he spoke. It involved a lot of shuffling. Hepzie was holding on to the moonstone buttons of his waistcoat and floating out waving her free arm in time to the music. Zebbie, upside down, was holding his hand.

The music finished.

Grandpa Culpepper sat down with a groan. The twins drifted off, singing bits of the tune.

'I was trying to cheer them up,' said Grandpa Culpepper. 'They don't seem to be quite themselves these days.'

'Perhaps it's the weather,' suggested Otto, chomping his sandwich.

'Perhaps,' said Grandpa Culpepper and he went into the kitchen, fetched a broom and began sweeping the ceiling.

Otto followed, stepping over lots of things on the floor.

'If you'd like to help,' said his grandfather, 'I won't stand in your way.'

Dolores' cat Wishtacka sat in her basket. She licked a small, grey, spotless paw. Helping didn't agree with her.

Otto, not concentrating, picked up one wooden brick and

put it on the table. 'Do you remember anything about someone called Roxie Lightning Needles Mook?'

'Yes, of course. WoolBandit. Helped a lot of people. Only a little girl. I was a child myself at the time. We were all, you know, rather fascinated and impressed. No one could prove anything, it seemed. No one could work out how they got the wool into the City. Bulky stuff, wool.'

'But do you know what happened to her?'

'Hmm?' growled his grandfather. He was getting something out from under something.

'Was she arrested?'

'No. No. I think the story was she just disappeared. Went into hiding for a while I expect. They stopped the Wool Tax not long after. I remember that. Big celebration.'

'So was there just her?'

'Forsoots, Otto, it's a long time ago.'

Otto picked up another brick.

'I do remember the talk about the man from the Excise. She made a bit of a fool of him. There were a lot of jokes in the papers and so forth. I think he resigned or something in the end. Good riddance. He had big ambitions to be Mayor. Bit of a doobeo. My father didn't like him at all.'

Otto picked up another brick.

Grandpa Culpepper had now filled a big wicker basket

with things. He carried it back into the living room. Otto, helping, followed with the brick.

'ZEBBIE! Get those off her, would you, Otto? I thought they were in my pocket.'

Zeborah was wearing her grandfather's glasses on her head. She hovered over the sofa and then allowed herself to fall on to it backwards.

Otto tried to take them from her. It was hard to do it without breaking them. She kept kicking. He started shouting.

'Ideally, Otto,' said his grandfather calmly, 'you shouldn't call your sister a skinking little git. The word skink—'

There was a crash from the front door.

Dolores. Carrying lots of parcels and packages. She didn't waste too much time saying hello or anything. The twins bounced around her as she came in and out of the living room, unpacking, taking off her coat. She was rushing about so much that it seemed as if she might rush right out of the flat again.

'It's dreadful out there, Dad,' she called. 'Has Al phoned?'

'No,' said Grandpa Culpepper.

'Well he's dreadfully late.' She bustled. Not quite looking anyone in the eye.

At this point Albert did come home, looking terrible, and Dolores immediately turned on the television, although they never normally watched it at this time.

There is only one television channel in the City of Trees. At that moment a discussion was in progress.

The presenter nodded into the camera.

A tidy man was sitting beside him. Face like clay. Moulded into an expression of concern.

'And now we have with us the leader of the Guardians of the Normal, the new Ultra-Normalist group—'

'Please,' said the guest in a low voice, 'we do not use the word "leader". The Guardians consider themselves a *family*, a family of peace and brotherhood—'

'Well, er, Councillor Bliss, I gather you have an announcement to make.'

'Indeed I have,' said Councillor Bliss, sighing deeply and shaking his head. 'I am sad to announce that Mayor Crumb, who has served our City so diligently over the last three years, has been taken ill. He is suffering from stress. He has handed over control of the Council to me. He—'

'He's resigned?' exclaimed the presenter. 'Has he made a statement to the people?'

'If you would allow me to finish. Ex-Mayor Crumb has not made a statement. He is too unwell—'

'He's in hospital?'

'He is resting at home.'

'He is too ill to make a statement, but he isn't in hospital?'

'PLEASE.' Councillor Bliss paused. A good man struggling

to do right in a harsh world. 'PLEASE, this is very, very distressing for all of us. Now that I am Acting Mayor I would like to reassure your viewers that we will do all we can to investigate the causes of this very worrying weather situation. *Unlike* Mayor Crumb who has not been well and has had rather strange ideas. I myself have a valuable contact in the mud towns. I can say no more at this time.'

'You are linking the Karmidee in some way to the extraordinarily cold weather and the destruction of crops which is taking place as a result? These are pretty serious allegations—'

Councillor Bliss placed his hand on his heart, looking shocked.

'PLEASE. I did not say that at ALL. The Guardians of the Normal do not *blame* people, we *help* them. For example, once this problem with the weather is resolved, with the help of my contact, then we will reach out to our poor Karmidee brothers and sisters. They're burdened with their unnecessary magical energy and their dangerous Impossible abilities, we will help to cure them of—'

The picture abruptly changed. The Town Hall crest floated into view. This always happened when there was a problem with transmission.

'Blister!' exclaimed Grandpa Culpepper. 'Mr Blister! I knew I recognized him from somewhere. He used to work in the Mining Department when I was at the Town Hall. Not the most honest of people either. He seems to have re-invented himself. Mind you, with a name like that—'

The television made a crackling sound and a picture appeared. There was one of the weather forecasters standing in front of a map of the City, wearing layers of extra clothes and holding a hot-water bottle.

The map was covered with symbols, many of them never seen before, including what seemed to be a cloud of rabbits. The forecasters had been looking more and more tired and anxious every night.

'We would like to reassure viewers,' she said, blinking a lot, 'that we are working round the clock to, er, clarify the pattern, as it were, in the pattern of chilly fronts, cold fronts, and downright freezing fronts sweeping in from the East, West, North and South bringing bands of much colder, er, things.

'All this can now be explained. A snow jinxer has been sighted over the City, coming from the direction of TigerHouse. It was first seen two days ago and I can now confirm that it has been seen again on three separate occasions. The Normal Police have been informed. There is no cause for alarm.'

Grandpa Culpepper turned the television off.

Everyone was staring at each other.

'What's a snow jinxer?' asked Otto.

'A sort of thing that goes in the sky,' said Dolores. 'Snow jinxers, storm jinxers—'

'You mean it's Impossible, Mum? A sort of Karmidee?'

'This is real life, Otto,' said Albert. 'Snow jinxers do not exist. If the Karmidee once controlled the weather it had nothing to do with wispy-looking characters flying about directing clouds. That's all Citizen superstition.'

'Well, they've found a way to blame the Karmidee,' said Grandpa Culpepper. 'And I presume we are all in agreement that Mayor Crumb is not so much resting in his home as imprisoned in it.'

'Oh, they're getting blamed all right,' said Dolores sharply. 'Did you see that public meeting outside the Town Hall today?'

'WE, Mum,' said Otto. 'WE, not THEY. Dad is the King—'

'And I don't suppose you've found out any more about where the weather comes from, Al, have you? I don't suppose you can stop this madness before anything worse happens? Before they come round here to arrest you like they did last time?'

'AND DON'T START ARGUING!' shouted Otto.

'It would be amazing if this Cure thing actually worked,' said Dolores after a moment.

Everyone else went extremely quiet.

She looked wistfully up at her two daughters, staring sadly down at her from the ceiling.

Alone in his room Otto looked out of his window at the snow. The moon was almost full. It shone through the edge of a cloud.

Then the cloud travelled on and the moon gleamed very bright and something small flew right across its face, across a space of sky and back into the shadow. Something which a Citizen might easily suppose to be dangerous and magical, a snow jinxer, perhaps.

Something which to Otto, with his knowledge of these matters, looked very like a long-haired girl on a carpet.

# Roxie

Roxie waited until the shop was quiet and dark again. Years of danger had made her very patient.

She waited until Mattie was asleep, curled up in her pile of wool, and then she crept out, dragging the present.

It was a pair of knitting needles. Each of them had a large, uneven pearl on the end. They were the most precious gift of all.

She put them next to Mattie.

Sween Softly had been right, very tiny people can't have conversations with anyone else. And since Roxie had never met another very tiny person, no one, except the rats, had heard her speak for over sixty years.

Nevertheless she spoke now.

'You are my blood, Mattie Mook,' she said, husky and harsh. 'More than my nephew Melchior, that pathetical weakness of a man. You're a fighter like me. That Marlene has tried to torment you and crush you into a nothing all your life. But you're still here.'

She coughed, scrunching up her wrinkled-apple face. 'Well I'll be introducing myself in personage now we've got the place to ourselves. When I'm feeling bold and brave enough.'

Her clothes were patched, torn, singed and blackened.

A bent nail was tucked in her belt like a dagger.

Her skin was scarred and wrinkled, her hair a frenzy, her broken fingernails and chipped teeth were stained with years of chewing bloodberry leaves.

She looked wild and dangerous.

She was.

Her parents, Honorine and Peabody, had loved Roxie. They had tried to persuade her to stop smuggling wool. When the Chief Excise Officer Roland Carmichael had finally surrounded the shop with his men, Peabody had poured shrinking mixture over her and put her in his pocket.

But it was Caractacus, the Unknown Boy, who had the antidote with him that night, the mixture that would restore the wool to its proper size once they had safely brought it into the City. The mixture that would have saved Roxie from her fate. And something terrible and unknown had happened to Caractacus between the twilight and the dawn and he had never been seen again.

Honorine and Peabody protected her as she grew up, trapped in her smallness, running with the rats through the walls of HighNoon. Later her brother, Melchior's father, had left food for her. Made her little bits of furniture. Always kept the stove warm through the night because he knew she slept behind it. And Melchior himself had been brought up to do the same. To keep this strange secret of the Mooks, never to be told.

But the people who had truly loved her were long gone.

Marlene had come to live at the Wool Shop. She had chased Roxie and cursed her. She had ripped the little carved doors off the wainscot. Forbidden Melchior to leave food. Cleaned and bleached and scrubbed. Roxie had even seen her steal the last phial of shrinking fluid, hidden for so long at the back of the safe. What nasty thing was she going to be doing with that, then?

Roxie crept back into the wainscot. She lit a taper and walked with her quick, limping stride along the dusty, crooked passageways in the walls. Past her secret store of gold and bits of jewellery, found under the many floors of HighNoon. Past a rat, dozing in his nest.

'Greetings, brother,' whispered Roxie.

She came to a place where there was a tiny opening between the timbers.

She put out the taper and squeezed through. She was outside, on the pavement in front of the shop, hidden in shadow. No moon now. Thick cloud, bringing more snow. Amber streetlamps.

She looked up at the HighNoon Hotel. The biggest building in HighNoon. Once the most grand and elegant hotel in the whole of the great City of Trees.

It was boarded up, of course. The doors had been nailed shut by the Excise men the night Caractacus had disappeared. It had been owned by his parents. It was common in those days for a business to be closed down if the owners were found to be Karmidee.

And his parents, like their son, were never seen again.

The streets around it had surged with life, children were born and grew up, carnival followed carnival, winter after summer after winter.

But the hotel remained completely silent, dark and still.

And now only Roxie Mook knew the strange secret in its heart.

# The Girl in the Tree

Then there was a scream, high enough for Roxie to understand, and a splintering crashing noise. Somewhere not far away.

Roxie had flattened herself against the wall, her hand on the rusty nail in her belt. Tense as a polecat.

There it was again. Another scream.

Something caught her eye. The Pearly Oak a little further up the street.

Something was moving in the branches.

Roxie, still close to the front of the shop, crept nearer.

Now she was outside the shop next door. Now the next.

There, where the lower branches reached past the streetlamp. There was something, someone, struggling up there.

The Pearly Oak is a great big bruiser of a tree. It is ancient and twisted and fears no one. When the winter wind howls up through HighNoon the Pearly Oak throws it around like a juggler and then sends it whimpering back the way it came.

Now its strength had saved someone. It had caught them as they fell from the sky. A younger more delicate tree with less experience would have dropped them for sure.

This made sense to Roxie.

'Well done, old Pearly,' she whispered. Not daring to cross the street. Waiting to see if the person had come to harm.

It wasn't long. There was a swinging and scrabbling in the lowest branches of all and a girl jumped down on to the ground. Her clothes, layers of them, were torn in places. There were twigs in her hair. She had blood on the side of her face and she was holding an arrow between her teeth. She stood for a moment and then sat down. She seemed to want to stand up again, but didn't.

Roxie watched her. Then suddenly she looked down at the frozen flagstones where she stood. Over the years she had learnt to understand the pulse of the City under her feet. The toiling of the trams. Even the reassuring murmur of the river and its many tributaries underground.

What she sensed now was not reassuring. It was running feet. A lot of them. A crowd. A mob.

They were some way off. Coming up from the Boulevard. All the time growing heavier and stronger and nearer.

Across the street, under the giant tree, the girl was holding the arrow in both hands. Turning it over, touching the silver feathers. She looked up and down the hill and wiped the blood on her cheek with her sleeve.

'Get up, little wench,' said Roxie, urgently. 'Arrows don't live in the sky. Someone shot at you. They're coming to look for you now.'

But the girl was not getting up. Slowly she began to crawl around where she had landed. She seemed to be searching for something on the ground.

A tram rattled past. She scrambled back into the shadows.

'That won't be enough,' whispered Roxie, feeling the pace of the hunters, slowed but relentless on the steep climb into HighNoon.

She didn't even bother with the taper. She could find her way through the walls and wainscots just as well in the dark. As fast as she could she went right back to the Wool Shop.

There lay Mattie, snuggled deep in her nest of wool.

Roxie hadn't planned to show herself for the first time this way. In fact she had been shy of the moment of meeting, had kept postponing it.

Now there was no time for fear.

She climbed right up to Mattie's face, tumbling about in the wool to reach her and gasping for breath. She tapped on the end of Mattie's nose and then slipped and only saved herself by swinging on a handful of Mattie's thick, curly, black hair.

Not surprisingly Mattie began to wake up. It was dark and she was half-asleep but she was sure that there was something jumping about on her face.

She scrambled to her feet, sending balls of wool skidding in all directions. Then she reached for the light switch on the wall near the photographs. Roxie didn't have time to let go and get safely to the floor. Mattie wore a nightdress she had designed and knitted herself. Roxie was now clamped desperately to the front like a barnacle.

Mattie looked down into her face and screamed.

Roxie screamed too, soundless, but scary to watch.

Then there was a silence and then Mattie put her hand around Roxie's middle and waited while Roxie, terrified, let go of the nightdress. Mattie put her on the floor, very slowly, and then knelt and folded herself down beside her.

They stared at one another. Two pairs of dark, bright eyes. Eyes that were different ages and different sizes, but like coals from the same fire.

Then Roxie ran to the glass door and began jumping about and pointing.

'Are you her?' asked Mattie, following her. 'Is this what you look like?'

Roxie kicked and hammered at the bottom of the door. Even through the floor of the shop she could feel them on their way.

'You've got so old-looking,' said Mattie.

Roxie bit her on the ankle.

Mattie unlocked the door.

Together they stepped out into the night. Mattie danced about on the frozen snow, hugging herself, teeth chattering. She could hear voices in the distance. It sounded as if people were coming up the long hill from the Boulevard. Quite a lot of people.

Meanwhile Roxie, who looked terrible and was possibly mad, continued to hobble about in front of her, pointing and waving, now towards the Pearly Oak, now down the hill, now the Pearly Oak again. Now the open door of the shop.

Then Mattie saw the girl.

She was standing now. Only just visible under the shadow of the tree.

Something was wrong with her.

The shouting grew louder still, echoing off the frozen buildings, savage and ancient. The words didn't matter. The meaning was clear.

Mattie looked down at Roxie.

Roxie stood still at last and drew her finger across her throat.

Mattie understood. Roxie was back. Very, very small and also old. And now they were going to help someone together. Just like the WoolBandits had helped people all those years ago. Good.

She strode across the street and the tramlines, grabbed the girl's arm and put it around her own square shoulders, stooped awkwardly to pick up an arrow, and then helped her back, slowly, to the door of the shop.

Roxie was waiting there, rocking about in anguish.

They stumbled in over the threshold.

Mattie could clearly hear what the people were shouting now.

She slammed and bolted the door.

The danger wasn't over. They were all three visible in the brightly lit shop. She let go of the injured girl and flung herself across to the till and the light switch.

Only just in time. A crowd of Citizens came round the corner of Pearly Needle Street. Their faces were drained by the streetlamps, Mattie couldn't see any colour in their clothes. The night, the lamps and their dreadful purpose made them all look the same.

'Find the jinxer! Magico scum!'

Mattie pushed the girl into the wool under the till and

crouched beside her, watching the street from around the side of the counter. Roxie had become part of the shadows.

The mob surged on, muttering round the Pearly Oak on the corner and then on up the hill.

It seemed to take a very long time but eventually the street was quiet again.

'Come through here,' whispered Mattie. 'We need to clean your face.'

She led the girl into the house behind the shop.

# The Searching Man

Roxie dithered. She stayed where she had hidden herself. She could see out of the glass door and the big curved windows on either side.

The moon and stars lit the edges of the drifting clouds.

The snow glistened.

Roxie sensed a new footfall. Someone else, alone, coming past the shop.

She saw a tall man, thin in a thick coat, walking slowly, looking everywhere on the ground. He was carrying a bow and a quiver of arrows with silver flight feathers. He found the confusion of marks in the ice on the threshold of the shop where the girl had stumbled. Now he was following the footprints back into the darkness under the Pearly Oak.

He jumped up and swung himself easily into the lower branches.

Icicles splintered on the frozen ground below.

Then he jumped lightly down again. He had something rolled up under his arm.

He crossed over to the Wool Shop and knocked on the door. He stared in. He had a quiet, still face and he looked as if he could wait for ever.

But Mattie hadn't heard the knock on the door. Roxie felt a whispering in the wooden bones of the shop. There were footsteps from way above. Mattie was upstairs.

The man took something from inside his coat, wrote on it and put it through the letterbox. Then, at last, he began to walk away.

But there was still something left to happen.

As he went slowly under the streetlamps he raised his hand.

And Roxie, still watching, gave a sudden cry. A cry of anguish and horror.

Something seemed to fall out of the sky. It circled the man as he continued to walk. Then it drifted down and landed on his shoulder.

Roxie, a statue, stared after him.

Finally, she crept out of her hiding place to look at the card. There was just enough light for her to read his elegant writing.

*Generous reward for lost arrow of sentimental value.*
*Diamond tip. Silver flight feathers.*

Slowly, she turned it over.

Arkardy Firstborn
Dealer in Fine Jewellery
255 The Boulevard

Shoving and scrabbling, cursing and spitting, Roxie dragged the card to the doorway in the wainscot. There, in the privacy of her labyrinth, she fetched a piece of sharp, polished stone and cut through the paper. Cutting, ripping, tearing. Until the message, the name and the address were all completely destroyed.

# The Castle

'And the headlines again,' said the newsreader. 'Fog, snow and ice continue to engulf the City. Food supplies are threatened. Panic buying is on the increase with some shops selling out of fruit, vegetables and other essentials. Rationing is being considered. Citizens are asked to report any sightings of snow jinxers to the Town Hall. Meanwhile the Bargain Hunters, responsible for numerous thefts of art works, remain at large.' She beamed into the camera and snuggled her hands into her outsized fluffy mittens.

'And we have in the studio Professor Gessing, an expert on, er . . .' much shuffling of papers on the desk, 'ah, yes, on *bees and bee-keeping*, who has kindly agreed to come along and talk to us today because we couldn't get hold of anyone else.

Well, Professor, thank you for joining us. As an expert on, er, bees, what are your views on how things must be for these daring outlaws at the moment?'

Professor Gessing had a neat and earnest face, partially visible behind his enormous red bow tie.

'They will undoubtedly be concerned by the recent very generous reward which has been offered for information leading to their arrest,' he said rapidly. 'They will undoubtedly be aware that the only real danger to them at the moment is someone who knows their identity deciding to, er, reveal the location of their hive. As it were.'

'Do you think it is only a matter of time before that happens?'

'Undoubtedly,' said Professor Gessing.

'I'm turning this off,' said Sween.

The long dark room grew longer and darker.

Sween put a log on the fire and blew on it with bellows. Orange flames danced up. He added another log and the wood began to crack and spit.

He sat down in his winged chair. Otto was in the one opposite, his knees pulled up under his chin.

Shadows flickered over their faces.

Despite the fire the room was still cold.

It had turned out that Max Softly and his son lived in an ancient castle on the mountainside overlooking BlueCat

Wood. It was partly built of stone, partly carved out of the rock.

It had taken Otto ages to get there and he had consoled himself on the long cold tram journeys with the thought that Max Softly, friend of the famous, would surely be living in luxury.

But no.

Expensive pieces of antique furniture stood like sentries on long grim stretches of wooden floor. There was one picture, an ancestor of Max and Sween's apparently, standing on the edge of a forest wearing, among other things, a gorgeous feathered head-dress. Like them he wore his hair in two long plaits. But even he wasn't smiling.

There were no soft things to sit on and, so far, nothing had been mentioned about eating.

Max Softly's last girlfriend but one, apparently, had been an interior designer who favoured something called Sternism.

'This girl at the shop might help us,' said Otto. 'I don't think she actually knows how you shrink people or make them bigger but I think she might actually know someone who does. Know, I mean.'

Otto had sworn the Oath of the Mountain. This was making things very difficult.

Sween hissed with frustration. 'Why do you keep talking

like this? Did you make an excuse to look around? Did you see anything that looked like a safe?'

'Look, I can't tell you why but I'm sure it isn't locked away in some safe,' said Otto, thinking of the doorway into the wainscot.

'Why the skink not? Because you're scared? Because it's not *your* dad who's going to prison?'

'I think there's someone else there who can help us and I'll go back tomorrow but I'm not breaking in and I don't think you should either. This girl's mum, Marlene presumably, is going to throw her out if anything goes wrong while she's looking after the shop. And she, she sort of needs the wool.'

'She *needs* the wool.'

'Yes.'

Sween leant forward and very deliberately spat into the fire.

'Perhaps you could ask Marlene,' gabbled Otto. 'Wouldn't she help now? Surely she wouldn't let them all, you know, get arrested.'

'NO, NO, YOU DON'T UNDERSTAND! There's something horrible she wants. Something horrible.'

Sween jumped up and began to pace up and down.

'She's my mother,' he said suddenly. 'I don't have anything to do with her. She walked out when I was tiny. I didn't even know she'd got this other kid. I used to write her these stupid

166

little letters for years but she never replied. She's my *mother* and this whole thing is to do with *me*.'

'How?' asked Otto. Trying to keep up with things.

'She wants me to go and live with her and her creep husband. I have to promise not to see Dad any more. I have to agree to let her be my manager.'

His eyes were bright. Almost crying.

'Look, I've got a sort of natural talent thing, OK? For the guitar. I play a lot. Flamenco. Jazz. All sorts. I make a bit of money, Otto. My dad banks it all for me for later. He won't touch it. I tried to get him to have some now to stop this cake business but he wouldn't.' He stopped speaking a moment. 'That's what she's after, you see. She wants me because she wants my money.'

Otto looked into the fire.

There was a silence between them.

'Well, anyway,' said Sween, in a different voice, 'it's lunchtime. I've got to feed the family.'

He walked to the door and Otto followed down a long, daunting corridor with animal skulls displayed at intervals along the walls. Otto prepared himself to meet a clutch of tiny brothers and sisters.

Then Sween opened another door and everything changed.

They were in a warm kitchen with a big stove. There were lots of cupboards and dressers and a big wooden table. Chairs with stripy cushions. A great deal of dirty dishes piled up by the sink. A dustbin overflowing. Nevertheless the whole effect homely and welcoming.

'That designer girlfriend was going to do this place next,' said Sween. 'She was going to make it even more Stern than the living room. But they split up, thank goodness, and the next girlfriend just liked reading poetry. She's gone too, now. He's always falling in love. Gets his heart broken all the time.'

Otto had found something. It was on the floor by the stove. A sort of dog basket, lined with blankets. Several strange little animals were curled up inside.

'Are those armadillos?'

They had heard Sween chopping food.

Daintily, with much stretching of paws, they began to uncurl.

'Yes, a kind of,' said Sween, pouring water into dishes.

'But why are they all painted brown like that? Did you do that?'

'They're five-banded pink foot rock nibblers. Very rare. They nibble rock to make their shells stronger. Impossible, presumably. They've started turning up in TigerHouse. They've been nibbling on something with precious stones in. They've got rubies in their shells and all the rich people are wanting them as pets. The VeryDoshs have got five.'

He put down the food dishes and the armadillos began climbing out of their box, making musical cheeping sounds.

'But they look after them. They've built them their own little garden place where they can make tunnels.'

He stroked the nearest one.

'Whenever my dad comes across one he brings it home and paints it brown. Some people try to trap them, you see. To get the rubies—'

'Help!' cried Otto. He jumped in the air and then reeled around, thumping at the pocket of his great coat.

'It's all right, they won't—' began Sween.

Otto staggered towards the door to the corridor of bones. Sween followed him.

There was a smell of burning. Otto needed room. He crashed back into the Sternist sitting room where he took off his coat completely and started stamping on it. One of the pockets was smouldering.

His crystal communicator, now luminous and lime green, was rolling across the floor. It seemed to be steaming slightly. Or possibly smoking.

'Don't!' cried Otto, as Sween reached to try and pick it up. 'It's really hot. It's overdone, you know, they've been trying to get through, it might be urgently important and urgent, I've never had a message before, I haven't been checking, it should be, you know, where I can see it . . .'

169

He was struggling back into his jacket and coat.

A face had appeared in the crystal communicator. Someone Otto didn't recognize, standing in a bush.

'Calling Otto Hush. Calling Otto Hush,' said an anxious voice. 'Hello, hello. Come in, come out.'

'I'm here! It's me!' yelled Otto.

'I can't see you, dear,' said the person in the communicator. 'I can only see a foot.'

Otto crouched on the floor, unwilling to touch the communicator just yet. Then he lay on his side.

'Ah! At last! Wonderful. Professor, we've made contact.'

Another face appeared next to the first. A man with a beard. A green beard. Or perhaps it was something to do with the glass.

'This thing is just so much more than somewhat,' whispered Sween.

'Otto, this is Madame Doriel speaking. And here is the Professor. We've met at your flat once or twice, haven't we, when the Professor's been to show your father some of his inventions. We've been trying to contact you for, er, some while. Your mother said you were visiting a friend. The Professor phoned somewhere, didn't you, dear, but he could only speak to a parrot and they didn't *relate* and it wasn't—'

The picture swerved to one side. It became all twigs. Then Doriel reappeared. Then it became clear that she was holding the communicator up, trying to show him something. The tips of her fingers could be seen around the edge. Otto could just make out a crumpled shape on the ground. It was a bird.

The bird suddenly flapped its wings, half rose up, floundered, crashed about, screaming.

'Can you come at once, Otto?' shouted Doriel, reappearing. 'We have an injured bird here with, er, *other problems*. We called your father and he thinks that you are the best person to help. He says to tell you it is serious, maybe a matter of life and death. You know where we are, don't you? It's a little hard to see from above because of, er, you know, special features, so come down near the street entrance and we'll let you in there.'

The bird gave a terrible screech.

'I'll leave now,' said Otto, as calmly as possible because of course Sween was listening and everything.

'Good, good . . .'

The screen became silvery white.

'What the—' began Sween.

'I've got to go to the Amaze,' said Otto, gingerly picking up the communicator and putting it back in his singed pocket. 'They always ask my dad if there's an Impossible animal with a problem. He's very good with, you know, dragons and things. And, um, he's sort of suggested me, apparently. It's in the Amaze.'

He put his coat on.

'He's never suggested me, actually, before.'

'An Impossible what? And you're going to the Amaze? It'll take you ages. It's miles away.'

'I know.'

'It'll be dark. It'll be more than dark. It'll practically be tomorrow.'

Otto hesitated. He hadn't told Sween about the mat.

'Does that open?' he asked, looking at the window. A narrow, sombre affair, all purple and red glass with a pointed arch at the top.

'Yes, but we're three floors up and we're on the side of a mountain. We have a satisfactory door downstairs, you may remember using it to come in.'

'Air currents, wind,' muttered Otto. 'Difficult to get the height.'

He unlatched the window. It opened outwards.

No difficulty about getting height here. The drop was horrific.

Wind and snow blew in his face. Below he could just make out the wall of the castle, then a steep rockface, disappearing into the tops of trees.

He was looking to the southwest. The City was hidden in a great haze of falling snowflakes.

To try and set off from this window, in this weather, on his flimsy little carpet, would be madness.

'This'll do fine,' he said, and began struggling into his overcoat. Then put on his extra scarf and extra mittens. Then he got the mat out of his bag and put it on the floor by the window-sill.

He was shaking with fear.

'I don't believe this,' whispered Sween.

It was satisfying to hear him so impressed but Otto didn't feel well enough to savour it properly.

He lay down on his front on the mat. He felt it lift a little.

'I'll go back to the Wool Shop tomorrow,' he said hoarsely. 'I'm sure she'll help us if she can. If it's there, the antidote.'

'It's there all right, it can't be anywhere else,' said Sween. 'And I'm going to the Wool Shop myself. After dark. Tonight.'

No time to argue now.

There was a blast of cold, savage wind through the window.

'Don't worry,' croaked Otto, terrified, and he tugged at the fringe without giving himself any more time to think.

The mat rose.

Sween seemed to scream.

The mat, buffeted by the wind, swayed in the air, it banged against the stone window frame, then it soared up, the wind lifted it higher, higher, back over the roof of Max Softly's castle, back into other great currents of air swirling off the frozen mountains.

It hovered. Otto, eyes barely open, crying, hauled again on the fringe. Then they plunged forwards at last, into the great sea of dancing snow.

# The Hat on the Tram

The Amaze must be as old as the City itself.

It is a great labyrinth, enormous and rambling, with unexpected places and things to find inside. Fountains, cafés, mulberry bushes (they always have fruit on), a machine which dispenses little wooden toys that walk on the ceiling, a boating lake and a small time machine (Pay in advance. Report any problems to the management last week).

There is a centre but most Citizens never reach it. Instead they wander happily all day in the sunshine and, when closing time approaches and they feel like going home, a helpful person, employed by the Amaze, finds them at once and shows them the way out.

The whole thing is looked after by Madame Doriel, a widge,

and Professor Flowers, Citizen, florist and inventor. They live underneath it.

From the outside the Amaze takes up only as much space as a small shop. Inside it is vast. This is Impossible, of course, and is one of the reasons, as Madame Doriel explained to Otto, why it is difficult to find from the air. Unless you know exactly what you're looking for. Which he didn't.

Otto flew on over the City for two hours. He went slowly, dropping from time to time to try and find somewhere he recognized and then climbing again, to hide.

He was very cold and although he was no longer terrified he was still afraid.

And now the winding streets of Cloudy Town were below him at last.

They were very busy. Trams, rickshaws and fierce shoppers battled through the snow.

He found the High Street and, at last, he spotted the door. Dark blue paint and gold writing, rather worn. A list of prices and opening times. A sign saying, *Closed due to inclement weather*. As a rule, of course, the Amaze was sunny and warm all year round.

The other side of the wall was mysterious. A small space, apparently filled with a green cloud.

A massive steam-driven doughnut engine rumbled past

below. The fire glowed at the back, great clouds of smoke and steam billowed up from the chimneys and the vat of oil bubbled and spat under its roof of gilded iron.

The doughnut woman was standing on the front in the open, snow sticking to her clothes, flapping her arms like wings to keep warm.

'Maintain your body heat!' she yelled. 'Get your doughnuts here!'

The engine stopped behind an open-topped tram. Understandably empty upstairs.

Otto circled anxiously.

Very afraid of being seen.

Maybe he could land on a roof.

In a great gust of snow he crashed into a young crate bird. Screaming and squawking they both tumbled and then saved themselves enough to land something like the right way up among the seats on the top of the tram.

The crate bird's head was under Otto's arm. Her wings flapped in his face. (Crate birds are a similar shape to storks, but much bigger.)

'Forgive me,' gasped Otto, bowing formally, as they disentangled themselves.

She replied with a courtly inclination of her head and a low cooing sound. Then she shook his mat out and folded it in half.

The snow was easing.

Unfortunately, as they recovered themselves in this civilized manner very uncivilized things were starting to happen down on the pavement.

'Snow jinxer!' someone shouted. 'Did you see it? FLYING? It's up there! Quick! It's landed. See! And the snow's stopped!'

The tram shook as people fought with the doors. There was an instant excited crowd. Growing fast.

'Go, go, you go!' cried Otto to the crate bird, trying to get ready to take off himself.

He reached for his mat and knocked his hat off against the back of the seat.

'Driver! Driver! There's a snow jinxer on the roof! Let us in, you skinking idiot!'

The driver must have decided to see for himself first. He was coming up the spiral staircase, grunting and muttering. The passengers from the lower deck were following him.

Otto grabbed up his hat.

He crammed it back on his head.

The crate bird hovered, clucking.

The driver loomed down the deck towards them.

Otto tried to get on to the mat but the gangway was too narrow to spread it out properly.

There was an evil crashing and the tram shook. They'd got the doors open.

'Don't move! Stay where you are! Freeze!' yelled the driver, skidding on the frozen floor. 'Magico scum!'

'Yeah, freeze!' shouted someone. 'We all are. Thanks to you, weirdo!' Laughter. 'Not much longer!' shouted someone else.

There were plenty of people up there now. Otto stumbled backwards. He was at the front of the tram. Nowhere to go.

The crate bird, beating her great wings, kept the driver back for half a minute. And Otto, at last, remembered what his hat was for. He had no idea what it would do and couldn't see how it would help him now but while he was trying to get the mat flat on the front seat he stopped long enough to tug on the brim three times.

Then he looked the driver squarely in the face.

The driver stopped shouting. He took a step forward, frowning, shook his head, looked quickly from side to side, then back to Otto. Finally he brought his hand up to his chin and touched his own face. His thick red beard. His nose. The gold stud in his nostril.

Otto, fascinated, kept still and staring.

Plenty of other people had piled up behind the driver, climbing on to the seats and over them to get to the front.

Those who could see Otto stopped climbing.

They were all silent now.

Otto could see their puzzled faces ranged in front of him.

The cold air began to crackle with fear.

On an inspiration he tilted his hat a little further back on his head. Making sure they could see all of his face. Or whatever it was they were seeing.

The crate bird circled.

Otto took a small step towards the driver and the crowd.

The driver and the crowd took a small step backwards.

'Get him,' said someone at the back.

'You skinking get him yourself,' snarled the driver.

Otto picked up his mat and began to walk down the tram. Turning his face slowly from side to side. Meeting everyone in the eye.

He had no idea why they were afraid. And surely he was the most afraid of all. But he kept walking. And they kept backing away.

He reached the top of the stairs and the Citizens who were there began to back downwards. There was thumping and complaining. Someone stumbled.

But he kept going. Desperate to get out. Fighting the need to shove his way through. So close to them. Feeling their heat. Smelling their breath. Face after face after face. One step. Another step.

He was on the pavement now. A child, a boy, much younger than he was, reached towards him. He was pale-skinned and had an old scar running down the side of his face. He touched

Otto's cheek. Then slowly traced a line from Otto's cheekbone to his jaw.

Otto's mouth was dry with terror.

Everything seemed suspended. At any moment something would break and they would be on him.

'It may give you time to escape,' Granny Culpepper had said.

May.

In this strange and desperate moment Otto smiled at the little boy, who was one of the people who had wanted to kill him.

Then he walked slowly backwards, still staring at them all.

A space cleared around him as he went. Passers-by, coming towards him on the pavement, doubled back, walked into each other, stood still. Someone muffled a scream.

Still backwards he made for the door to the Amaze. He put his hand on the handle. Would they all follow him in? He opened it, stepped quickly through and slammed it in their faces.

'Ah, excellent, good, you're here,' said a voice behind him.

He took off his hat and turned round.

# The Amaze

Madame Doriel wore very large boots and a brown boiler suit, scarves, shawls, mittens, leggings and other woollen things. Only her round earnest face was showing. Very dark, like Grandpa Culpepper.

There was a small kiosk and a brass turnstile.

'Do come through,' she said. 'And thank you so much.'

'I had a bit of trouble,' said Otto, 'outside.'

He listened. It was hard to believe that the High Street was just the other side of the door.

Madame Doriel unwound her scarf and fiddled with buttons. What he had thought was a furry part of her clothes turned out to be a small black and white cat.

'Hates the snow,' she said.

She went to the wall with the cat perched on her head. Then she tapped on a brick, which became transparent.

'Oh, I see what you mean. They all look a bit shocked, dear. Did you do something to puzzle them?'

'Just a little trick my gran gave me,' said Otto, casually, hoping very much that she wouldn't ask what the little trick might be.

'Well, I think the best thing would be some sort of distraction.'

Doriel and her cat prepared themselves to amplify a spell.

Doriel stared very hard at her cat, frowning with effort, and her cat stared through the transparent brick at the crowd of people milling about outside. Otto watched over her shoulder.

He couldn't hear what the people were saying but he saw how they kept looking at the door of the Amaze. Someone tried the handle. A man pointed up at the top of the wall. Planning a climb?

Then, it seemed, the door and the wall and even the evil snow jinxer were driven clean out of everyone's minds.

They all sank into the pavement as far as their knees.

Other people, coming down the street, began falling over each other trying to get away. The pavement seemed to be melting. The snow had turned to steam.

'You go in, dear,' said Doriel, brightly. 'Just follow the string.'

Otto pushed his way through the turnstile, burning with frost, and stepped through the opening in the towering wall of hedge. Everything in the Amaze is on a grand scale. The enormous hedges grow naturally along the top into the shapes of animals and birds. The paths between them are wide enough for a tram to drive down (although, obviously, they don't).

Eventually he heard a familiar voice. Professor Flowers.

'Not long now,' the Professor was saying on the other side of the hedge. 'We're just waiting for Otto Hush. I have great faith in his abilities, he is exceptionally gifted.'

Burning with pride, embarrassment and anxiety, Otto Hush the Exceptionally Gifted rounded the last corner.

He was shocked by what he saw.

Professor Flowers was standing next to a statue of a unicorn. His face was shiny with cold. His beard really was green.

There was a bird on the ground not far away, almost under the hedge. It was sitting awkwardly with its wings partially outstretched and it looked disconcertingly like the grey and brown falcon thing which had attacked Hepzibah on the Town Hall roof.

'Oh, Otto, good, you're here,' said the Professor. 'This

bird seems to have damaged its wing . . . come and see . . .
not too close . . . there.'

The snow around the bird was churned with footprints and
the sweeping blows of its wings. There were flecks of blood
there too.

Otto crept forward.

He was sure it was the same bird now. He was the one who
had injured it. He had thrown the piece of slate.

'Professor,' he began, 'I think—'

'Now,' said the Professor, 'this is a merlin, a kind of falcon,
but we believe it is also a dammerung, Otto. It is obviously
hurt there on the wing but that is, er, superficial and not the,
er, main problem—' At that moment the bird, its eyes fixed
on Otto, gave a hoarse, painful cry. It tried to lift itself into
the air and then, as it floundered horribly, it suddenly became
indistinct. The light and the cold and the snow seemed to
merge and shimmer. Otto saw a glimpse of something else,
someone else, and then the bird was there again, collapsed in
the bloodstained snow.

'Skink,' he whispered.

'We believe it has been the victim of a Bird Charmer,'
said the Professor quietly. 'It has escaped somehow. See that
gold chain around its leg? Bird Charmers especially prize
dammerung. A bird that is part human can be charmed
to do many more things. We think it is trying to make

the change from falcon to human. But something is preventing it.

'The dammerung have never told other Karmidee very much about themselves. As you know they carry a carved familiar when they are in their human form, where their animal energy is stored. In order to change back into their, er, creature, they must bring their familiar to their lips.

'But we don't know as much about the other change, from animal, or in this case, bird, to human. All I can see here is that this bird is trying to change and something is stopping it. We need you to use your heartsight. See if you can find out what is wrong, Otto. Then perhaps we'll be able to help. Otherwise I think it will just go on until it dies of exhaustion.'

The falcon looked at Otto. He knew it remembered him.

He stared back, into its bitter eyes.

'Nice bird!' Hepzie had screamed. 'Don't hit bird!'

And for a moment he saw other eyes, wide, full of pain, frightened, defiant, a child's eyes.

Then again, the falcon.

'This wing can easily be mended,' said the Professor. 'The other problem is much more serious.'

'But I've never made a heartsight happen. It just happens—'

'I am quite certain, Otto, that if we leave you here together then your ability will manifest. Your father has told me about your ability.'

'But—'

'We'll leave you now,' said the Professor calmly.

He nodded politely and then crunched away through the snow. He was wearing what looked like big pieces of basket tied under his shoes.

# The Bird Charmer

They were alone. The merlin and Otto.

Surrounded by walls of frosted leaves under a piece of pale winter sky.

Everything was very still and strange.

Otto had folded himself into his overcoat. His mat was still jammed down his front. It felt a little warm, as such carpets do.

Nevertheless he was very cold.

But the bird was colder. It barely moved now. Its eyes opened, flickering, as if it knew it must stay awake. Then closed. Then opened again.

Otto rocked to and fro.

Tears which he had ignored were on his cheeks. Cold on cold.

'I'm sorry,' said Otto, who had said this a number of times already. 'I'm sorry. Maybe you didn't attack her.'

The bird didn't move.

'On the roof,' said Otto sadly.

The silence and the snow seemed invincible.

Then suddenly the bird began to struggle all over again. It began to blur. It was trying, one last time, to change.

'What happened?' whispered Otto.

He screwed up his eyes and clenched his fists, willing the heartsight to appear. He could hear the rush of his own blood.

A scene opened up before him, fast, like flinging open a door.

The giant hedges and the broad snowy path were gone. He was in a narrow street at night. The streetlamps were reflected in puddles. It was raining. Big heavy drops. A summer downpour. And the air was sultry, despite the rain.

There was a carriage standing on the cobbles. Black and gold. Otto could hear the rain on the canvas roof.

Then, suddenly, he seemed to be inside it.

Two men were sitting in there together. One wore some sort of uniform, partly hidden by a long coat. The other was dressed in black velvet. Intricate lace flowered briefly at his throat and on his wrists. Heavy gold rings gleamed on his fingers. His hat, which was purple, was decorated with a single grey feather.

Money was involved, it seemed. Money and a bird.

'Well, I thought you had an exaggerated idea of your abilities, Mr WellBeloved,' said the man in the uniform, counting coins into the other man's palm. 'But you have been as good as your word. I've been trying to get my hands on him for months and you've done it in one evening.'

'That's why they call me a Charmer, Mr Carmichael,' said the man in the purple hat. 'Some say that I am the greatest there has ever been. It is not for me to judge and it ill becomes me to speak of my fame. Let us simply say that I can call any bird I like. Except the crates, but they are of no use to me anyway. I value the hunters, the masters of silence. And those who feed on carrion and live by their wits.'

He was holding a bird by the legs.

Otto recognized the merlin.

'And a dammerung of this age is especially valuable to me,' continued the Charmer. 'As I'm sure you realize. We mustn't forget that you are a Respectable gentleman of the Law, Chief Officer Carmichael. Although recently I have heard other names for you. Bagsey, was it? Inspector Squirm? It would seem that you are something of a figure of fun. I imagine your difficulties with these little WoolBandits have cost you your ambition to stand as Mayor.'

Otto gasped. Roland Carmichael himself, the Excise Officer who had hunted down Roxie and the Unknown Boy!

But it was hard to think. The bird in Daedalus WellBeloved's hand was terrified and now Otto's own heart was beating faster and faster, and the terror in the bird was becoming his terror too. The bird's mind was racing, searching, desperately trying to remember something. The fear was so bad that for a moment Otto wanted to let go of the heartsight, felt it begin to slip away . . .

'Not after tonight,' said the Excise man. 'I'm settling all my scores tonight. His parents have already been dealt with. Their place is being boarded up as we speak. And after this I'll be arresting the girl. I know who she is and her home is surrounded by my men. She can't escape.'

'Well, you're a ruthless man indeed, Bagsey,' said the Charmer. 'With you, I realize, it is a question of revenge, even against children. How did you get out of that sack? It didn't say in the paper.'

'Never you mind, my good man—'

'Professional secret, is it? Did you require assistance?'

'Tell me how you will stop him changing back into a boy,' said Carmichael, his handsome face ugly. 'I must know that it will never happen. He must disappear for good.'

'Oh, I've already stopped him,' said the Charmer. 'Ever

wondered how dammerung change from one thing to another, Chief Officer?'

'When they're a person they have a familiar, a carved animal, where their animal energy is stored,' said Carmichael smoothly. 'They carry it with them. When they want to change they bring it to their lips . . .' he mimed, kissing his fingertips, 'and it disappears and they become an animal . . . or a bird.'

'Well, they do teach you people something at the Town Hall after all. But what about the other way . . .?'

Carmichael smiled angrily. 'Tell me then.'

'It's all to do with the name. Their name. Their human name. They keep it in their little animal heads. As long as they know it they can always return to their human form. That's where this comes in.'

The Charmer held up a glass jar. There was something brown and withered inside. Tree root, perhaps, or mushrooms.

At that moment the bird struggled in the Charmer's grip, blurring, almost changing, it flapped its pointed wings, threw back its head. Screamed.

'You feed them that? They eat it?'

'Let's just say they will swallow anything with enough persuasion.'

Carmichael's face changed.

Otto saw him hide his thoughts.

'It would be greatly to your advantage, would it not, to carry out your work with a dammerung who chose to be your partner and who could change back into their human form.'

WellBeloved looked at him for a moment. A quiet look.

'That would indeed be an excellent business proposition,' he said softly. 'But the dammerung are so private. It is hard to see how an introduction would be arranged.'

There was a silence.

Then the stricken merlin gave a tiny cry, desperate and lost.

'Poisons the memory,' said the Charmer, laughing. 'Steals away the soul.'

Otto felt as if he were falling. He couldn't see the carriage and the men any more.

Only the bird's anguish stayed with him now. He, too, had screamed.

He was cold through his clothes. Someone was bending over him, they had their arm around him and he was sitting in the snow. Ah. He had his head between his knees. That's what they did if you were fainting. Why? Because knees smell reassuring.

Doriel's face. Eyes full of concern.

'He just needs to know his name,' whispered Otto. 'And

I think I know it. He's the Unknown Boy. He's in a photo at the Wool Shop. He was a WoolBandit. His name is in this private book thing I saw. It's Caractacus.'

# Caractacus

Madame Doriel was holding the merlin now.

Otto and the Professor stood at a distance, watching.

Otto could hear Doriel whispering. Telling the dammerung his name. Over and over again. Caractacus.

For the last time the falcon became indistinct. A changing shape. Doriel opened her arms and she too seemed to be inside a cloud of rain.

Then the bird was a boy.

The boy from long ago, in the photograph at the Wool Shop, his coat still tied with string. Trapped in their human form a dammerung will grow old. Trapped as an animal they barely age at all.

He looked at them all, from one face to another.

As a human he still had the sure gaze of a falcon.

He held out his hands, palm up in front of him, and stared at them.

Then he turned to Otto and spoke for the first time in sixty years.

'You . . . threw . . . something . . . hard.'

'No! Yes!' exclaimed Otto. 'My sister, I thought you were hurting my sister—'

'She helped me,' said the boy. His voice was amazing, a husky whisper.

His skin was creamy and freckled, like the speckled feathers of the merlin. His hair, like the merlin's back, the colour of wet slate.

'She helped me. There . . . were . . . no chances . . . I was . . . chained . . . then this little child . . . out of the sky . . . magical . . . hair like flame . . .'

'I'm sorry,' said Otto, miserably, his voice sounding loud and clumsy in all this poetry and snow.

'Please do come inside—' began Doriel kindly.

'I've got to go . . . home,' said Caractacus, suddenly younger. 'I need to see them . . . my mother . . . my father . . . they'll be worried—'

'Please, before you go, a warm drink—'

But he was backing away from everyone. He started to stumble and run, his coat flapping, his feet turned slightly outwards. He skidded at the corner.

'Follow the string!' yelled Doriel.

Those left behind stood in silence for a moment.

'I should go home, too,' said Otto, not meeting anyone's eye. 'I did see that bird before. It was awful . . . I hurt him, but I thought—'

'You tried to protect your sister, as I understand it,' interrupted the Professor.

'That is hardly a crime, Otto,' said Doriel.

# BirdTown

Otto was once more high up in the numbing air.

It was getting dark.

The streetlights lay like necklaces below him.

He banked round, following the line of the Western Mountains. If anyone shouted 'Snow jinxer!' he didn't hear them. He went as high as he dared, steering by landmarks. Then he turned towards BlueRemembered and saw the dim shapes of the Karmidee Tower and the Town Hall.

He let the mat climb and drop again and weave from side to side. It wasn't that difficult really, not when you were experienced and kept your nerve. Shame Mab couldn't see him now, he was becoming quite an artist of the air.

Then he lifted abruptly back to the southwest, not the way he wanted to go at all.

He was fighting with the wind, trying to get back on course, going very fast now, much too fast, on and on, dipping and rising, soaring up, shaking with cold, struggling with the fringe, the wind pushing and pulling.

He won the battle suddenly. The mat shuddered to a stop.

It was poised in the sky.

Otto looked directly below. Terrified.

Among the white rooftops he could just make out a square and some trees.

The wind dropped and so did the carpet. Like a stone.

And hovered again.

This was dangerous. He was far too low.

Nevertheless something about the square below held his attention. The sounds of the City were everywhere muffled by snow. Here, however, it did seem especially quiet. Only one trail of footprints meandered across the square. A man, wrapped up against the cold, disappeared under the trees.

There were shapes in the trees, in among the frozen branches.

Otto dared to drop a little lower.

Then, staying low, he set off once again, setting his course by the shapes of the mountains, keeping down in the slower, steadier air.

He was remembering a story.

BirdTown was not always called by the simple name it has today. It was once a bustling place full of workshops in basements and children running with messages and urgent packages.

Then a great many stone birds appeared on the rooftops of the buildings in the square. Others stood on the pavements and some, as if sleeping, roosted in the trees.

These birds all appeared on the same night. When people tried to move them in the morning they discovered that they were stuck fast wherever they stood.

So the birds stayed. And a sort of stillness gathered around them. Even many years later, when Otto Hush, artist of the air, made his unplanned visit, anyone walking through BirdTown Square always lowered their voice and spoke softly. Without knowing or asking why.

# The Twins at the Flat

'You're very late,' said Dolores, meeting him in the hall.

'I had to go and help Madame Doriel and Professor Flowers with a bird, Mum,' said Otto. 'And the wind was terrible on the way back.'

'Yes, well, they were trying to find you but I don't think your father should involve you in these things at the moment. Or at least you should get a tram. You could have had an accident. Or been seen. People are out everywhere looking for these snow jinxers, it's on the telly, in the papers.'

She was sorting through bags of shopping.

'And I found this in the living room. Is it yours?'

It was the bag with the sign of the crossed knitting needles, containing wool for Granny Culpepper.

'That was a present for Granny.'

'It's beautiful, Ottie, but you know she doesn't knit?'

'I'll probably be going back to the shop anyway,' he said, weighed down with secrecy. 'There's a girl who works there, her parents are away, she's called Mattie, she knows everything about wool.'

Then the door to the sitting room opened and there was Albert, still wearing his coat.

'What's wrong with the girls?' he asked.

They followed him back into the sitting room and there were Hepzie and Zebbie and amazingly they were doing just that. Sitting. Neither of them had bounced up through the air to meet Otto. They were on the sofa with their legs stretched out in front of them. They looked like dolls.

'Oh yes, I was going to mention that,' said Dolores, in a sort of pretend casual voice that made Otto stare at her. 'I think they've grown out of it, Al. You said they might.'

Hepzie stood up on the old saggy sofa. She swayed awkwardly, took two steps and *fell off* on to the floor with a thud. Her small face contorted with shock.

She screamed.

Dolores scooped her up.

'What do you mean, they've grown out of it?' asked Albert, very quiet and serious.

'Come to Ottie,' Otto whispered to Zeborah, holding out

his arms. Now she just looked, sadly, flapped her arms like a baby bird and then gave up.

'There, there,' Dolores was saying busily to Hepzie.

'What do you mean?' repeated Albert.

'They've stopped floating about, obviously,' said Dolores. 'And it's much for the best.'

'Oh no!' cried Otto. 'No! Zebbie, Zebbie come here!'

He picked her up. How heavy she felt. He took a step back into the side of an armchair and stumbled. Automatically, he loosened his grip to let her fly. But she didn't.

Instead he almost dropped her and she clung on tightly to him and stared around with big woeful eyes.

'Do you know why this has happened, Dolores?' asked Albert, in this voice that was cutting through everything.

'I keep telling you, Al, they must have just grown out of it. They had a little sleep after lunch. Then when they woke up they were like this.'

Otto put Zeborah down and she began to walk unsteadily out of the door. He followed. She swayed down the corridor as if she was on the deck of a rolling ship. After nearly a year of flying, walking was unfamiliar to her.

'You've got to agree,' Dolores was saying in the background, 'it's all for the best. The Normal Police were round here this afternoon. Asking for you, trying to get me to talk about those wretched Bargain Hunters, as if we would know something.'

Zeborah wandered into the kitchen. Otto followed her miserably. She looked up at her unfinished drawings on the ceiling, made a sad snuffling sound, tried to jump into the air and fell over.

Otto picked her up. Were all little children this heavy?

There was a parcel with one end undone on the fridge. Something was sticking out, a glass bottle, the top of a glass bottle with a cork.

The parcel was addressed to Dolores. Wishtacka sat next to it and for the first time ever she hissed at Otto.

Then Dolores herself came in, followed by Albert, now holding Hepzie.

There was a terrible hissing and snarling from Wishtacka. Albert, however, picked up the parcel and took the bottle out.

'What is the problem, Al?' continued Dolores, putting on the kettle as if everything was all right. 'I thought you'd be pleased. Now they can have a proper life. Like Normal children. You want them to have a life, don't you? Like everyone else?'

Albert put Hepzie down very carefully on the floor.

'I need to speak to you alone, Dolores,' he said.

He walked out of the room. Dolores followed. Both the twins turned to look at Otto. There was something frightening in the way they stared. They seemed old and sad.

Dolores had not closed the door properly behind her. They

seemed to be having some sort of conversation by the coat hooks in the corridor.

It very quickly grew louder.

'How dare you even think I would do such a thing!' shouted Dolores.

'You have made it very clear that they are unacceptable to you as they are. You want them to be Normal. You have said so many times.'

'I would never, never mess around with—'

'The evidence is in front of me, Dolores. As their father I insist that you do nothing more. I insist. I have that right, I believe.'

'But Al—'

'You think I don't know what this is? Is that why you didn't hide it? It was on the fridge. Just sitting there on the fridge! It is nothing but poison. People took it in the mud towns when I was a kid. There is no antidote. This seems to be practically full—'

He must have been holding up the bottle.

'At least you haven't given them very much. One dose should wear off. Although they may never fly again so you've probably got what you wanted. And now, if you don't mind, I'm going to dispose of this . . .'

Albert's voice receding into the kitchen. A gurgling in the sink. The tap turned on at full blast.

Albert, now shouting above the noise, 'Meanwhile I will stay at the library tonight.'

'AL!'

Finally the front door clicked shut. It didn't slam, it just closed quietly, which seemed worse somehow.

Otto could hear Dolores crying.

He picked up Hepzie and Zeb and stumbled into his bedroom to look out of the window. He just caught sight of his father striding away under the trees with his hands jammed in the pockets of his flimsy winter coat.

Otto stayed looking out a while longer. The twins sat silently on his bed.

The lime trees were covered with blackened frostbitten buds.

'Ottie?' whispered Dolores behind him.

He turned and looked at her.

'I didn't give them anything, Ottie, I didn't give them anything to stop them flying, you do believe me, don't you?'

Otto looked back down through the deadened branches of the trees. At that moment it began to snow again and the night became full of flickering shapes and shadows.

It was hard to see what was real.

# Mattie and Mab

The girl who had fallen out of the sky was called Mab and she was angry.

She kept asking Mattie questions. She had rested now, she had slept almost all day, but that was only her body. Her mind couldn't rest. Even in her sleep she muttered.

Now it was evening again. Outside more snow was falling.

Trams with snowploughs on the front laboured along the streets.

The girl sat huddled on the bed of blankets Mattie had made for her by the till. Asking things.

'Don't you read the newspapers? I thought everyone read the newspapers. Haven't you got a television? I thought all you people had one. You do realize I'm a Karmidee, don't you? Or do I need to prove it? I've been looking at all the weird names you have on your wool. *Lemon* Dawn. Oranges and *Lemons*. *Lemon* Flower . . . what else is there . . .'

Mattie was knitting. She speeded up. She was trying out the pearly knitting needles. They were fast.

'Which of the *lemon* coloured ones is your favourite *lemon*?' demanded Mab, snarling with frustration.

(The word lemon is of great importance in the City of Trees. Anyone brought up in the mud towns can learn to speak like a Respectable Citizen if they have to, but they will never be able to pronounce the word lemon the way the Citizens do. Meanwhile the Citizens, should they wish to pretend to be Karmidee, will always give themselves away if they try to speak of this troublesome yellow fruit.)

'I like Lemon Dawn,' said Mattie simply.

'I'm a Karmidee! They shot me out of the sky because they think I'm making all this snow and ice! Are you going to call the Normal Police? They're out and about, you know. You do know? Don't you, Citizen?'

Mattie's needles were a blur.

'I only really know about wool,' she whispered.

'The spring hasn't come,' said Mab, in a deliberate, slow, clear voice. 'Everywhere is covered in ice and snow. It is very, very cold. The Citizens are blaming the Karmidee.'

Mattie had finished a jumper. It was in a purple mixture

with yellow and orange flecks called Monday Morning Headache.

The good thing was that she had never got to such a high speed before. The bad thing was that the jumper had three arms.

'OK. OK,' said Mab. 'I'll try something else. Have you heard about the Bargain Hunters?'

Mattie selected a more relaxing shade, Blue on Bluer. Perhaps that would help her to concentrate.

'The Bargain Hunters are these amazing people. They're Citizens, at least that's what everybody thinks down in the stilt houses. No one knows who they are. They take things that Karmidee artists made years ago out of the museums and galleries and things in the City and they sell them. Then they give the money to this hospital in TigerHouse. They built it. Except they were nearly caught and now there's a reward. A huge reward. And they've stopped sending money.'

Mattie knitted.

'If you had a TV we could find out if they've been caught. The hospital would have to close and my granny is in there now. She's been very ill.'

Mattie, knitting, peeked at Mab from under the brim of her hat. Mab didn't sound quite so cross any more.

'I've got a sort of granny,' she offered.

'Here? Living here?'

'Yes. No.'

Mab hissed quietly through her teeth and rolled her eyes.

'How nice for you,' she said. 'A yes, no, sort of, granny. Sounds quite a character.'

'Oh she is,' said Mattie solemnly. 'She's wild.' She glanced quickly at the little doorway in the wainscot. She had seen no sign of Roxie since the wonderful moment when they had rescued Mab together. Not that Mab had seemed all that grateful so far.

'You're good at that, anyway,' said Mab. 'You're good at knitting. I suppose it takes up all your brain. None left for anything else.'

'I'm working on accuracy while also trying to build up speed,' said Mattie, staring at her flying needles.

They were going faster and faster now, almost impossible to see.

'It's best if it only has two sleeves,' she explained, gritting her teeth with effort. 'But at this speed it's hard to keep track of where I've got to.'

The giant ball of Blue on Bluer bounced and danced on the floor in front of her, getting smaller by the second. Now the only sound in the shop was the pearly needles, buzzing in their cloud of smoke. A spark flickered.

'Done it!' breathed Mattie. Never before, in her whole life, had she dared to be truly proud. The sweater was finished, with two sleeves and a fringe effect on the cuffs and neck.

Blushing with delight, Mattie picked it up. It was beautiful and soft and faultless. She held it out to Mab.

'For you—' she began.

But Mab didn't take it. A tear had left a pale streak in the grime on her face.

Mattie stared at her, horrified.

'Don't you understand?' said Mab savagely. 'Don't you see? I'm trapped here. My granny is sick. She needs the medicine and MY MAT IS GONE.'

'Gone?'

'Lost. My carpet. Someone shot at me and I came down. I couldn't find it. Then you made me come into your stupid shop. There were only about six left in the whole of the mud towns and now there's five. It's dead and my gran is sick in the hospital in TigerHouse and I can't get there. And I've got these medicines for her. Fresh. From the cavers in SmokeStack. I've been going backwards and forwards getting them.'

'Could someone else take the medicines for you?' asked Mattie.

Mab gasped.

'That's it!' she exclaimed, wiping at her face. 'Can I use your phone?'

This, at least, was easy. The phone was in the parlour, the first room at the back of the shop. Mattie guessed that Mab would not mind that the phone smelt so strongly of disinfectant that it made your eyes run or that the spotless furniture was protected by dustsheets.

'I've got this friend. He's a, a sort of Citizen,' continued Mab, excitedly. 'He'll help, I know he will. I'll phone him.'

She walked slowly, leaning on Mattie. Then Mattie tactfully left her alone and went back into the shop.

Outside the snow fell steadily. It was dark. Each streetlight seemed to be surrounded by its own cloud of tumbling flakes.

It must be very cold now inside the walls.

Mattie picked up the beautiful pearly knitting needles and the Blue on Bluer wool.

'He's not THERE,' said Mab, limping angrily back. 'No one was THERE. The operator says there's something wrong with the phone lines. Icicles. Pulling them down.'

Mattie nodded, concentrating on her knitting.

'Well, I'm going. I'll get trams and things,' said Mab. Although it was obvious that she could hardly walk.

She looked at Mattie who lifted her needle to her face and deftly bit through the wool. She had finished. She had made a dress with a large useful pocket at the front.

Mab looked at it without speaking for a moment.

'Look at you,' she whispered at last, 'all cosy here in this mad little shop. Not knowing anything about anything.'

This was beginning to sound like Marlene. Mattie frowned anxiously.

'You're a freak!' Mab shouted suddenly. 'That's what you are. You don't care. Making dolls' clothes when my granny's going to die!'

Mab wasn't really like Marlene, Mattie was sure of it. Mab was just frightened and upset. Nevertheless it was hard for Mattie to stop her thoughts from splintering and swirling away. Just the way they did when Marlene called her names.

With a huge effort she managed to speak.

'I've had an idea about wool,' she said.

Mab snorted.

'About wool and your carpet.'

'Don't you even speak about my carpet.'

Mattie stood up, picked up her long pole with the hook on the end. She crossed the shop, rolling a little from side to side. She was holding on to Roxie so tightly in her mind, Roxie who loved her, that she walked with Roxie's walk.

Then she began swinging the pole through the air. Flicking different coloured balls of wool down on to the floor so that they landed right in front of Mab in a neat pyramid.

Mab watched, her face full of miserable disdain.

'All the wools in this shop have names. Except two,' said Mattie.

She didn't look at Mab.

'They are very, very old. A lot of them. Although we add new ones. We never discontinue. It says on the advertisements "Mook's Family Wool Shop No Variety Ever Discontinued".'

Mab sniffed. A prisoner.

'Some of the names are just about the colours. Some are sort of jokes, to do with the time of the WoolBandits. And some are just names. And no one knows why.'

Mattie paused. Then she sat down opposite Mab and carefully dismantled the pyramid.

'There are two colours which we must always sell together,' she said. 'They are so old, no one even knows their names. They are Impossible. No one knows why.'

'So what? Are they in this lot here?'

'No. These are the Forbidden Six.'

'The what?'

'They must never be sold together. They must never be knitted together. Never.'

'So?' said Mab.

'Well, they've all got names. This brown is called Feet on the Ground. Then you've got the green, that's Treetop. Then the grey and white mix, that's a strange name. Can't See. Then the blue. Dancing.'

'Dancing?' exclaimed Mab.

Mattie went on in the same thoughtful voice, putting together a puzzle.

'Then you've got the purple and silver, we've always called it Owl Eyes and then this very dark purple, almost black, is called No Moon.'

Mab was listening fiercely now.

'I think,' said Mattie finally, 'that these are all to do with flying. I've always wondered about them. Feet on the Ground might be like a beginning, then, over the Treetops—'

'Dancing,' said Mab, 'yes, dancing is what we call it when it's sunny, blue sky, a good journey, and owl eyes, that's what we say if there's a good moon, you know, so people can see, and then, no moon, you see, when they can't. At night.'

'So this one,' said Mattie, picking up the grey and white, 'is like a fog.'

'Yes. A cloud. Flying in a cloud. That's horrible.'

They both looked down at the wool.

Mattie knew she had done something extremely useful and clever. She looked quickly over at Roxie's doorway. Just darkness.

'I think that's why they're called the Forbidden Six. It's because if we knit them all together, like in your carpet, they'll fly. People don't want their clothes to fly about.' She said this very seriously and then, when Mab laughed, she laughed too.

And soon, taking a little of each colour, and sternly instructed as to the design of butterflies, Mattie started to knit a flying carpet.

# The Cloak

It was almost midnight.

The carpet was ready. Mattie had made it very slowly, with Mab leaning over her saying be careful, be careful, be careful.

Even Mab couldn't fault it.

It was time to fly.

'Turn the light off,' said Mab.

'But you'll bang into the walls.'

'Wait and see.'

Mattie turned off the light and then watched as Mab stepped on to the mat, sat down and tugged at the fringe.

The carpet rose timidly into the air. Mattie flattened herself against the nearest wall: Rose Pink, Raspberry

Ice, Itchy Rash. Two silvery beams of light swept across the shop.

'It's called lamp-eyes,' said Mab, from just under the ceiling. 'That's how my energy manifests. I can see in the dark. Impressed?'

Mattie watched the carpet dive and bounce, a shadow plunging through shadows. Beautiful, impossible, alive. And all because she, Mattie Mook, had understood the secret of the wool.

Mab spiralled down and landed silently. The Little Moth.

'You're good at that,' said Mattie, feeling heavy all over.

'You're good at knitting,' said Mab.

Mattie began to blush.

'You and those needles,' added Mab, 'thunder and lightning.'

And for a moment the sharp angles of her face were softened by a smile.

'Thanks,' she said abruptly. 'I've got to go now.'

Mattie wanted to say lots of things. She wished Mab would stay. Mab was still stiff and bruised from the fall. There were circles under her eyes in the shade called Summer Lavender. The rest of her skin was the colour called Ghost. 'Would you like some more food?'

'Another broccoli sandwich? No thanks. Anyway, it's better not to eat too much before a long flight.'

The door was open.

The street, the buildings, the Pearly Oak, seemed changed by the snow. Even the HighNoon Hotel. Its awful cavernous silence muffled and softened.

But the air and the sky were cold indeed.

'Wait!' cried Mattie and ran back inside.

Her footsteps thudded through the tiny, cramped, antiseptic rooms. She flicked the light on but the furniture, crouching under its dustsheets, still frightened her. Up the steps that sounded hollow, up another flight to her crooked bedroom in the attic.

There was her bed, the dolls' house, which Marlene hated, and the chest-of-drawers.

Mattie had brought her books down to the shop and had hidden them under the till, too precious to leave in this harsh little room. *A Guide to the Dangers of the Wool Trade* and the ancient, much damaged and barely legible *Wool: Colour, Texture, and Cosmic Energy*.

Mattie pulled open the cumbersome bottom drawer of the chest. It was packed with clothes, old and beautifully made. They had always been there and now they were just about the right size for her. They should fit Mab too.

She chose a cloak, three layers thick and very, very soft. Beautiful abstract designs covered the outside. It could be buttoned up, there were six obsidian buttons.

She rushed downstairs again, thump, thump, thump, her

serious face lit up with excitement. She had made a friend at last and now she was going to give the friend a marvellous present. And she would invite Mab to come back soon. Perhaps Mab would take her for a ride on her carpet. Mattie had never been further from HighNoon than the Boulevard.

She burst into the shop and as she did so the door to the street creaked a little way open and then, creaking, almost closed.

A gust of wind skimmed over the snow on Pearly Needle Street. The door rattled.

'Mab?' whispered Mattie, walking across the polished floor, hugging the cloak.

Somewhere outside a clock chimed. Nine o'clock.

Of course. Mab had gone.

# Homecoming

Mattie opened the door and stepped out into the snow. No new footprints. Not with a carpet.

She looked up into the dense darkness above the streetlamps.

Then she turned to go back inside and all her excited ideas, including the gift of the cloak, seemed immediately and definitely stupid. Stupid to think that anyone as beautiful and mysterious and weightless as Mab would ever want to be her friend. Stupid, as Marlene would say. Stupid, stupid, stupid.

Out of the corner of her eye she caught sight of someone labouring up the hill.

The wind blew again, more savagely this time, and a cloud

of snow was lifted up, swirling into her face, making everything white. She shivered. Something about the figure made it hard for her to look away. It was visible again now, small and hunched over. Still watching, she unclasped the cloak and slipped it around her shoulders. It reached almost to the ground.

The figure came nearer. Perhaps it was not an adult. No, a boy, wearing a big coat. On the far side of the street.

Mattie screwed up her eyes to see better.

Another gust of wind.

He was much nearer now. She could see the string around his waist, his thick, straight spikes of hair, blown back away from his face.

A tram was coming slowly down from the top of SteepSide. The plough on the front sent great chunks of snow into the air, showering the pavements.

But Mattie noticed nothing. She did not see the tram, or the flying snow, or the driver, his teeth clamped ferociously together as if this might help the brakes on the long descent to the Boulevard.

She saw only the boy.

He crossed the street in front of the HighNoon Hotel. He went right up the steps, despite the boards nailed over the windows and the broken balconies and the heavy iron grille bolted across the doors.

Chief Excise Officer Carmichael had painted a sign on the wall sixty years before. A clumsy 'K' for Karmidee. A warning. To let everyone know why the Hotel had been so suddenly closed down.

The boy seemed finally to see this sign. It was faded and rusted brown like blood.

Mattie heard a terrible scream, half-human, half-bird. She put her own hands to her mouth with the pain of it.

He stood there a moment longer and then turned and walked back down the steps like a very old man. Then he looked up and saw her and began to stumble and skid across the cobbles and the tramlines.

He reached her at last.

He was weary and hunted and everything about him was strange. She held out her arms to help him inside and he grabbed hold of her and wouldn't let her go. She who was never hugged by anyone.

'I'm back, Roxie,' he said, in his shy, harsh voice. 'Is it really you?'

# Otto and the Beetle

Otto woke suddenly and sat up, flailing his arms. Something small and hard was on his face, had hit his face.

Now it had fallen off. He felt a tiny thud on the bedclothes and then, as he scrabbled for the light switch, he heard a feeble buzzing . . . On the bed? He'd knocked the lamp on the floor. Now, suddenly and very alarmingly the buzzing was RIGHT IN HIS EAR.

Finally he was sitting on the bedroom floor, where it was surprisingly cold, and holding his lamp, now lit, like some sort of shield.

Mab's beetle. Creeping wearily around on the carpet. Its beautiful green carapace dusty, scratched and stained.

He had left the window open very slightly of course, in

case, but he hadn't expected to see the beetle again.

He hurried about fetching cabbage and water and he made a nest of socks on top of the radiator (large, ponderous, like all radiators in the City of Trees).

'It's all right,' he kept muttering. 'I know you did your best.' The beetle lay down on the cabbage. It looked awful.

'Don't die,' he added. And he prodded it very gently to make it move and it didn't move at all.

Well, he was very much awake now. He had that sick, churning feeling which comes when you wake up and remember something horrible.

Then he remembered another horrible thing. He suddenly started grabbing clothes and pulling them on. How could he have forgotten? Tonight, Sween had said, tonight he would be going down to the Wool Shop to try and get the shrinking mixture.

Otto thought of Mattie, alone there, and Sween, desperate, doing . . . what? Smashing windows? Descending on ropes?

He reeled around the small bedroom accumulating layers of clothes on top of his pyjamas. Then jammed on his hat, opened the window further and unrolled his mat.

# Mattie and Caractacus

The Wool Shop was warm and he was wrapped in blankets but Caractacus still shivered.

Mattie had fussed about, fetching drinks and things. She had washed and bandaged the cut on his forearm while he blinked at her and said nothing.

Now she was sitting beside him on the floor, knitting slowly and quietly because she didn't know what else to do.

Roxie was hidden among the Squashed Orange. She had been watching everything all day. She had seen Mattie make the carpet. Good work, for a beginner.

She had also seen the proud-faced girl with the long, fair hair leave while Mattie was upstairs. No goodbyes there.

'Good riddance!' she had screamed, angry to see Mattie

stand, lost and clumsy, on the doorstep. 'Mooks don't beg for friends!'

But then, just as she was about to swing down on her rope of wool, something else had happened.

Caractacus had come back.

And he wasn't even old. He looked exactly the same. Just as she had known him and kept him in her heart all these long barren years.

And Roxie, overcome with longing and fear, stayed hidden a little while longer in the wool.

Caractacus hadn't taken off his gloves, or his coat, or anything else. His gloves stopped at the first knuckle on each finger and his fingers were scarred and some of his nails were bruised blue-black. One thumbnail was gone completely.

'Roxie?' he whispered after a long time. 'Are my mum and dad dead?' And he turned his sharp face to the windows and the HighNoon Hotel beyond.

'I don't know,' said Mattie.

'You're sure it's all locked up?'

Mattie nodded. 'For a very, very long time.'

He seemed to ponder.

'Did Carmichael get them?'

'I don't know,' said Mattie.

'Where is Carmichael?'

'I don't know. No one talks about him now.'

'And where's Honorine and your dad? Why are you all by yourself?'

'My parents are away,' answered Mattie, very quietly. She put down her knitting.

'I got caught. A Bird Charmer. He stopped me changing back. I had to pick locks, get in through windows. Jewel thief. Chained up . . . Then he sold me to another Charmer . . .'

He pulled up his trouser-leg a little way. There was a gold chain around his ankle and scabs and scars where it had cut into his skin.

He shrugged his shoulders up and his coat rustled like feathers.

'Caractacus—' began Mattie.

'Did you try to find me?' he asked suddenly. 'Did anyone try to save *them*?' and he jerked his head towards the hotel. 'Did anyone try to do *anything*?'

'I don't know.'

'Roxie?'

She walked over to the till. She picked up a duster from the counter and began to fold it. Smoothing the edges, folding and smoothing again. She looked up and saw him staring at the faded photographs on the wall behind her.

'I am a dammerung,' he said slowly. He seemed to be talking more to himself than to her. 'We grow old if we are trapped in our human form. But if we are trapped in our other form. Our animal. Our bird. When we change back we're the same. A long time can pass,' he paused. 'Years. Many, many years.'

Mattie went on folding the duster. She stared at it with a terrible concentration.

'You look different,' he said. And he sounded afraid. 'You look different. And you act different. Why aren't you talking? Roxie's always talking. Roxie's a real fiery one. Roxie would be pleased to see me back, that's for sure.'

'*I'm* pleased,' said Mattie miserably.

He looked hard at her now and his eyes were ruthless.

Eyes made to scan the ground from high above, to see tiny, hiding things.

'You're not Roxie. You're not Roxie at all. Why are you wearing her clothes?'

Of course, the cloak. The cloak that had always been in the chest in her room.

'I'm Mattie,' whispered Mattie.

To be Mattie was nothing, she knew. Caractacus' family were far away indeed. Far away across time.

The duster was now folded very small and tight. As if all the hurt of the world could be trapped inside.

Caractacus had started to weep silently. He didn't move. The slow tears trickled down his face.

'But she's here,' said Mattie.

'Who?'

'Roxie.'

'WHERE?'

'But she's very small—'

'SMALL?'

'And my mum's going to put poisonous gas under the floor.'

'WHAT!'

'And she's older now. And she keeps hiding.'

# Picking the Lock

There was a knock on the door. A tall boy was outside in the dark, looking in at them.

He wore a long coat with the collar turned up around his face. His hat was pushed back on his head. His face was white with cold and he was carrying a very old guitar case. He raised his hand and rapped on the glass again.

Caractacus and Mattie both stood up. So did Roxie, now a little further up the wall, concealed in a yellow and green mix known, alas, as Where's Your Hankie.

'We're closed,' shouted Mattie through the letter box. Wool was essential, of course, and usually she would not have turned him away, but this was not a usual situation.

'Open the door,' called the boy outside.

Caractacus narrowed his deadly eyes.

'What do you want?' asked Mattie at the letter box.

The boy had got something out of his pocket.

There was a tiny rattle at the keyhole.

'He's picking the lock!' whispered Caractacus.

Roxie, unnoticed, swung out on a long rope of wool and landed on the brim of Mattie's hat.

Before they could do anything the door opened, the night poured into the shop, and the boy walked in, swaggering a little. He stood in front of them, looking from one to the other.

Caractacus took a step forward.

He said something very quietly.

Who knows what he was going to do.

But he didn't have time to do anything at all.

Mattie was suddenly engulfed in smoke. As Roxie screamed unheard encouragement, sparks flew, the boy yelled, there was a great scuffle of limbs and needles, more cries, muffled now—

And there was the boy, all knitted into a big sack, writhing on the floor.

'Sweet shade of trees,' said Caractacus. 'You're almost as good as Roxie.'

Mattie coughed. She started opening the windows and flapping her arms. All this smoke was bad for the wool.

'She's my great auntie,' she said, too proud and pleased to meet his eye.

How long they would have left Sween in that horrible situation it is hard to say.

At that moment, when the door was still open, Otto Hush the Remarkably Gifted, son of Albert the Quiet, King of the Karmidee, landed his mat backwards on the pavement and fell off sideways into a pile of muddy snow and ice.

# Discussions at the Wool Shop

'Shut the door!' cried Caractacus. 'He's an enemy!'

'HUUHLP! HUUHLPEE!' cried Sween, rolling about on the floor.

Mattie recognized Otto, hesitated, and Otto stomped in through the door, chunks of snow and ice falling off his boots, coat and hat.

He had been chased by a crowd near the Boulevard, blown badly off course over WorkHouse where some people had thrown things at him from on top of a roof. Over Harms Way, going out of control in the wrong direction, he had, he was sure, been shot at with at least two arrows.

He was not calm.

'I'm not an enemy!' he yelled at Caractacus. 'I'm the one

who got you out of it, don't you realize, the business about them giving you that mushroom thing—'

He stopped. A large wriggling sack had rolled out from behind the till and caught his eye. It was pink and knotted closed with a tasselled drawstring. Someone was shouting inside.

'What the skink—'

'OHO, IZZ DAT OO?' shouted the person.

'Is that Sween Softly in that bag thing there?' demanded Otto. Bricks, arrows, jeers, shouting and now MORE nonsense.

Mattie was holding up her needles dangerously, a ball of Vampire Red at the ready.

'Don't DO that!' shouted Otto, who had discovered that he couldn't get his voice any quieter. 'And he needs HELP!'

'You tried to kill me on the roof, Normo,' said Caractacus, in his grating voice, 'and he just tried to break in here.'

'And what exactly were you doing to my sister on the roof, Birdman?' enquired Otto. Arrows! One had only just missed him. Someone really had tried to kill *him*.

'She was trying to undo the chain. Her fingers were small enough. He was out of sight. You don't often meet people on roofs. It was my first chance in, in . . .'

Caractacus didn't finish the sentence.

He still looked terrible, Otto now noticed. And Mattie

234

didn't look too good either. Then she suddenly took two steps towards him and raised her hands, her fists were clenched around the pearly needles.

Otto backed against the nearest wall of wool with his hands in the air.

'OHO, AR OO AIR?' shouted the sack.

'I'm sorry he picked the, the lock,' said Otto, trying to sound calm. 'But he's desperate. You might be able to help him. To help us. Both of you. And I'm sorry I threw the slate. But I did help you too. In the Amaze.'

Mattie didn't lower her needles. He didn't lower his hands.

'So how do you claim to have helped me, Normo?'

'Your name,' said Otto. 'I saw something. A heartsight. Carmichael and a man with a purple hat. He said he was a Bird Charmer. He poisoned you so that your forgot your name and you couldn't change back. But I recognized you from your photograph. The Unknown Boy. And then, in the Privat Booke, I realized that your name must be Caractacus.'

Caractacus flinched. Memories crashing in, perhaps.

'Someone tried to shoot me down,' added Otto to everybody, 'with arrows, when I was on the mat just now.'

'OHO! ET EE OWT!'

'Please, Mattie, put those needles down,' said Otto. 'And please let him out.'

So Sween was released from the sack and Mattie unpicked

it almost as fast as she had knitted it and quickly made him a waistcoat, which he declined to accept.

Then Otto explained about Marlene and the tiny Bargain Hunters and Sween let him do the talking.

'We need the mixture, or whatever it is, and we thought it might be here. If we don't manage to get some for this Firstborn person then Sween's dad will go to prison.'

'So where is the safe?' interrupted Sween, who seemed to be recovering fast from the knitting experience. 'Unless you don't want to help us, that is, with Marlene being your mum.'

Caractacus had said nothing for a long time. Now, however, he spoke. Two words.

'Be polite,' said Caractacus.

'And who exactly are *you*?' demanded Sween. 'Mattie's the one I'm talking to,' and he added, as if the words hurt him, 'Marlene's daughter.'

'The thing is,' cried Otto, 'we won't get anything done this way. This is stupid. The thing is—'

'The thing is,' interrupted Caractacus suddenly, 'that you have to talk to me. I invented the mixture. I know the ingredients. I can make some more. Both sorts. Big and Small as me and Roxie call it. This Marlene person probably found the last little bit of Small. She's tricked your Bargain Hunters or whatever they're called. There's no chance of her having any Big. We'd run out. I was going to make some more Big that night.'

'What night?' spat Sween.

'The night I was caught.'

'Well make some, what are we waiting for?'

'It's not that simple, Normo.'

'Why not?'

'Because my place is all locked up, by people like you, no doubt, Citizens who think they have a right to do anything they want and that everything belongs to them. And my laboratory, and all the chemicals, are inside. Underneath. In the cellars. Carmichael may have been down there and wrecked it. But I doubt it. The entrance is well hidden.'

'It's a matter of life and death,' said Sween.

'Well someone else needs my help too,' continued Caractacus. 'Someone I knew a long time ago.'

Roxie, on Mattie's hat, couldn't understand anything they were saying. But she was watching Caractacus all the time. His face, his sharp hooked nose, his eyes that gave nothing away. Caractacus was back and he would save her. She was sure of it.

'Do you want money?' asked Sween suddenly.

Otto groaned out loud.

'Only a Citizen would speak of money at this moment,' said Caractacus. 'I will help you, when I have completed my own business, as a matter of honour.'

'Where is your home, and the laboratory, Caractacus?' said Otto quickly, before Sween could make everything worse.

'You can see it out of the window.'

Everyone went to look. Their breath immediately began to steam the glass. There were several shops on the other side of the street and then, alone, the HighNoon Hotel. Taller by at least five floors than anything nearby. The Pearly Oak stood on the corner. Everything, everywhere was glinting with icicles. Like diamonds, like daggers. Waiting to fall.

'That one?' asked Sween, pointing to a bakery.

'Too far to the left,' said Caractacus quietly.

'The Pearly Oak Tea Rooms? The china shop with the little pink doggies in the window?'

But Otto had guessed. He understood that Caractacus had fled from the Amaze, his heart screaming to be home. Expecting what? Who? Finding this. Everything boarded up long ago, terrible and silent.

'It's all right, Caractacus,' he said. 'It's that big hotel place isn't it . . . I'm sorry . . .' He put his hand out to touch Caractacus' shoulder, or at least where his shoulder should be, deep inside the ancient, too-big coat. Caractacus jumped sideways away from him.

'THAT GREAT BIG—'

'SHUT UP, SWEEN.'

Mattie raised her needles dangerously.

No one spoke for a moment.

Then Caractacus, expressionless, said in his strange dry voice, 'You, memory thief, go into the tunnels tomorrow evening. The best way is through Matuschek and Outhwaite's. There is a secret entrance there. A hidden switch. Go down into the tunnels and find the entrance to my cellar. There should be a sign on the door. HighNoon Hotel.'

'But what about you and Mattie—'

'We will meet you there.'

Otto tried not to look as scared as he felt. The tunnels could be dangerous. He had only been down there once. Not by himself either.

'But how will you get in? Can't we come in with you—'

'I'm sorry. I have my reasons.'

'Well I'm going with Otto,' said Sween.

'No,' said Caractacus. 'One person. One person is not so likely to attract attention down there in the tunnels. You are noisy. You must have things you are supposed to be doing. Do them. Our first rule. Everything must seem to go on as usual.'

'Our first rule?'

Caractacus stared at him, unblinking.

'I'll explain,' said Otto hurriedly.

'I don't want to go home!' yelled Sween. 'I can't stop thinking about my dad. I can't sleep. What do you mean GO ON AS USUAL? You don't care about my dad. How do

I know you're not just going to pack me off and then go and get the stuff without me?'

'As a matter of honour,' said Caractacus, in the formal manner of the Karmidee, 'I give you my word. We will help you.'

# The Forbidden Six

It was the middle of the morning. Caractacus was asleep, sitting in a chair in the parlour. Mattie went and checked on him again. He was sitting straight, with his knees up under his chin and his arms wrapped around them. He still had his coat on.

She went back into the shop.

She had almost finished a new piece of knitting. It had been a difficult project involving a lot of different colours. Extreme care rather than extreme speed was needed.

There were no customers. A blizzard had left drifts of snow halfway up the windows.

She put down her knitting for a moment and it shot up into the air, hit the ceiling and stayed there. The pearly needles glinted down at her like mischievous eyes.

Mattie was trying out the Forbidden Six. It was hard to know exactly how much of each to use. Maybe the mixture needed more Feet on the Ground.

And then Marlene walked into the Wool Shop, followed, as always, by Melchior.

# Marlene at the Wool Shop

'Just calling in,' said Marlene. 'I need some of my fur coats. We didn't expect this strange weather.'

Mattie looked at her mother and felt herself become clumsy and sad. This always happened.

Marlene wore high-heeled pointed boots made from scarlet snakeskin with gold fur trim. Her ankle-length coat was knitted of the finest black wool. It was covered with tiny red beads that glistened like drops of blood. Her sky-blue hair hung to her waist in a plait wound through with gold thread. Her gloves matched her boots. Under the coat, Mattie noticed lumpily, she wore a simple gold dress, unadorned, faultless, following the curves of her slender body, emphasizing their perfection.

Melchior brought his manicured hand out of his pocket and consulted his fob watch. 'Taxi's waiting, darling,' he said. A shaggy white camel stood gloomily outside, knee-deep in snow.

'I'll get the coats,' cried Mattie, jumping down from her box.

'In my dressing room,' said Marlene. 'Run along.'

Mattie certainly ran along. She ran into the parlour. Melchior's voice followed her. His footsteps followed his voice.

'I'll just check the safe,' he was saying.

Mattie seized a dustsheet off a little table and threw it over Caractacus, still, it seemed, deeply asleep. The sheet covered him. He made a noise a bit like a sneeze.

'Making plenty of money?' asked Melchior as he walked in.

She nodded. He had his back to the chair. Now there came the sound of a tiny croaking yawn.

'Lots of money,' she said.

'I'll take it now, then.'

Mattie hurried upstairs. Through her parents' room, all piled and draped in purple and white, curtains, covers, cushions, a mirror as big as the door.

Into the huge dressing room. Full of costumes. Sets of false nails fanned out on the walls like spears.

She seized three fur coats and wrestled them down to the kitchen.

Melchior was closing the safe, concealed behind a cupboard.

He returned to the shop and Mattie followed into the parlour. A small snoring had started under the sheet.

Then she heard her mother laugh. This was always very high-pitched, of course, the sharp, metallic laugh of a born High Frequency Voice Artiste.

Caractacus stopped snoring and twitched the sheet off his face. Mattie put her finger to her lips.

She crept nearer to the door into the shop.

'Of course it's perfect,' said Marlene. 'It's only a matter of time before the boy gives in. He'll do anything to help his daddy. And anyway, if he doesn't I'll just tell the Town Hall that he's living on his own and that I'm his mother. That's why he can't ask anyone for help, you see, because they might tell the authorities . . .'

Mattie stayed still.

Her father said something which she didn't hear properly.

'Have you any idea how much he makes playing that guitar thing? And he could make a lot more. Half the time he doesn't even ask for money. I can only do a few screams a year. The voice is a delicate instrument. But that guitar thing, it's just a wooden box really.'

And here Marlene burst into unpleasant laughter.

'We're going to be outrageously rich. We can sell this place for a start. Lumpy can go to my cousin in boiling, skinning and scumming.'

'I have to admit your ideas are very elegant,' said Melchior. 'One small thing, did you remember to call the pest control about—'

He stopped abruptly as Mattie came in, dragging the coats.

'Well, Mattie,' he said, with a small, polished smile. 'Well, we'll see you after the Tour is over. I think we may have some interesting news.'

Mattie saw something move, quite high up in the greens.

A shower of Snot, Lettuce and more Snot burst off their shelf and landed on Marlene.

She screamed. Not her full velocity, maximum-volume, high-performance scream, but a scream nevertheless, and Melchior and Mattie both frantically ducked and covered their ears.

More wool, a lot of it, landed on Melchior too.

A family of innocent customers came in.

Marlene picked off a ball which had caught on the gold wire in her hair. She spoke in a controlled whisper. 'I have already spoken to the pest control agency. They are sending someone round very soon and that should put a stop to this sort of ridiculous *accident*.'

The customers, clucking pleasantly, helped Mattie pick everything up.

Marlene and Melchior opened the door on to the street, where their taxi had started to shiver.

The customers chose lots of different wools. There was a little girl much the same age as Mattie.

'I'm going to go to the carnival,' she said. 'My daddy's getting the costume tonight. He got me a brilliant costume last year. All sparkly and—'

Mattie nodded abruptly and tried to smile. She felt cold with shock and fear. Her face exactly matched the wool called Tiger Tooth White.

As soon as they had gone, in a flurry of cheery goodbyes, Caractacus came through from the parlour. He was walking stiffly. He stretched the arm that had the bandage on it and rubbed it.

Mattie had begun tidying the counter, although it was perfectly tidy already.

'Who was that?' asked Caractacus. 'I don't mean them, I mean the thing that was in here before. I had a look around the door.'

'My mother,' muttered Mattie. 'And my father . . .'

Caractacus gave a long soft whistle. 'Are you crying, Mattie?'

'She's a High Frequency Voice Artiste,' continued Mattie,

looking at her hands. 'She's so beautiful she's been on the cover of *Fashion Victim* two months running. People have their hair dyed to look like hers. But hers is natural. There's a special diet too, Scream Yourself Thin—'

'I don't think she's beautiful at all,' said Caractacus. 'And she won't get what she's wanting, none of it. Me and Roxie'll see to that.'

A ball of Squashed Orange flew off the shelf and bounced on his shoulder.

He turned round extremely fast and held up his hands, all in a moment. His fingers had curled into claws.

'It's her,' said Mattie.

'WHERE?'

'She's hiding.'

He scanned the rainbow walls.

Everything became very still. Only the sheep, revolving on the till.

'Oh, Rox,' he whispered. 'I'm so sorry. I should have given some Big to your dad. He could have hidden it somewhere. You must have poured Small over yourself. You must have been so sure I would make everything all right.'

'They're coming with the poisonous gas,' said Mattie. 'It's on the calendar.'

# State of Emergency

Otto had slept through the morning.

The twins were sitting in the hall by the door, singing mournfully.

There was no bread or strawberry jam in the kitchen. The fridge smelt funny and the kettle had exploded.

Dolores seemed to be sorting out everybody's clothes. There were piles of things all over the living room. (Except on the table. Now cleared of half-made mobiles and instead weighed down with books, charts and manuscripts, all concerning the weather.)

'That's to throw away,' she muttered, 'and that and that and these and those . . .'

She looked up at him and her eyes looked big and dark and smudged.

In the background the twins finished their dreary song and began again at the beginning.

'That Gorm man who's made himself Mayor has just been on the radio,' said Dolores. 'Councillor Bliss. Councillor Bliss and the Gorms. They want to declare a State of Panic.' She scrabbled ruthlessly among the socks. 'No, no, not Panic, Emergency. They want to declare a State of Emergency. Your father is staying over at the library or somewhere. Your granny's coming round today. I have to go out.'

'You're always going out,' said Otto.

# Big Mo's

Matuschek and Outhwaite's Toy Shop is so devastatingly large, so monstrously vast, that very few people really know their way around it or can claim to have seen everything it contains.

It is in its own separate and ancient building with spiral spires on the top and undulating rows of windows along the front, all different sizes and shapes. As soon as it gets dark, every night, very beautiful fireworks are set off from the roof garden. They do not bang. They sing.

Everybody calls it Big Mo's, after the giant illuminated letters M and O over the doors.

Otto went up in the lift to the high balcony running around the walls of the central hall. The stained-glass dome glowed above him, crowded with suns, moons and golden stars.

He stopped for a moment and leant on the polished wooden rail and looked out across the great space.

An immense figure of a man, almost as tall as the balcony itself, raises his hat every half hour and releases a flock of mechanical birds. Despite the fact that he didn't really have time, Otto waited to see this happen, as he had done so many times with Albert on their expeditions to buy things to make into mobiles.

The air was packed full of sounds, voices, music, sudden bangs. There was a smell of sawdust and wrapping paper and new things about to be tried out.

Silvery acrobats spun from the trapeze.

He unfolded a piece of torn paper, already slightly grubby. Lost Property Cupboard No 27. Green switch.

Then he took a cushion down the helter-skelter into the pet department.

He entered a dark maze of fish tanks.

Someone had just chosen a fish, it seemed.

The assistant was balanced on the top of a towering stepladder, waving a net on a stick, while the customer, a boy, perched a couple of steps behind him.

'. . . that's how they get their name,' the assistant was saying breathlessly.

'It's just that if it's so good at changing colour and, you

know, blending in,' said the customer, 'how do we know when you've caught it?'

'The purchase of a chameleon fish does involve a certain amount of trust, sir,' gasped the assistant, lunging dramatically with the net.

'Excuse me,' said Otto, down below.

'I just mean, if you can't see it and I can't see it . . .'

'Can you tell me the way to Lost Property Cupboard Number 27, please?'

'Perhaps sir would like to consider a more visible pet?'

'No, no, my mum doesn't want me to have any pets at all. This way she'll think I've just got a tank—'

'I looked at the list of departments and things by the front entrance but I couldn't see anything about Lost Property,' persisted Otto.

'I fancied a chameleon rabbit but I thought she might see the lettuce, you know, disappearing, not to mention—'

'North Wing, via Knights of Old and Mechanical Toys,' snapped the assistant, who had just got his sleeve extremely wet.

A few minutes later Otto side-stepped two heavily armoured children who were fighting a duel with cumbersome swords. Much clashing, crashing and squelching. The blades passed harmlessly and dramatically clean through anything – or anybody – they hit with horribly realistic sounds. Very popular. Quite Impossible.

He hurried on through the Bargain Practical Joke Department (just boring ones that everyone knew like slug-slime slippers, melting clothes and those evil alarm clocks that climb up on to the pillow during the night).

'Big Mo regrets to inform customers that the emporium will close one hour early due to heating difficulties,' said a sorrowful voice over the loudspeaker.

Then a clown walked past handing everybody whistles. Children started blowing them, making piercing sounds and sending out streams of foul-smelling purple smoke.

Otto sighed out loud, bumped into someone and almost fell flat over someone else, or possibly two people, who were crawling along the floor in a crocodile costume.

This was horrible. He'd never find this cupboard in time. If it existed at all.

He was on the edge of Mechanical Toys – Find It, Wind It and Stand Well Behind It. A large metal dragon came lurching towards him. It seemed to be leading some sort of parade.

'I should go the other way round if I were you, sir,' said an assistant pleasantly.

There was a pile of wooden packing cases round a corner away from where everyone was walking. Otto ducked towards them. A moment later he was sitting on the top.

Ah, the Spring Biscuits. A few left in the bag.

He paused to get his breath back. Mechanical creatures, life-size and larger, plodded past below. Smooth-spoken announcements rang through the air.

'And now, Citizens, our latest addition . . . the TRAM . . . one fifteenth of actual size . . . delightful green and purple, authentic City crest . . . can carry three children . . . or possibly two partially folded adults . . . can reach speeds of . . . clockwork mechanism . . . excellent for parties . . .'

Otto, starting to relax, unwrapped his biscuit.

'MAKE WAY!' yelled the announcer, suddenly not smooth at all. 'MAKE WAY! WE ARE EXPERIENCING A STEERING PROBLEM! RUN!'

Otto looked at the message in the biscuit. Very short this time.

## MOVE!

He stared at it, blinked, and then flung himself sideways off the pile of packing cases, hit the floor badly, stood up, stumbled and then looked wildly around him.

There was a terrible whirring noise. Also people screaming. Also splintering and grinding. The pile of packing cases collapsed. The tram, purple, green and out of control, rode right over them immediately. Otto scrambled out of its path as it ground ruthlessly on, demolishing numerous other things, including a large display of something and a counter. He caught a glimpse of a man in Big Mo uniform, presumably supposed to be driving but, regrettably, running along behind, waving part of a steering wheel. Security Persons blowing whistles charged past.

'CUSTOMERS ARE REQUESTED TO REMAIN CALM,' said the announcer breathlessly. 'PLEASE AVOID THE MECHANICAL TOY DEPARTMENT WHERE THERE HAS BEEN AN UNPLANNED OVER-PERFORMANCE REDUCED-CONTROL INCIDENT.'

Otto wandered off in no particular direction. His hands were shaking. He didn't feel well. He clutched the bag of Spring Biscuits and then sat down unexpectedly on a seat. The seat began to play nursery rhymes, which he ignored.

He decided to unwrap another biscuit. He seemed to have dropped the other one somewhere.

He looked at the message. After all, everyone always looked at the messages, it was supposed to be a comforting, harmless tradition.

## LOOK BEHIND YOU, DINKTOSH!

He spun round with a yell.

And there was Sween Softly with a grin as big as a dinner plate.

# Lost Property Cupboard Number 27

'Greetings,' said Sween.

'You're not supposed to be here. What are you doing here?' gabbled Otto. 'You're supposed to be playing the flamingo. Everything's supposed to be going on as—'

'Cancelled it,' said Sween, still grinning. 'Followed you. Saw you escape serious injury. How did you know that tram thing was going to crash like that? Impressive.'

Otto opened his mouth to say something and then didn't.

'So where are we going now?' said Sween.

'Where are WE going?'

'Yes, you know, *we*, as in *you* and *me*.'

'Well, I'm just off now to find the, er, Lost Property, you know, Cupboard. But you should—'

'Look no further,' said Sween. 'I've already done that. I came here first thing and found it. Allow me to escort you. And hurry up, they're closing in a minute.'

He led the way, walking purposefully, swinging his guitar case. And Otto followed, trying not to be pleased.

The Lost Property Cupboard was behind the Rocking Horse Department. Life-sized rocking horses bucked and kicked. Big kids swathed in protective clothing bounced, yelled and fell off.

The cupboard door was painted blue and gold to match the wallpaper. There was a sign saying 'Strictly no entry unless accompanied by a member of staff'.

'Big Mo's will close in five minutes,' said the announcer. 'Customers who cannot find a door are advised to stay where they are. Our specially trained Rescue and Security staff will be along to assist you shortly.'

Otto tried the handle.

It was locked.

'No problem,' said Sween cheerfully. He pulled two bits of bent wire out of his pocket and began fiddling with the keyhole while Otto sweated and jiggled beside him.

'Done it!'

The door swung open and they pushed each other inside.

The cupboard was packed with umbrellas. They hung densely from the ceiling and were stacked against the walls.

Carved handles. Jewelled handles. Gold and silver handles. And the umbrellas themselves striped, spotted and plain. Fringed. In some cases furry. There was just enough room for Otto and Sween to stand in the middle.

'*Shut it*,' hissed Otto. '*Quickly.*'

Sween shut the door, the lock clicked into place and everything was immediately totally dark. They didn't move.

'Can you see any switches or anything?'

'I can't see anything at all.'

'I thought you might be able to see in the dark or something.'

'No, no. Not me. That's just the lamp-eyes.'

'Well, there must be a trap door in the floor somewhere.'

They stamped.

'Sounds hollow,' said Sween.

They shuffled about, stamping. The floor sounded hollow all over.

Then the door handle rattled.

'Seems to be locked,' said a voice just outside. 'Definitely saw some kids sneaking in. Have you got the master keys?'

Tension mounted in the cupboard.

'Here's a switch!' cried Sween.

'SSSH!'

There was a click and the light came on. They both started frantically pulling umbrellas out of the way to search the walls. Clouds of dust. Now they started coughing.

'Thanks,' said the voice again. 'Here we are, must be one of these.'

The lock rattled.

The light switch was the only switch to be seen. Otto and Sween were floundering in a pile of umbrellas. The ones at the back were all incredibly old.

'What's that?' exclaimed Sween.

'What?'

The lock rattled again. 'Tut, tut,' said the voice. And then, more loudly, 'I know you're in there. We don't bother with the police here at Big Mo's. We've got our own ways of sorting out little problems like you.' The person speaking sounded about the same size and shape as a gorilla. 'And believe me, when I've finished with—'

'There, in your hand, look!'

Otto looked. He was holding a particularly ancient and ragged umbrella with a carved wooden handle in the shape of the head of a crate bird. On the top, where the crate bird's crest of feathers should have been, there was something that really did look like a switch. A green one.

'You don't really think—'

'JUST TRY!'

'. . . begging for the police,' concluded the voice.

Otto pressed the switch. There was a sudden sharp noise,

like bolts thudding into place. The lights went out. The whole cupboard shuddered. Then, with a tremendous grinding sound it began, unmistakably, to fall downwards.

'Stop grabbing on to me!'

'Well stop standing on ME!'

Without any doubt they were going somewhere.

'It's a lift!' yelled Otto, falling over.

They were speeding up. Surely they must be at the ground floor by now.

But they weren't going to the ground floor. They were going much further than that.

Faster and faster, rocking and lurching.

All around umbrellas were springing open dangerously by themselves.

And then, finally, they stopped suddenly and dramatically. Silence.

The light came back on. They had a moment to stare at each other.

The door had been left behind in the Rocking Horse Department. There was another door there now. Scratched, worn and painted with a faded tree. Before Otto had time to disentangle himself and stand up, it suddenly opened. Warm air rushed into their faces.

They were looking into a stone passageway. A worm lantern glimmered on the wall.

# In the Tunnels

A huge figure walked past with the swaying stride of the cavers, claws scratching on the floor.

'More than somewhat!' exclaimed Sween. 'Did you see that?'

'Caver, ancestor,' said Otto. 'Look like giant lizards. Walk, talk, live in SmokeStack, play billiards. Have been known to eat people.'

'Eat people!'

More footsteps and a rattle of wheels.

'Look, just keep your voice down,' muttered Otto. 'And don't say anything.'

Two men appeared, pushing a rack of clothes on wheels. Carnival costumes. Even the most Respectable Citizens buy their carnival costumes from the Karmidee.

'Honourable greetings,' said one of the men.

Otto raised his hat.

Sween opened his mouth and managed to shut it again in time.

They stepped into the passageway and Otto closed the door carefully behind them. Bolts snapped across somewhere. There was a loud grinding noise from the other side. The Lost Property Cupboard was going back to Big Mo's.

'Now,' whispered Otto, 'we're looking for a door marked HighNoon Hotel.'

'But that's an incredible long way!'

'Ssh!'

They started walking and the City rumbled above them.

Sometimes there were mosaics on the walls and floor. Sometimes paintings. In places initials and messages had been scratched on the stone.

They went past doors and gates with signs that made no sense to them. Drinking fountains. Benches. A stall selling ice cream. Stairs leading off here and there. Other passages leading downwards.

This passage, however, was going steadily uphill.

It was growing warmer.

Then, at last, after a very long time they found themselves walking on pictures of birds. And painted birds covered the walls. Not crate birds or the little birds that eat seed off window-sills. Eagles, kites, merlins. Birds like Caractacus.

'Somewhere here,' said Otto.

A door with carved birds all over it and a faint sign underneath.

## HighNoon Hotel
### Premises closed. Proprietors missing.

### Please do not enter until further notice.

'This is it, then,' said Otto.

# The Armadillo

And then they stared at each other in alarm.

Something was definitely coming towards them along the tunnel. They were close to a corner. Whatever it was it was about to scratch and clank and boom and echo into sight. It was an especially dark section of tunnel. Several of the worm lanterns appeared to be dozing.

The scratching grew louder. They moved close together.

Otto was in front and was the first to see the little armadillo. He accidentally jabbed Sween in the ribs with his elbow.

The armadillo's tail was caught in a trap which was dragging along the stone floor behind it. It was dirty and bloodstained but, despite the gloom, its back twinkled with sparks of rose-coloured light.

Sween immediately dropped his guitar case, leapt forward and grabbed hold of the trap. The armadillo skidded on to its side and curled up. It was clear that it was little more than a baby.

'Help me!' commanded Sween. 'Hold this bit.'

The trap was like iron teeth. Somehow, it seemed, the armadillo had managed to pull it out of the ground. But its tail was hurt; the teeth of the trap were locked almost shut, embedded, piercing its dainty shell, caked in blood.

Otto reached to touch it and it tried to drag itself along faster and began to make a horrible high squealing noise. He jumped back.

'Does it bite?'

'Grab the trap,' said Sween. 'And don't be skinking ridiculous.'

Otto, not reassured, did now manage to get hold of the trap, his fingers sliding in rust and blood.

Sween wrenched at the trap's jaws.

The armadillo screamed.

The trap didn't move.

'Don't let go, Hush,' said Sween.

He spat some curses, the jaws shifted, and there was just enough room for Otto to edge the armadillo's tail free. It turned round and he thought it was going to bite him for sure but he didn't let go, although he did scream.

'Don't hold it so tight,' said Sween. 'Put it down.'

The armadillo didn't go anywhere.

It looked at Otto with surprising eyes. Large, gentle and thoughtful.

He could clearly see something twinkling on its shell. Not even on it, no, not stuck on. Part of the shell itself. Chips of bright, glowing stone, all different sizes. The armadillo was surrounded by a haze of warm, pinkish light.

'This is what they look like,' whispered Sween. 'You know? TigerHouse armadillos. The ones at our place. The ones we've painted. Those are rubies. Very valuable. That's what we paint them for, to cover them up. People do very nasty things to get their hands on precious stones. Like setting these skinking traps, for instance.'

He wrapped a handkerchief thing round its injured tail and it curled a little way in his hands, holding all small paws in the air.

Otto stroked the armadillo's nose.

'Let's get out of here,' he said.

Sween unbuttoned his coat and the lining gleamed unexpectedly in the gloom. It was blue with silver clouds. He snuggled the armadillo inside against his chest.

Then Otto opened the carved door which would lead them to the HighNoon Hotel and they saw a flight of narrow steps winding upwards into the darkness.

Dense blue dust covered these steps. As they opened the door the draught lifted this dust and it swirled in the air, stinging their eyes, making them cough.

# The Handprints in the Cave

Not far away Caractacus and Mattie were standing in Marlene's rehearsal room. The cave underneath the Wool Shop. Mattie had only been allowed in there once, when she was very small. Marlene had been trying to find out whether Lumpy had inherited the Scream. Mattie couldn't remember much about what had happened. She did know, however, that she had not inherited anything of use or interest and had never been allowed into the cave again.

Now she gazed at the luminous blue stalactites hanging from the roof and the several pairs of jewelled ear-protectors, made from coiled stuffed snakes, which Marlene wore to protect herself from spontaneous vomiting should a Scream bounce back off the walls at too sharp an angle.

There were paintings everywhere, older no doubt than the City itself. They were faint. Green, black and orange against the blue rock. Mattie could just make out unicorns, crate birds, a dragon, some merpeople, several trees.

In one place, also faded and seemingly ancient, there were a number of small handprints.

'My mum and dad had this fixed up for my birthday,' said Caractacus. He was pointing at the handprints. 'It's a passage through to the hotel. So we didn't have to cross the road when we were small. It was our secret. Me and Rox. And we were the only ones who could open it. We did new ones each year, as we got, you know, bigger. This was a storeroom then.'

He put his palm against one of the prints.

Mattie jumped back.

A door swung open in the rock. It led to a narrow, low-roofed passageway. The right size for children.

'I didn't tell those other two,' said Caractacus. 'This is private stuff. Family.'

He uncovered a worm torch and Mattie stumbled behind him. The idea that she was being included in some sort of family affected her balance.

'Have you got your needles?' he asked. Of course she had, they were tucked into her belt.

'Just in case of problems,' he added. 'See if you can make it work too. This is one of Roxie's, the last one she did.' There was another collection of handprints, this time on the wall of the passage. He pointed to an orange one, slightly higher than the others.

Mattie put her own square palm on the print. Her fingers were shorter and broader than Caractacus'. Her hand was exactly the right size.

The door swung shut.

'Good,' said Caractacus.

He led the way and Mattie followed. The passage curved round to the right, under Pearly Needle Street, towards the HighNoon Hotel.

At the other end a spark of fear jumped silently between them.

They were right underneath the hotel now. The last place where Caractacus had seen his parents.

'You open it,' he said.

The door swung very slowly, with a long whispering creak.

Caractacus stepped into the darkness and Mattie saw the light of the worm torch tremble as he cast it around the walls of the cellar. She realized that they were both holding their breath.

Whatever Caractacus had feared he might find was not here.

The walls were lined with brick. There was a long wooden table in the middle of the room and what looked like an oil lamp hanging from the ceiling. The air was warm and dry. Various bottles and packets and so forth were lying around. There was a large wooden rocking horse.

'That's Roxie's,' said Caractacus quickly. 'She kept it here.'

He took a knife out of his coat, climbed on an unsteady chair, and was beginning to trim the lamp when Mattie, standing beside him, felt her hat tilt suddenly to one side.

She grabbed at it to stop it falling off.

Then she swallowed a yelp of surprise as something burrowed under the collar of her silver and black dress, wriggled rapidly down her sleeve and jumped off her hand on to the dusty table. Sounds of scuttling.

Of course, once Caractacus and Roxie were re-united they would both forget her. She reached into the darkness, sweeping the tabletop with her hand, making the little footprints go away, just for a few moments longer.

Caractacus, muttering, managed to light the lamp. Everything jumped into view and at that moment another door opened and in came Otto Hush and Sween Softly, coughing, sneezing and covered in cobwebs.

'Greetings,' said Sween. A strange little curled-up animal was peering out of his coat. It glittered. 'We found her near the door from the whatsit, the tunnel,' he announced. 'She needs love and attention.'

Otto was rubbing at his face with his scarf.

The same dust covered everything in the cellar.

'So have you got the ingredients?' asked Sween.

'Nothing has been touched,' said Caractacus. He glanced at the short flight of wooden steps which led up to a trap door in the ceiling.

'So how did you get in? Did you come through the hotel?'

'I need to concentrate,' said Caractacus coldly, reading the labels on bottles.

Sween frowned and began to stroke the armadillo. She uncurled a little, revealing a crimson, velvety stomach and four pink feet.

Mattie could see Roxie now. She was standing between two jars. She had something in her hair. A comb. Part of a comb. Mattie watched her. She knew that this was the last moment she would have Roxie for her secret own.

Roxie dug the comb into her hair and tugged so hard that she fell over.

She rolled right into the middle of the table under the oil lamp, a ball of rags and filthy lace, fighting with her hair, knocking into things, kicking her legs, waving her arms.

Everyone stared at her.

'It's her!' cried Otto.

At the side of everything, away from the pool of soft light, Mattie watched Caractacus hold out his hand, with his matted fingerless gloves and his wrecked fingernails.

She watched Roxie hobble on to his palm with the piece of comb still tangled into her hair. Saw him shake his head, disbelieving. Saw him touch Roxie's leather face and pull a lump of knotted hair away from her eyes.

Heard him say for the second time, 'Roxie, is it really you?'

# Small Becomes Bigger

Otto, Sween and the armadillo were sitting in the corner of the cellar on a great pile of sacks. These were not empty. They were full of wool, all ready, dyed and wound into balls.

There were more such sacks next to them. But these were very small. Extremely.

They knew more about the Bandits now. Caractacus had explained how he and Roxie had walked many miles along the Karmidee tunnels to a distant entrance on the edge of PasturesGreen. This was close to where the sheep dyed the wool, in strange, curved, wooden sheds which looked like upturned boats and were said to be as old as the City itself.

Roxie and Caractacus had shrunk the wool there and brought it back through the tunnels to the cellar. Sometimes they had made it big again there. On other occasions, daringly, they had made it big again at the last minute, in the street as close as possible to the customers' house. That way they could carry enough for many blankets hidden in their pockets. It was dangerous work and Carmichael had come close to catching them many times.

'But the people needed us,' explained Caractacus simply. 'And we couldn't let them down. Before we started smuggling, whole families were freezing because they couldn't afford enough clothes and blankets. Little kiddies getting sick. Normos, Karmidee. The cold isn't proud, she goes under any door.'

He was boiling a lump of raw wool in a little pan.

'Wool can shrink,' he said. He had been talking all the time since Roxie appeared. He frowned into the saucepan. And he added, as if this made everything obvious, 'And it can grow, of course. It grows on the sheep.'

Otto and Sween looked at each another.

'Is a sheep needed at this stage?' asked Sween.

Caractacus sighed like an adult and shook his head. Gently, because Roxie was sitting on it.

The saucepan continued to bubble.

Caractacus added grass seeds from the pocket of his coat. Then a number of other things from jamjars. Everything was covered in bluish dust.

'Stand back!' he said suddenly, pouring things through sieves back into his pan. There was an extraordinary smell. Sween and Otto began coughing.

'Of course, all these ingredients are so old . . .' He went to a tap on the wall and turned it on and there was a tremendous clanking and rusty water came out, full of bubbles. This went into the pan.

Perhaps he was about to do more. Certainly he had put some little bottles ready on the table. He had already explained that only a small amount of the mixture was needed.

But he didn't have time. Roxie, with a silent war cry, leapt off his head and jumped into the pan, sending up a great splash.

Everyone yelled. Purple steam belched out of the pan. Caractacus, still holding it, staggered and fell to his knees. It had become very heavy. Roxie had become heavy. She bounced up, steam hissing and roaring around her, and up and up. The pan was too small. She was standing in it.

It was stuck on her foot.

She gave a ferocious kick and it flew across the room, crashing against the wall, spilling the rest of the mixture.

She stood before them, dripping, steaming and grinning. All wrinkles and triumph.

# The Sinews of the Sky

Caractacus, who had stood up, suddenly fell forward again. Otto and Sween, right by him, caught him halfway. He was rigid. He raised his arms, beating at the air.

'It's him!' cried Roxie.

Caractacus seemed to be trying to walk. Perhaps to fly. Now he was grabbing at his neck. Glint of silver.

'Don't let him!' cried Roxie. 'Don't let him get his bird thing!'

Otto saw the familiar, the bird carved from blackglass, little emeralds for eyes. Caractacus had it clenched in his hand. Roxie jumped at him, wrenching at the chain.

'He's trying to make him change. Then we'll lose him! We'll lose him! Don't let him do it!'

Mattie stepped out of the dark and raised the pearly knitting needles.

Caractacus was crying out, the familiar was almost at his lips. He had kicked both Sween and Otto very hard on their legs. Roxie was swinging on his arms.

All this disappeared in smoke for a moment.

Mattie hadn't knitted Caractacus into a sack. Instead the little carved bird was now inside a strange woollen ball which was at least as big as his head. Tightly knitted. He was ripping at it with his fingers. No good.

Then he stopped.

Roxie helped him to sit down.

'He's gone now,' she whispered. And added, to Mattie, 'Fine knitting, niece child. You are a true Mook.'

Even the dim light could not conceal from the others that Mattie was blushing deeply and profoundly. In fact there was actually no shade of red in the entire Mook Family Wool Shop that was as red as she was at that moment.

Very slowly she held out the pearly needles.

'No, no, they're yours now,' said Roxie, waving her crabbed hand. 'You're blood of my blood. Bandit blood. You're a Bandit same as us.'

'Who's gone?' whispered Sween to Otto. 'What's happening?'

Roxie pointed at the ceiling.

'*He* was up there somewhere close. Looking for Caractacus he was. Hunting him down. Pulling on the sinews of the sky.'

'Pulling what?' said Sween.

'You know,' muttered Otto. 'Like clouds.'

'CLOUDS!' crowed Roxie. 'They ain't *clouds*. He's not interested in *clouds*. I'm speaking of the great and mysterious magneticals that wrap around the earth! Migrational magneticals that reach into a bird's heart, fill the mind with the music of the journeying, whisper to the soul! That's what he's tugging on—'

'Would someone please explain who he—'

'The Charmer,' said Caractacus softly, as if he was naming death itself, 'the Bird Charmer.'

# The Charmer and the Kite

Everything Roxie had said was true.

Not far above them the streets around the HighNoon Hotel were quiet in the cold of the evening. A wind, sly and biting, tried its strength against the scornful Pearly Oak.

From time to time the man known as Arkardy Firstborn stopped and ran his fingers through the frozen air.

He sent tiny, strange disturbances from his fingertips. Into the streams of magnetic energy that flow between the poles of the turning world, the invisible mystery which speaks to the birds and guides them on their long and ancient journeys.

Karmidee energy does not always stay in the confines of the body. And Mr Firstborn was a Karmidee.

A cloud of small birds surged silently above him. They

could not stop following as he went on down the hill, although they were dangerously far now from the safety of their roosting places.

He looked over the lights of the Boulevard and he called his lost captive for the last time. The merlin had been of immense value in the business of stealing small and valuable things.

Arkardy cursed softly.

But there were other, greater matters which needed his attention. He sent a different message from his fingers and a shape came swooping down over the rooftops.

The red kite.

From wingtip to wingtip he spanned Otto's height. His shadow fell like a piece of the dark sky. Soundlessly, he landed on the Charmer's shoulder.

They did not greet each other. Such things were unnecessary between them.

And very soon they turned off into unlit streets. They lived a secret life and did not wish to be seen.

# Sween and Otto Arrive at the Flat

'He doesn't want to go home tonight,' explained Otto. 'His dad's away and he keeps worrying—'

'The armadillos will be fine,' interrupted Sween in a rush. 'I always leave them plenty of water and stuff and they're very self-efficient. Except this one is hurt. I've got it in my coat.'

'Proficient,' said Otto.

Dolores was already wearing her carnival costume. Why? Perhaps she was trying it on to make sure it fitted all right. She always went as Midsummer Night, one of the Mountain Spirits, and her costume was in floating layers of green and gold. (Costumes are expensive and can be used for many years. Sometimes they are inherited.)

The mask was under her arm.

She stood back to let them into the flat. She smelt lovely. Otto led the way and Sween followed, blushing. There was a bag in the hall, packed tight and all done up. The twins sat next to it wearing all sorts of clothes.

'There's some sandwiches in the kitchen,' said Dolores. 'Please do make yourself at home, Sween.'

They seemed to have been eating sandwiches for every meal.

'Great, thanks,' said Sween, tripping over Otto.

'I thought you'd be back before this, Ottie,' said Dolores. 'It's very late.'

She sounded like someone in a play.

Otto looked in the kitchen, where there were a lot of sandwiches, far too many, even with a visitor.

Then he checked the bedrooms and the bathroom and finally the living room. All the weather maps and things were still spread out on the table. No sign of Albert then.

'This is so soft!' said Sween, sinking into the collapsing sofa. Sternism had not reached Parry Street yet.

'I'll get you something to eat,' mumbled Otto.

He went back to the kitchen to find Dolores putting on several scarves. She had covered up the costume with her thickest coat. He now noticed that she was also wearing a pair of very old boots.

'They're my strongest ones,' she said, when he pulled a face.

Two small, sad voices began to sing in the corridor.

'I'm going away, Ottie,' said Dolores. 'I've made a lot more sandwiches. There's peanut butter, peanut butter and pickle, bean curd and mustard, sardine—'

'GOING AWAY? WHERE?'

'I have to go.'

He stood still. He wanted to scream at the twins to shut up. Any minute now Sween would come through.

'Your father knows. He's coming back tonight. I want you to stay here with him.'

'But Mum—'

'I have to go, Ottie. It's very, very important.'

She suddenly pushed a chair out of her way, stretched out her arms and hugged him to her. He hugged her back.

'I love you,' she whispered.

Then she let go.

Sween came to the kitchen doorway and immediately went away again.

'But the twins—'

'I'm taking the twins, Ottie. But you stay with Dad.'

'Please, Mum—'

'It'll be all right—'

'*Please Mum*—'

Now she was twisting her hands together.

'I *must* do this, Otto, and you must *stay here*.'

She looked strange and fierce. His beautiful mother.

The twins had stopped their horrible singing. Everything was very quiet.

'I'll just finish getting them ready,' said Dolores.

Or something like that.

He was alone in the kitchen, everything broken, hollow with fear.

# In the Night

Much later he woke in the night. Sween had fallen asleep on the sofa and had a blanket over him. Otto himself was in a chair. Someone had put a blanket over him as well.

Albert was there, he was at the table. The lamp was on and he was reading. All those papers and things.

There was a tiny rattle from the floor and Otto looked down and saw the injured armadillo, all neatly bandaged, eating something off a saucer.

Otto knew that something very bad had happened. He wanted to speak to his father, although he felt very, very tired.

Albert turned a page. The paper rustled. Something else rustled too. Then Otto saw that there was a bird sitting on some books on the table by the lamp. It was a big bird. Albert reached out, without looking up from his reading, and stroked its chest.

He was silhouetted in the lamplight. The bird, which had a long sharp beak, was silhouetted too.

Otto wanted to say something. He wished Albert would turn round and see him. But all the time he was wanting and wishing he was falling back into a horrible sleep.

# Morning in Herschell Buildings

When he woke again it was morning.

Now he remembered immediately that Dolores had gone. She had taken the twins. She and Albert had stood by the front door not saying anything properly. Dolores had been crying most of the time, silently. The tears just came down her face and she ignored them.

Otto felt his stomach churn. His heart pounded as if some danger was circling the room.

Now he remembered that Sween had been there. Was here somewhere, presumably.

He sat up. Then he stood up.

Wondered whether the twins were awake. Remembered again that they were gone.

Some sort of conversation was going on in the kitchen. Low voices, one of them his father. A gentle clatter of china.

'. . . and the bacarolle,' said Sween.

'. . . and the pavanne and the dumka,' said Albert.

Sounds of pouring tea.

'. . . and the bergamasca and the bolero and the fandango and the gailliard.'

'Yes. And the unbearable power of the flamenco——'

'And the boogie-woogie and the birth of the cool . . .'

Otto stomped into this harmony of beautiful, unknown words.

Albert was dressed to go to work. A shadow in clothes.

Sween, of course, had slept in his.

'Sween's just telling me about the music he plays at his concerts,' said Albert.

'Your dad knows a lot about music,' said Sween.

'Has Mum phoned?' asked Otto.

Albert shook his head.

Sween picked up his mug of tea and walked quietly out of the room.

'So what are you going to do?' asked Otto.

'Well, no one can tell me anything about this mysterious person that Councillor Bliss claimed to know in the mud towns. The one who is going to help the Gorms to persuade the Karmidee to take the Cure. And I have investigated everything I can find about the weather.' Albert's voice was flat. As if he was reciting something. As if he no longer cared about the weather and his duty as the King. 'I've a feeling the answer might be right in front of us. Too familiar to see. I intend—'

'I MEANT what are you going to do about Mum and the twins?'

'*I know what you meant*,' said Albert.

Sween had started to play his guitar somewhere in the flat. Something very slow. A lullaby perhaps.

Otto and his father both stared at the things on the table.

A haze of colours began to spread around Albert. Karmidee energy. A sign of pain. Otto's energy had never manifested that way. He wished it would.

Right now everything was trapped in his chest. Feelings began exploding in there like firecrackers.

He picked up a cup and threw it across the kitchen. It smashed into a cupboard. Fragments of china ricocheted through the air.

The lullaby stopped.

Otto began to shake all over.

Albert, however, remained completely still.

Later, when Albert had gone to work, Sween made Otto something a bit like scrambled eggs, which Otto couldn't eat.

Otto phoned Granny and Grandpa Culpepper, hoping to speak to Dolores, but there was no reply.

The armadillo, who was now called Rosie, sat on Sween's shoulder.

'Have you got any other relations? Would she go to them?' asked Sween.

'My dad's parents live in TigerHouse,' said Otto. 'We never see them. My Grandfather Cornelius, my dad's father, won't have anything to do with us. He despises my dad for living in the City and being a librarian and talking like a Citizen and changing his name to Hush.' He paused, remembering the only time he had seen Cornelius. 'He's pretty scary. They call him Cornelius the Lion. I don't know if there's any other relations. I haven't met my grandmother. My dad hardly ever talks about any of it.'

'Albert the Quiet,' said Sween.

'She's taken her cat,' added Otto, walking from room to room now, opening cupboards. 'You don't understand. My mother's a widge. They have cats. Hers is called Wishtacka. Not all that friendly actually. Always has her nose in the air. Now why would Mum take Wishtacka if she's trying to get rid of the twins' Karmidee energy and everything?'

Otto had told Sween about the twins and how they had suddenly stopped flying and how it seemed that Dolores had given them something to stop them.

'I thought she wanted us all to be Respectable and Normal . . . that's why Dad's so upset, he thinks she's, you know, harmed them, sort of . . . It's very dangerous apparently . . .'

Otto stopped talking. The worst morning.

'Mothers are hard to understand,' said Sween. 'But she didn't seem to me to be the sort of person to do anything that might hurt her kids.'

'Not deliberately,' said Otto, miserably. 'She thought she was helping them, you see. To have a Normal life and good jobs and all that.'

They were standing in the corridor. Otto suddenly remembered something else.

'Last night, did you see a bird? Did my dad have a bird with him? At the table? A really, you know, big one?'

Sween shook his head. 'I didn't see any bird. I just saw your dad. He came and put a blanket over me.'

Otto suddenly flung the nearest door open, and stood, breathing hard, on the threshold of the living room. There was a shocked stillness and silence in there. The absence of his mother and sisters. The table was spread with papers and books. There was a pile of books by the lamp.

'There! It was sitting there! I saw it. He was working. And it was sitting there. And he, he . . .'

They examined the table. The tall windows, all closed.

Otto searched for feathers, scratches. The struggling radiator gulped and gurgled.

'You had a bad dream,' said Sween. 'I have loads of them.'

Otto went back to the table and stared at it.

'We should really go now,' added Sween. 'Or there'll be none left.'

They were going to try and buy carnival costumes to wear for the meeting with Arkardy Firstborn. It was very important.

Shouts from the outside made them both hurry to the window.

Yet another fog, freezing and wailing, was churning down Parry Street. It was full of flying chips of ice. They rattled on the windows like claws, like something evil, trying to get in.

# In Deux Visages

Sween and Otto struggled down the streets, using a large umbrella of Albert's as a shield. At last the fog began to roll back, leaving pools and puddles of watery ice starting to freeze on top of the snow. They found what would be the first of several tram stops. They were going to Deux Visages, near Cloudy Town, at the foot of the mountain called The Rainmaker.

The frightening weather and the food shortages were not going to stop the people of the City from celebrating their week-long Spring Carnival. Everyone goes to the carnival, even though many, many Respectable Citizens claim that they stay at home. Everyone must have a costume and the best costumes are magical and Impossible and are made by the Karmidee.

Citizens want to wear these wonderful costumes. But they do not want to be seen buying them.

They arrived in Deux Visages in the late afternoon. It was already going dark. They felt damp and squashed on the tram. When they got out they immediately felt cold as well.

Streetlamps on spiral posts glowed red in the twilight. The shop windows were brightly lit, many of them with candles. There were balconies and hanging signs and arcades leading out of sight, inviting and busy.

Traders wandered the pavements selling the new and popular hot-water bottle mittens, also scarves and boots and heated umbrellas (*Beat that troublesome build-up of ice. Taller hats may catch fire*).

'What now?' whispered Otto. Deux Visages had been Sween's idea. He remembered his father talking about getting a costume there the year before.

At that moment two members of the Normal Police, Mr Six and Mr Eight, came out of a nearby shop and started towards them down the snowy pavement.

Otto grabbed Sween's arm and backed him into the entrance to an arcade.

'What's the—'

'They know me. Really. They don't like me.'

Mr Six and Mr Eight had stopped in front of a sweet shop. Musical gobstoppers were at half price.

'Don't you know about them, Sween? DON'T run. They'll SEE us—'

'They're only Normal Police. The Gorms have let them out again, now that Mayor Crumb's not in control. They're supposed to stop anyone who looks like a Karmidee, give them educational leaflets—'

'Oh, screaming trees, Sween, they're *arresting* people, trying to keep them in the Muds, getting information about the snow jinxers, arresting people—'

'Calm *down*, Hush, you're usually so—'

Otto pulled Sween further back, out of sight. They banged into a number of shoppers, all so bandaged with scarves, only their eyes were showing.

Mr Six and Mr Eight, now sucking their gobstoppers, swung impressively out of the sweet shop.

Something strange happened to the people on the pavement. A space opened up around Mr Six and Mr Eight and travelled with them. Citizens walked into lampposts, blundered through piles of snow, were nearly hit by trams. All in badly failed attempts, it seemed, to make themselves inconspicuous.

Otto, despite the need to move, couldn't help stopping to watch in amazement. Respectable Normals behaving as if *they* were about to be arrested . . .

'That's why they're all wrapped up with their scarves over their faces,' whispered Sween. 'False beards, false ears, anything not to be recognized. They don't even want their friends to recognize them, let alone those Police whatsits. They're here for costumes. Same as us.'

There would still have been time for them to merge away into the crowd.

Then a handcart loaded with Spring Carnival presents skidded, fell on its side and sent a lot of things flying everywhere. The special dolls, sugar cherry blossom and musical boxes spilt among peoples' feet. Someone tripped over something. Then someone else tripped over something too.

A tram stopped, blocking the road.

It all happened very fast. Otto and Sween, ridiculously, were trapped by the contents of a gift shop.

Briefly, but not briefly enough.

Mr Six saw Otto, jumped at him and grabbed him by the arm.

'Hey yoosh!' he shouted. 'Haltsh!' He was shouting round his gobstopper, which was living up to its name.

'Itch himsh!' he explained to Mr Eight. 'Remembersh?'

The tram moved on, grinding through dirty snow.

'Howsh yoursh daddysh?' asked Mr Eight into Otto's face. His breath smelt terrible. Like some kind of sinister sweaty strawberries.

Otto felt his heart thumping like a hammer. He tried to pull a face at Sween, telling him to run. Then he'd turn his hat round. Or maybe just do that now. Nothing to lose. He took hold of the brim with his free hand—

However, Sween had no intention of running. He was a Child Prodigy. He had given concerts for the Mayor at the Town Hall, in the sparkling glass houses in the Winter Gardens and in the deluxe invitation-only tea rooms on the top floor of Banzee, Smith and Banzee. Rich people, and their ways, were very familiar to Sween.

'May I ask you what you are doing, my good man?' he asked, in a clear, ringing voice.

Otto let go of his hat for a moment.

'Thish ish the son of the librariansh whosh . . . SHRING! IING!'

Mr Six stopped. The musical gobstoppers had started to work and it was obvious why they were half price. Instead of the soothing noises usually produced they were making horrible shrill and ear-splitting shrieks. Especially ear-splitting for Mr Six and Mr Eight.

The heads of both Normal Police were visibly vibrating, like bells on top of alarm clocks. This caused them to jump into positions of alert readiness. Each looking in different directions up and down the street for the approaching enemy.

'Clearly there is some mistake here, which I am willing to overlook, Chief Inspector,' continued Sween, generously. He had to raise his voice because of the noise. 'I am Sween Softly, Child Prodigy. Perhaps you would be kind enough to let go of my cousin, Cesario VeryDosh.'

He opened his coat. There was a glimpse of the lining, the blue sky and the delicate, sunlit clouds. It didn't look like material at all. As he did so Rosie the armadillo climbed into view and sat on his shoulder.

Otto saw Mr Six's eyes widen. Reflecting the light of so many precious stones.

'My card, Commissioner,' said Sween, holding out one of Max Softly's Agency cards.

A small seabird flew out of the sky in his coat and wheeled up into the real sky, now dark, above the chaotic street.

At this point Mr Six experienced a moment of insight. Unusual for him. It led him to remove his gobstopper. He threw it into the gutter where it continued to shriek angrily by itself.

'Is that coat totally Respectable, sir?' he asked Sween, polite and doubtful at the same time.

'Absolutely,' Sween assured him. 'I'm sure my father could get you one, Senior Constable. Just write your telephone number on the card.'

Mr Six let go of Otto and produced a pen.

'Is it *lemon* flavour?' Otto yelled to Mr Eight. '*Lemon*'s my favourite.'

There was a startling crunch. Mr Eight had cracked his gobstopper in half and swallowed it. Terrible piercing sounds were coming from his stomach. Nevertheless he was still a professional on duty.

'Over there!' he cried to Mr Six, pointing at a man walking along with a unicorn. 'Impossible animal. Should be confined to the mud towns for its own safety! New Rule Number 17 Part B!'

The unicorn gleamed blue-black under the streetlights. It tossed the beautiful waves of its mane.

Mr Six and Mr Eight rushed to the opposite pavement, scattering shoppers.

'Oh no,' said Sween.

But as they watched the man and the unicorn changed. There was the man, there was the unicorn. Then, there was the man and there was a woman, looking rather shocked. She had long black hair. It was moving as if she had just been spinning around.

'More than somewhat,' breathed Sween.

There was a pause while they both stared across the street.

'You were pretty good yourself,' said Otto gruffly.

Sween continued to stare at the woman who had been a unicorn.

He didn't look at Otto. But he gave one of his clown smiles, crinkling the corners of his eyes.

# The Sign of the Cat

'So, er, where's the shop?' asked Otto.

They had walked briskly round a number of corners.

'It's not like that. No one will admit they're buying costumes, let alone look at windows full of them. And then you've got those two jokers, prowling around. They're multiples, aren't they? My dad told me about them. All the Mr Sixes know everything that happens to the other Mr Sixes. There's really only the two of them but they multiply together. Six eights are—'

'Forty-eight,' said Otto grimly.

'And then at night when they finish work there's just the two of them again, one Mr Six and one Mr Eight.'

'That's right. Karmidee doing dirty work for the Town Hall.'

'Anyway, the point is if we just stay still a moment someone will come and tell us. About where to get costumes. Somehow.'

They stayed still. Otto started shivering.

'Well, I don't—'

'Ssh!'

Two men collided nearby. Neither could see properly where they were going. They both jumped. They recognized each other.

'Good evening,' said the one with the enormous false moustache to the one who was wearing glasses which didn't seem to fit. 'I'm just looking for a, um, a *jigsaw* for my wife. I've heard they have excellent bargains up here.'

'So am I.'

'Such lovely Respectable little shops. She needs a *jigsaw*, you see, to occupy her during all this carnival rubbish. We never go, of course.'

'What carnival?' blurted the man with the glasses. 'I didn't know there was one.'

'Absolutely. My words exactly. What carnival? Absolutely. Exactly . . .'

Otto and Sween grinned in the shadows.

Twenty minutes later they were both nastily cold.

Then a man stopped next to them under a streetlamp. He lifted his foot as if to scrape something off his shoe.

Sween nudged Otto and they crept forward together.

There was a picture carved into the sole of his shoe. A cat's face.

Sween and Otto held their breath.

The man put his foot down. It seemed that his other shoe needed attention now. He lifted it up, brushing snow off with his hand.

There was a number there. Not easy to see.

The man had finished cleaning his shoes. They watched him walk slowly away. He stopped on a corner near a family who were loitering there. Then he began to clean his shoes again.

'I've got it!' said Sween. 'It's the Sign of the Cat, right, and the number 32. The Sign of the Cat at number 32!'

There were wooden signs hanging at intervals outside the shops in all the streets of Deux Visages. Some were cut out in the shapes of animals. Long ago, very few people had been able to read.

The Sign of the Cat was not far from where they were standing. There was no window beneath it. Only a door with a number.

'Well, there you are,' said Sween.

Otto knocked with his cold hand and the door opened at once.

They were in a neat shop, softly lit. Polished wooden floors.

A row of fitting rooms with gold-embroidered curtains. Large gilt-framed mirrors.

And oh the costumes. All along the walls. Not crammed together on racks but displayed like pictures. Like beautiful and strange and in some cases dangerous works of art. Which they were.

Otto and Sween stood close together.

Another customer was just leaving with a large parcel. He held up his hand to hide his face as he passed.

A woman in a grey velvet dress walked softly over to them. Her flawless skin was many shades darker than Dolores'. She wore a net of pearls over her hair.

'Can I help you, gentlemen?' she asked.

A Citizen. The accent of the Heights. Yet Otto had no doubt that the costumes she was selling were wildly Impossible.

He recognized the Ice King, blue and silver. A mixture of velvet and metal, sparkling with its own frost. The mask grave and aloof.

Next to it was Midsummer Night. He felt a pain tighten in his throat. Dolores had been wearing her Midsummer Night costume when she had said goodbye.

Except this one was far more beautiful than hers. It too was green and gold but blue butterflies spread their wings on the shoulders, flying up, shimmering, settling again.

'Midsummer Night is popular,' said the shopkeeper. 'And the price includes your own pool of moonlight which goes everywhere with you.'

At the mention of the word price Otto and Sween looked anxiously at each other. But the shopkeeper was all unhurried assurance. Encouraged by Sween's clothes. Also the stunning jewelled accessory on his shoulder.

The Midsummer Night costume and the Ice King were, of course, named after mountain spirits.

There were others.

SmokeStack, with its own drifting smoke and showers of sparks.

The Rainmaker, all shifting greys wound round with mist and rainbows. Real rainbows which striped the spotless floor and rippled on the wall like reflections on water. This was the costume, or some version of it, that Arkardy Firstborn would be wearing.

CrabFace. Desolation and rock. A faint mutter of thunder. The mask without expression and a worrying sign underneath. *Warning – Lightning Can Kill.*

Someone came out of one of the fitting rooms.

Sween, Otto and Rosie all gasped.

The person seemed to be made of flowers. Their mask was lost in petals. A number of hummingbirds hovered and circled around them. Sipped from the flowers. Hovered again.

The person walked over to a mirror. Even their hands seemed not to be hands. They seemed to be leafy and woven with tendrils.

'I'll take it,' said a woman's voice decisively.

The shopkeeper smiled. She walked over to the counter. Velvety slippers soundless.

'Say something,' Otto suggested quietly to Sween.

'In a minute,' muttered Sween.

They began to creep casually down the shop. Two confident customers who knew exactly how to behave.

'WOW!' burst out Sween. 'LOOK AT THAT!'

They looked.

'My dad always wears that one,' added Sween, reverently.

It was the Blue Hare. The spirit of BlueRemembered Mountain.

'Would you like to try this one, sir?' asked the shopkeeper.

A moment later they were in an Impossibly large fitting room. Rosie sat on Otto's head while Sween slipped off his beautifully tailored coat. The lining of sky and clouds briefly dazzled as he folded it up.

He wrapped the Blue Hare costume around him. On the hanger it had looked flimsy and shapeless and much too big, but once it touched his shoulders it began to change. The baggy sleeves seemed to close around his arms. The legs, which were very long, became exactly as long as his own.

And as he did up the buttons on the front they disappeared one by one.

Otto handed him the mask.

Sween had soft blue fur, frosted with silver. He had large ears. His eyes . . . or were they part of the mask? No they must be his eyes, because he was looking out of them, and blinking, but his eyes were so large, and set on the sides of his head.

'How do I look?' said Sween's voice, coming from somewhere.

He had long black whiskers, very delicate.

He took a step, turned and walked about.

Except he didn't walk. He hopped, or sort of walked and hopped. He moved with a sort of clumsy grace.

The way hares move.

Definitely his legs had got longer. Otto realized that they had not only got longer, they were a completely different shape. In fact Sween was a completely different shape all over. He was the shape of a hare.

Otto felt himself starting to sweat. There didn't seem to be enough air.

They went out of the fitting room. Sween swayed over to a mirror.

Once there he gave a cry of shock and leapt extremely high, banging his head on the ceiling. Then he sat still for a moment, twitching his nose.

'How much is it?' said someone. Sween, in fact.

The shopkeeper named a sum of money slightly larger than three months' wages for Albert Hush, Senior Librarian.

'Take it off,' whispered Otto.

'It's incredible, isn't it?' said Sween, doing a sort of twirl.

'*Take it off, Sween.*'

The shopkeeper pursed her lips. A delicate and fleeting frown disturbed the tranquillity of her face.

She selected another costume for Sween to try. It was slightly cheaper. It was a small dragon and was supposed to be fire-breathing, although that feature wasn't working very well. Dragons had been very popular the year before last.

When they heard the price Sween and Otto decided that it was too scaly.

The shopkeeper, now somewhat stony, offered to take Sween's coat in part exchange. She showed them a costume that might be within their means. It was a crate bird outfit that Otto suspected had previously belonged to a City Guide. One of the legs had darns in it.

Sween wouldn't part with his coat.

An hour after they had arrived they finally left the shop. They had one large package. It was the only costume they had been able to afford and both of them had to wear it at once. There was no money left.

The shopkeeper escorted them to the door, weaving

through the many other customers who had now arrived and had been waiting for them to make up their minds.

It turned out that her beauty wasn't real. Now that she was angry it had disappeared altogether.

They stood on the pavement and the cold rushed over and hugged them.

'How are the WoolBandits getting there?' asked Sween.

'The trams, I suppose,' said Otto vaguely. 'They said something about buying jackets, at least I think that's what they said . . .'

He was squinting nervously into the sky. The plan was to use the carpet now. It was just starting to snow again.

'Someone was coming to the shop today,' he added. 'Something to do with the floor. Roxie was very keen to meet them.'

The three WoolBandits were all coming to the meeting with Arkardy Firstborn. Caractacus was bringing the shrinking mixture, known as Small. Mattie and Roxie were determined to be bodyguards.

'So,' said Sween. 'This is it then.'

'Let's have a biscuit,' said Otto. 'I've got one left.'

He broke the biscuit in half, gave a piece to Sween and then casually squinted at the message.

# GOOD LUCK, DINKTOSH, AND DON'T BE DECEIVED.

'Do you know what Dinktosh means?' he asked Sween, trying not to look interested.

'Of course.'

'So what does it mean then?'

'Oh, you know, it's what a brother would call you. Sort of rude but, you know, sort of on your side.'

Otto made quite sure there were no more biscuits in the bag. Then he folded up the message and tucked it behind the shell on the brim of his hat.

They found a quiet square, away from the shops, and Otto unrolled the mat.

# Under the Stage

The Wastelands Arena was a temporary yet imposing affair, ringed with high fences. Marlene the Scream's concert would soon be starting. Crate birds, dogs and wolves had been leaving the area all afternoon. Children were not allowed.

This year the unexpected and relentless cold was a problem. Any sort of roof was out of the question. The consequences of a confined Scream would not be covered by insurance. Instead six hundred heated umbrellas were available for the audience to use at their own risk.

Melchior Mook, in a luminous blue costume and wearing a badge saying 'Manager', rushed around organizing and annoying the large, silent Security Guards (hired from Snoop and Swoop), the conspicuous medical support teams and the people pushing the trolleys selling hot-water bottles.

All these personnel wore full carnival costumes, including masks. The medical support teams were dressed as skeletons. Their masks were skulls.

Gradually the Arena became crowded. Groups of persons who had positioned themselves close to the stage, laughing and making loud jokes, fell silent.

Some people decided that they wanted to be near the back after all. In some places the back became very crowded. Meanwhile everyone kept glancing at the stage and straightening their masks. It was tense.

It was also tense *under* the stage. The time had finally come to meet Arkardy Firstborn.

Otto, Sween and the WoolBandits were just behind the painted canvas panels that hung down at the front. They could see out through the narrow slits between them.

Despite the snow and ice outside Otto felt very hot. This was because he was inside his carnival costume. This costume, much to Roxie's delight, was the back of something called a pantomime camel.

Sween was the front.

There was nothing Impossible about this costume. It was old, heavy and enormous and involved a very large number of buttons.

The hump, which was Otto's responsibility, kept slipping to one side. When this happened the whole camel lurched after it.

The head, neck and front legs now contained Sween and, predictable but uncomfortable, his guitar case. He was looking out of one of the camel's nostrils. The eyes could revolve and blink. It was all a question of pulling the right string.

'You two were supposed to be looking majestical,' said Roxie. 'The bee's knees, you were going to be—'

'We couldn't AFFORD IT,' said Otto. He had to shout. No one could hear him otherwise.

'We offered,' continued Roxie, gleefully. 'But oh nose. We offered to knit something but oh no indeedy, you wanted—'

'ALL RIGHT!' yelled Sween. Very loud from Otto's perspective.

Roxie and Mattie were wearing tree costumes. Small trees with lots of branches. They had knitted them themselves, of course, and Otto had to agree that they were very good. Light and functional. Formidable. Also, a hint of mystery created by the fact that other people couldn't tell which way they were facing.

Caractacus wore a simple, expressionless grey mask and his usual long dark coat. The string was gone from around the waist. He had a habit sometimes of being very still and quiet. He was being them now.

'Do you think he'll show up?' asked Sween. 'Do you really think he'll have my family? And the photographs and everything?' Lowering his voice so that it stayed in the privacy of the camel.

'Yes,' said Otto.

'It was on the radio again this morning – Bargain Hunters this, Bargain Hunters that—'

'He'll bring them. He wants the shrinking stuff.'

'And Caractacus has really got the stuff?'

'Yes,' said Otto.

'You think that's it's really the real stuff?'

'Relax,' said Otto. Tensely.

Marlene the Scream, glittering and terrible, was coming down the Arena towards them. Her audience shrank from her as she passed. The paramedics and the Security Guards hurriedly put on their ear protectors.

She grew bigger and bigger and then disappeared. Now she was climbing the steps on to the stage.

Otto looked round through the spyholes in the other side of the hump, checking the way they had come in, which was now their escape route. They had left the canvas folded back.

Someone had arrived. A tall person. Fantastically dressed in a costly and thoroughly Impossible costume. The Rainmaker. Partially hidden by mist.

'I think he's here,' whispered Otto, nudging Sween.

The Rainmaker wore the traditional mask. Benign, very slightly smiling. His thoughts on finding a shrubbery and a camel among those waiting for him could only be guessed.

He bowed, shimmering with rainbows.

'I have come here to meet someone,' he said. Or possibly shouted. 'I have some items of value to them which I wish to exchange.'

The gentle mask face turned. Taking them all in.

'He hasn't got the basket,' hissed Sween.

The Rainmaker swept one arm from under the storm cloud of his cloak.

He held out his hand. An envelope.

The camel swayed forwards. Sween stuck his hand out of one of the ears.

He took the envelope, dragged it back in and handed it, very crumpled, to Otto.

Otto opened it, staggering and wriggling, trying to hold it near a spyhole to get some light. It was the photograph. And some others too. And some negatives.

'It's them,' he whispered.

'My confederate will be here with the other items, as soon as I have witnessed the process,' said The Rainmaker.

'Let us proceed,' said Sween, all elegance.

Otto sneezed violently.

Sween had been willing to use Rosie to demonstrate the

Small. However the Bandits, especially Roxie, had insisted that they would bring a rat from HighNoon. Roxie, apparently, had a number of friends who were rats.

'*My* confederate will now demonstrate,' said the front of the camel grandly.

Sounds of someone blowing their nose from the hump.

Caractacus stepped forward, produced a velvet bag from inside his coat, unfastened it and tipped the contents on to the ground.

Both ends of the camel yelped in surprise.

There were no rats in the bag. Instead there was a tiny man and a tiny woman. They were wearing blue overalls with City Rodent Removal embroidered across the back.

They wandered in dazed circles.

Caractacus held up a small bottle of blue liquid and sprinkled the City employees with a few drops.

Immediately they began to grow. Bewildered, hanging on to each other, they expanded both upwards and sideways.

The Rainmaker stepped towards them.

The shrubbery flexed its branches menacingly.

Caractacus waving another bottle, flicking drops of purple liquid.

Before they had time to do anything sensible, like run away, the man and the woman began to shrink again, yelling horribly for help.

The shrubbery stamped and cheered.

Smaller and smaller. The yells also smaller.

Until they could not be heard.

'Surely he's not going to leave them like that—' hissed Otto to Sween.

But Sween was too desperate to care. And the rodent removal operatives didn't wait to find out. They ran, rat-sized and holding hands, across the freezing ground and out under the canvas wall of the stage.

'He hasn't got them,' whispered Sween. 'He hasn't—'

And then Arkardy was seen to remove a glove and, with his hand newly freed, he stretched up and plucked at the air.

Caractacus staggered. But the summons was not for him. In an instant a great rust-red bird burst in upon them all. The wicker basket swinging like prey in its grasp.

The bird lowered the basket to the ground.

Sween, necessarily followed by Otto, stumbling, rushed forward and knelt down causing Otto to fall sideways, almost twisting the camel in two. Sween lifted the lid of the basket, and Otto, now kicking about on his side, managed a glimpse of the cake decorations, all tiny indignation, swarming about over the rim.

At a sign from Sween, Caractacus gave Arkardy the second bottle.

All would have been well.

Marlene always opened her concerts with a long, nerve-racking warm-up phase. That was now finished. Up above them, in the centre of the stage, she began her Scream.

It hit Otto somewhere just above the navel.

He struggled to get his hands free to try and block his ears. He felt his sternum and ribs start to vibrate. A new and terrible sensation. All his other bones joined in almost at once.

He and Sween both lurched to their feet. The whole stage was shaking.

Arkardy Firstborn, with the red kite on his shoulder, was silhouetted against the opening in the canvas. He, too, had his hands over his ears.

The Scream was now indescribably appalling. Otto's teeth were chattering. His hair was standing on end. His eyelids were stuck at open.

There were lots of other sounds. Splintering and crashings. Creaking. Rending. Human screams from the auditorium. The whole stage was leaning to one side.

The stage was breaking.

Arkardy stepped sideways out of sight.

They all tried to follow him outside.

Caractacus went first. Then Roxie and Mattie, sideways, with Sween, his arm stuck out of the camel's ear clutching his basket of relatives, and finally Otto, who had just been sick inside the hump, being dragged along, urgently trying to de-camel.

Marlene continued the Scream. It wasn't the first time a stage had fractured. She kept her balance and simply climbed to the highest point of the wreckage. The audience lay flattened and splattered in front of her like a field of wheat in a storm.

Then suddenly she stopped. She always ended the performance abruptly.

She stepped daintily down into the Arena and swept off, shimmering, shaking hands here and there with persons able to move.

All this could clearly be seen by Otto, now staggering about in the fresh, freezing air behind the crumpled remains of the stage. There was frenzied action all around him. Caractacus had sprinkled the Bargain Hunters with Big. Handsome Max was hugging his son. Roxie and Mattie were lost in a cloud of smoke, knitting costumes for the newly enlarged.

Arkardy Firstborn was there too.

A little distance away. Unnoticed by the others.

His mask was at an angle. Probably something to do with trying to block his ears. Hurried and clumsy, he took it off to straighten it. No one chooses to be seen without a mask at a carnival.

There was just enough time for Otto to see his face.

The Arena, on the Wasteland, was on the edge of the carnival itself.

Stalls, rides, acrobats, dancers, bands and bonfires stretched in all directions. Back into the City. On into the mud towns.

The sky was lit with fireworks. Everything was beginning.

Caractacus walked over to where Otto was standing.

'Are you all right?' he asked.

Otto stared at him. Then back at Mr Firstborn. Who had gone.

'Are you all right?' asked Caractacus again. Softly.

'I've got to go,' said Otto.

He looked back at Sween, the Bargain Hunters. At all of them.

Then he turned away, walking. Then he started to run. Into the crowds.

No direction.

Faster and faster.

He had seen Arkardy Firstborn clearly.

Arkardy Firstborn was Albert.

# Into TigerHouse

Otto Hush was invincible, unstoppable, he ran like a wolf, a tiger, tireless, nameless. On and on and on through the crowds.

A face among thousands of masks, alone.

Glimpsed for a moment, running on, forgotten.

Now he was going down some sort of track between wooden houses.

He was in TigerHouse. He had been here on the mat to visit Mab. But she had always come to meet him.

Not tonight.

Now he could see the frozen river. People skating.

The sky was ruthless. The moon like a scream between the clouds.

He would never go home.

There was no home.

Stopping finally, doubled over, gasping for breath, he saw the dark shape of a bird against a snow-covered rooftop.

The red kite?

He moved on and the bird wheeled. He looked back and knew that it was following him.

'I can see you, skinking scavenger!' he shouted.

He remembered the bird he had seen in his home, *in his home* in Parry Street. The bird that had watched from the pile of books while Albert had sat working.

Some people banged into him, their arms linked. They were all wearing cat costumes. 'Ooo-EE!' they cooed, leaning over him. 'No mask, my dears. No *costume*, how *daring*, how *naked*—'

Otto pushed past them.

The bird kept its distance.

'Go back to him!' yelled Otto. 'Keep him!'

The crowd surged and dragged. He almost fell over.

'Are you on your own, green eyes?' whispered someone, very close by. 'Cover your face. Cover your face.'

He was lost. Which was fine. He had just enough interest in his own welfare to turn his collar up and pull his hat down.

He climbed down towards the river. He had noticed an island. There didn't seem to be much happening there.

# On Rose Island

He skidded and stumbled and ended up half walking, half skating, hunched over.

He scrambled up the bank, through thick snow and frozen undergrowth, and came into a small forest.

There were lanterns here too.

But only round the edge. Further in among the trees he saw a painted sign. A picture of a unicorn's head with a broken horn. Otto happened to know that this was a Karmidee symbol meaning DANGER – KEEP OUT.

He didn't even have time to get his breath back.

There was tremendous crashing and crunching. A massive figure was looming and swaying towards him, waving a worm torch.

He backed against a tree and pulled the brim of his hat down three times.

The person stopped. He hadn't noticed Otto yet. He took off his mask and wiped his face.

It was Councillor Bliss, who had recently made himself Mayor and was leader of the Guardians of the Normal, also known as the Gorms.

He was wearing an elaborate, Impossible chocolate-cake costume. A real chocolate cake.

'Hello,' he exclaimed suddenly, delighted with something or other. 'What a splendid mask. I didn't know they were making any like that.'

He shone his worm torch full into Otto's face.

Otto, of course, was not wearing a mask.

'How very flattering,' crooned Councillor Bliss. 'But no costume, how very unusual.' He smelt of bloodberry concentrate. It was making his face blur. A common side effect.

'It looks exactly like me. Exactly. It's even got the spot on my nose, and that only came up this morning. Incredible. I was going to use the pimple-popping powder but the neighbours keep complaining.'

He had bent down. The nose in question was almost touching Otto's. Councillor Bliss belched. Otto was nearly sick.

'Incredible,' repeated Councillor Bliss fondly. 'Splendid. A mask of my face already for sale. And I haven't even got rid of Crumb yet.'

He broke off a piece of his icing and handed it to Otto. Then he almost fell over. He was very, very dazed-out indeed.

'Just checking on my little property,' he confided, as if they were old friends.

Otto at last understood what was special about the hat his grandmother had so wisely given him. 'Who are you looking at?' it said on the lining.

Good question. Themselves. When people looked at him, that's what they saw. Their own faces. Looking back at them. Right now Councillor Bliss thought Otto was wearing a Councillor Bliss carnival mask. Of all things.

Otto was just working out how to wander away, because Councillor Bliss was not good company, when something stopped him.

The Councillor seemed to have a pocket in the cake. He was trying to pull something out. Something that was stuck. It was an armadillo like Rosie. But not quite like Rosie.

This one did not have rubies on its shell.

Instead, in the wavering light of the worm torch, Otto clearly saw that there had been rubies there, or stones of some sort, and they had been gouged out.

One of the wounds still bled. Others had partly dried into

weeping scabs. Councillor Bliss started giggling. He tried to speak through his giggles. He clamped his hand on to Otto's shoulder.

'Rock nibblers . . . rubies here . . . they've found them . . . must have been some sort of fall in the old mine . . . right under where we're standing . . . opened it up . . . old name for this dump is Rose Island . . . understand?'

Otto understood.

'This place has been given to me personally for me myself for my own,' added Councillor Bliss. 'I come down here whenever I like. The magicos leave me to it. Stay away completely . . .'

Well they would, thought Otto, they can understand the unicorn sign. The ground could probably collapse at any minute.

The good Councillor nodded his head solemnly, at nothing it seemed, and tapped the armadillo, who screamed.

What next?

But Councillor Bliss apparently had places to go. He let go of Otto. Then, slowly, he held out the armadillo, now crying quietly. Cake crumbs showered the snow.

'Got to meet some friends,' he said, running all the words together. 'Love the mask you have this few more bits if you dig around. They make horrible noise budizworthit.'

Otto clutched the armadillo under his coat.

Councillor Crumb slid slowly sideways and then set off through the trees, banging into most of the ones along the path.

# On the Ice

Otto was trying to climb back down the bank. Now, still clutching the armadillo, he was shooting out across the ice, spinning on his back. The clasp of his bag sprang open, the crystal communicator bounced out, reflecting lantern light. He struggled to his feet, caught it.

Too late.

'Now *that*,' said someone, 'is *nice*.'

A person in the costume of the Blue Hare. Not the gorgeous Blue Hare that Sween had become. A horrible joke Blue Hare, with great curved yellow teeth, matted stained fur. And a tar flare, burning and dripping, held over Otto's upturned face.

The hare's other paw was clamped around the collar of Otto's coat.

'I really don't think you should be here with nothing on your face,' said the hare. 'And where's your costume? Are you trying to attract attention?'

It blinked its red, glowing eyes. 'I'd really like that shiny thing.'

Otto held the communicator in one hand. His other remained clamped on his chest. He could feel the armadillo's heart beating.

'And what's so special inside your coat?'

Skaters were crashing together. Dazed-out. Not looking. Anything could happen now.

A spark fell off the torch on to Otto's hair and there was a fizzing sound and a terrifying smell.

'Tut, tut—' murmured the hare.

And then, as Otto began to scream and struggle, something came skimming across the ice, scattering everyone. Something white and streaming and full of fury.

This thing hit the hare with great force, knocking its big back legs right out from under it. The hare crashed down on its side, letting go of Otto. The torch flew through the air. The thing spun round, eyes blazing.

'Stay away from him, Demetrius, or you know what'll happen,' said the thing. An unexpected whisper, full of contempt.

The hare heaved itself up on to all four paws and stared out of its nasty eyes for a moment. But then it turned and loped slowly away.

Otto, who had fallen yet again, decided to remain seated.

'Hello, Citizen Hush,' said Mab.

# Under the Moon

Although he was in the form of a merlin, Caractacus felt the cold that had crept so deep into the heart of the stilt houses. Dammerung, even in their creature form, are still partly human. And Caractacus, as a human, disliked the cold.

He had left the rejoicing Softly family and Mattie and Roxie and he had followed Otto through the crowds. Otto, he knew, was in some sort of pain.

He saw him climb on to the island. Waited. Saw him come crashing out, flightless and clumsy, making a fool of himself on the scratched glass of the river.

Then something big had attacked Otto and Caractacus had been lining up to dive. But someone else, a long-haired girl, had saved Otto first.

Caractacus followed them as they hurried through the narrow streets. They reached a house further down the river and went inside.

And even though he was cold Caractacus stayed a while longer. Sometimes resting on the frozen rooftop. Sometimes circling, scanning for danger. Gliding under the moon.

.

# At Mab's House

'I don't believe it,' said Mab, through the steam from her mug of raspberry reviver.

Wood cracked in the stove. The injured armadillo dozed quietly, swathed in antiseptic bandages.

'Well, it's true,' said Otto. 'I saw him. It was my dad all right. And it all makes sense. He's got this other name, Arkardy Firstborn, and he's going to go and start a new life, just like he put in the letter to Sween. Think what you could do with that shrinking stuff. Make yourself tiny. No one would ever find you, never ever, ever . . .'

Outside, the carnival surged and roared and sang and drummed around the streets and jetties.

Mab's plain, oval mask was still slung around her neck.

She had slipped it off her face so that her cousin Demetrius would recognize her at once. She wore a blue and brown dress and necklaces of velvet leaves, the Forest Spirit costume.

'He always goes as the Blue Hare in that horrible outfit,' she had told Otto. 'That was my uncle's, I believe. He was a thief too.' She blushed. 'But he was scared of my gran. And so is Dem. A lot of people are. Even these days.'

Otto knew now, because Mab had told him, that her grandmother was in the hospital, here in TigerHouse. The one which the Bargain Hunters had built and which might be saved after all, now that Max Softly and his family were no longer tiny and working as cake decorations. Now that they might start Bargain Hunting all over again.

Mab poured yet more tea.

'And I don't believe your mam would dose the twins up with the Cure like you said either.'

'But you believe me about Brother Bliss, the extremely dazed-out chocolate cake, who believes that he owns a collapsing ruby mine—'

'I believe in Bliss and I believe in his secret mine, although I can't imagine why he thinks he owns something right in the middle of TigerHouse. And I believe in those skinking Gorms. They've been here for the last week, handing out their evil Cure. Did you see the posters? "You too can be

Normal. The Guardians of the Normal Party will provide medicine to drain and contain your magical energy. Free of charge." Some people are taking it too.'

She caught his eye. 'There's a reason . . .'

Otto sipped the tea.

He looked around the warm room. The floor was bare except for the shabby cushions they were sitting on and the low table. The walls were covered in pictures of figures, all painted straight on to the wood.

'They're taking it even though everyone knows it's dangerous,' said Mab suddenly. 'They're taking it because they think we're coming to the end.'

Otto had realized that the people on the wall opposite were all mountain spirits. CrabFace. TumbleMan. The Rainmaker. And here, holding hands, Midsummer Night and the Ice King. She was all in green and gold and he was in blue and silver.

Looking at them like that, side by side, where had he seen those colours before? That was it. The Wool Shop. And what had Mattie said? 'They are only sold together. At this time of year.'

'Did you hear me, up there in your palace in Parry Street?' asked Mab, suddenly harsh. 'The Karmidee, your people, believe that it will soon be finished for us here. That's why they're all being so wild.' She nodded towards the noise of the carnival. 'Nothing left, nothing to lose.'

'Because of the Gorms, the Cure—'

'No, no, you stupid idiot, because of the weather. The Citizens are all upset. Rushing around. Talking rubbish about snow jinxers. Shooting at people on mats. Stocking up with extra dinners. But they can leave. If they all decided to go, even Araminta's Gates wouldn't hold them. They can go to the Outside. It wouldn't be what they expect but they can probably live there. They are Normal. But the Karmidee . . .'

Otto put down his comforting cup of tea.

'The Karmidee have nowhere to go,' she whispered. 'The Outside is dangerous for us. Hospitals, freak shows, prisons, laboratories. People trying to use us as weapons. That's why we built this City in the first place . . .'

She paused.

'You know what they're saying?'

He shook his head.

She was smiling a grown-up, weary smile.

'People are saying that he's angry.' She pointed at the pictures on the wall. Otto realized that she meant the Ice King.

'You mean the spirit of the mountain?'

'Maybe, whatever that means. There are stories about them. All of them. Maybe they're named after the mountains, or maybe the mountains are named after them, whoever they are. People are saying that something has gone wrong and he can't find her. He's angry and sad. Maybe he will never find her again. And they should be together now, you see. This is the beginning of their time. When the trees throw their blossom. These are their dancing days.'

'What the skink are you talking about? Mountains dancing?' She rolled her eyes.

'No. I just said, maybe *they* are named after the mountains. Or maybe the mountains are named after them. They're in stories. You people do have stories, don't you?'

Otto stared at the pictures on the wall and frowned.

'I didn't say it made sense,' said Mab.

He looked down into his tea.

'Also, I don't believe for one minute that your dad would threaten to get the Bargain Hunters arrested, or plan to run away and start a new life, or whatever you're thinking,' she added, practical and stern again. 'He wouldn't leave you and hc wouldn't leave his people. Even if he couldn't do anything to help them.'

'Perhaps that's why he's running away,' said Otto, still staring into the tea. 'Because he can't save them this time. And he can't bear that.'

'Not them, Otto,' said Mab. 'Us.'

# The Secret of the Dancers

The music outside was very loud now.

'When he was talking about the weather once my dad said he thought the answer was probably all around us. We've just forgotten what it looks like,' said Otto. Although speaking of his father was terrible.

Was Mab even listening? She was tapping her foot on the floor.

Fireworks lit up the window. He waited, feeling very tired, to see if she had anything to say.

Suddenly she jumped up, clutching blankets around her.

'Let's stop breaking our hearts!' she exclaimed, lamp-eyes glowing. 'Get up! We're going dancing!'

Absolutely not. 'I don't think—'

But she had grabbed up her mask. Now she was scrabbling in a cupboard. Oh no. She had found another one. And a black-embroidered cloak, the Sleeping Prince costume. For him.

'Everyone dances after midnight. And anyway, your mother is a dancing teacher so it's in your blood.'

She unbolted the heavy door and freezing air blasted into their faces. There was a grinding sound as she lowered the ladder, into the music and colour and chaos below.

He put on the cloak and mask.

Exhausted, he followed her.

Mab had told him that she had fallen, something to do with a tree, and hurt her leg and the side of her face. She ran unevenly but it was still hard to keep up.

Round several corners, right through the middle of a crowd wearing firework hats, across a bridge and they were there, on the edge of one of the stilt platforms over the river.

He stood next to her, out of breath.

Musicians with flutes and pipes and small drums bobbed and swayed under a giant umbrella, fringed with icicles.

Lines of dancers, each facing a partner, were beginning the stately, gracious dance called the pavanne.

'Go on, join on there,' said Mab in his ear. 'Opposite me. You know this one, don't you?'

She took her place, and Otto, who did not know this one, or any one, took his.

Everybody bowed, Mab bowed, Otto bowed and his hat fell off.

Up and down the courtyard, animals, birds, giants, troll-trees, mountain spirits and various types of food began to sail towards their partners holding out hands, paws, wings and things.

Otto fixed on Mab. Whatever she did, he did too. Like a mirror.

Now someone else was joining the musicians.

This person was dressed as a patch of night sky, invisible in a blue-black absence and clouds of twinkling stars.

The music stopped. Otto retrieved his hat.

Then the skinking business immediately started all over again.

A different tune.

After a while Mab waved her arms.

Otto waved too.

She waved again, pointing her fingers, bouncing up and down. No one else was doing all this, nevertheless he tried to copy her. She waved again, hopping on her good leg, he waved, he hopped and she rushed at him and grabbed his arm and hissed, 'Listen, it's the music from your clock thing!'

The singer suddenly threw his voice up into the ruthless dark. High, eerie and wild.

A number of the dancers joined in, in various keys, a few notes behind. They were singing words unrepeatable here, which didn't fit the tune properly but which meant they kept laughing very loudly.

The singer's voice dipped and soared. He knew other, much older words. Otto tried to hear them.

> 'Fingertip to fingertip
> Palm to palm we meet
> And green the bud and green the shoot
> And something blossom sweet
> The ice and sun will join as one
> When palm to palm are we
> The something brings the something spring
> Beneath the blossom tree.'

Mab was dragging him to the edge of the dancers. She pulled off her mask.

'*Listen to the words.*'

Otto listened. There weren't many. The singer had gone back to the beginning already.

'It's them. They're the *real ones. The two people on your clock thing.* You know. What I said about the stories about them dancing and he's angry and she's not there and—'

'The Ice King? Midsummer Night?'

'Yes, Mr Brain. They really exist. They're the people on your clock. And someone has tied that stuff round the rail to *stop them*—'

'You mean—'

'To stop them from meeting! They're supposed to meet. They're supposed to dance. And they can't. And that's why the spring hasn't come.'

'You mean the clock controls the weather?'

She nodded, the beams from her eyes dancing across his face. 'So let's go and find your dad—'

'I'M NOT GOING ANYWHERE NEAR MY DAD—'

'OK, OK, FINE,' screamed Mab. 'WE'LL GO IN THE MORNING AND WE'LL MEND THAT SKINKING CLOCK OURSELVES!'

# The WoolBandits at Home

Roxie Mook had collected a great many tiny fragments of gold from under the wooden floors of HighNoon during her decades among the rats. She also had a number of rings, a small bag of diamonds and some jewelled hatpins.

It had been a very busy night at the Wool Shop.

Roxie and Mattie had visited gold and gem dealers (they often work at night in HighNoon). They had also visited the Mook family solicitor (who pretended that she had been asleep but had, in fact, just come home from the carnival).

The Wool Shop had been left to Roxie by her parents and, according to the laws of property in the City of Trees, it had continued to be in her name ever since. It is accepted in the City, although not spoken about, that adventures can happen to even the most Respectable of persons, even adventures which last for sixty years.

A locksmith had been summoned through the snow to change all the locks.

Now the WoolBandits were sitting in the parlour having breakfast. Marlene's dustsheets had gone. So had her furniture. The Bandits were sitting on new chairs, very soft, in Turquoise Ocean, Snake-eye Jade and Cosy Rose.

All Marlene and Melchior's possessions were piled up outside in the snow. The dustbin was full of frozen broccoli sandwiches.

'It's a matter of honour,' said Caractacus. 'He saved my life in the Amaze. He is in some sort of trouble.' He lowered his voice. 'When he spoke of the man's face—'

'We knows—' said Roxie.

'Whoever this man was, when he saw him it was as if he was pierced to the heart. He did not return to his home. He ran deep into TigerHouse. At one point he was attacked—'

'We knows—' said Roxie.

'Someone helped him. She took him in. They seemed to be friends—'

'So he's safe,' growled Roxie.

'Yes. No. I don't know. I would like to be sure.'

'But could we find him?' asked Mattie. Making the others jump.

A pause.

'I can find anyone,' said Caractacus quietly. 'Anyone that moves.'

And the Bandits fell silent. Reminded of the two people Caractacus had lost, and that he might never find again.

'Do you want to be hunting round some more in there, with us with you this time?' asked Roxie. Caractacus had chosen to go into the HighNoon Hotel alone. He shook his head.

The fire crackled.

'Well,' said Roxie, cheering up, 'I suppose we'll be utilizing those flying jackets again, that clever Mattie has made so dextricus.'

# Skull

Soon it would be dawn.

A grey wolf with dark markings around his eyes came down from the Heights and crossed the southern end of the Boulevard. Steady, swift.

On into streets of unlit shops, curtained windows, squares piled with glittering drifts of snow. Street after street. Square after square.

Now through districts where dancers were still wandering home.

Now, again, through silent places.

He reached the edge of the Wasteland as the pale sun washed the rooftops behind him. Then he stopped.

His name was SkullFace and he was a friend of Albert the

Quiet. He was hunting for someone. Someone Albert needed desperately to find.

Skull raised his muzzle, searching the wind.

# Albert Arrives at Mab's

Otto was sleeping on a pile of blankets on the floor.

The light didn't wake him. Nor did it wake Mab on her bed in the next room.

TigerHouse murmured around them.

Then there were voices raised, outside. Some sort of commotion. Very near the house.

Then a rap on the door. This sound was loud and insistent. It could not be ignored.

Otto opened his eyes. Mab was already in the doorway to the bedroom, staring at him, frightened.

Rap, rap, rap on the door.

She had wrapped herself in a blanket.

He stood up. For the second night running he had

slept in his clothes.

'Open this door,' shouted a hoarse voice.

Mab had crept to the window. It was small and high. She stood on tiptoes, looking sideways from behind the curtain of shells. Bands of light on her tense white face. Then she went to the door and opened it.

Albert Hush, librarian, King of the Karmidee, was standing on the threshold. He was wearing his carnival costume, the Ice King. His mask was in his hand. He was dishevelled and dirty. His hair stuck out. He had shadows under his eyes. He needed to shave.

But all this was irrelevant.

He was electric with energy.

'Otto,' he said, speaking very loudly, 'why did you not come home?'

Otto stumbled in the nest of bedclothes around his ankles. For a moment he felt scared.

Then he didn't.

'I'm never coming home you two-faced lying skinker!' he yelled. 'I don't have a home. My mum's gone. And you, you are going to make yourself tiny and run away too! You pathetic useless coward! You're leaving the Karmidee to die! Well you can't leave me now whatever you do. Because I've left you! So go away!'

'Be quiet, Otto,' shouted Albert.

'Go away, Mr Firstborn,' screamed Otto.

He could only see Albert.

Mab, however, still existed.

'Mr Hush,' she said, and her voice shook, 'please don't—'
She stepped between them.

'Firstborn?' said Albert, loud but no longer actually shouting.

'You blackmailed Sween and pulled the sinews—'

'What? Who is Mr Firstborn?'

'You are. You are. I saw you, Dad—'

'Sinews?'

'Mr Hush,' said Mab, painfully, 'Otto thinks that as well as being a librarian and King and everything you are really also a Bird Charmer who plans to shrivel—'

'Shrink—' yelled Otto.

'Excuse me,' shouted someone. 'Is this dragon with you? Only he's gone through the ice with his feet. He's stuck.'

There was a sudden roaring, like the blast when a furnace door is opened.

'Now he's melting the whole river—'

Albert turned away for a moment, calling something to FireBox outside. Much thunderous flapping and scorching sounds.

'I saw you, Dad,' said Otto. 'And it was you on the roof and you had your bird monster in the flat. I saw you and then—'

'Tell me it all,' said Albert. 'From the beginning. Tell me about the Bird Charmer.'

'Tell him, Otto,' said Mab.

Otto glared at her.

'This person, this Mr Firstborn—'

'HE KNOWS—' yelled Otto.

'This person, this Bird Charmer, found out where the Bargain Hunters were hiding. He found out who they are, he had photographs, and he found out where they were hiding. Which was on a cake. And he threatened to tell the Art Police—'

'*On a cake?*'

'Yes, Mr Hush. They were very, very small. They were decorating it.'

'Decorating a cake?'

'They *were* the decorations.'

'Ah.'

'Stop looking so puzzled, Dad,' said Otto.

'Mr Firstborn arranged to meet the son of one of the Bargain Hunters. And Otto and, er, some other people went too. It was under the stage at Marlene the Scream's concert. Mr Firstborn wanted something called shrinking mixture in exchange for the Bargain Hunters. And these friends had some shrinking mixture and they gave it to Mr Firstborn. And in return, he gave them the Bargain Hunters. In a basket—'

'Shrinking mixture,' repeated Albert.

'Yes, but they're big again now, aren't they, Otto—'

'And this man, this Mr Firstborn, you saw him, Otto, and he looked just like me,' said Albert carefully.

Otto, his anger used up for a minute, just felt very miserable.

No one spoke.

Albert looked down at the mask he was holding. He ran his fingers along the edge, decorated with silver beads.

When he turned to Otto his eyes were full of tears.

'Do you know his first name, Otto? Is it Arkardy?'

'You know it is, Dad,' said Otto.

'I don't believe it,' whispered Albert. 'I don't believe it.'

Otto couldn't look at him.

Another long moment passed.

'There's somewhere I have to go,' said Albert. 'You must come too. Now.'

# Arkardy and Cornelius

'I'll come with you,' said Mab, pulling on her costume and wrapping a heavy patchwork shawl around her shoulders.

Otto found himself following them out through the door.

FireBox was waiting below. Soon he was labouring into the air, coughing smoke. Otto, almost on his neck, was squeezed awkwardly between two massive triangular spines.

This was even worse than his mat.

It was a short journey.

FireBox landed at the end of a track which faded away into the Wasteland and the many tents of the carnival.

They all scrambled down to the ground and he took off again, belching smoke.

'Now,' said Albert, coughing, 'it seems I will have to speak about my older brother—'

'You've got a brother, Dad!'

'Yes.'

'You've got a brother and you never told me! Just like you never told me you are going to leave and start a new life! Just like you never told me any skinking thing about anything!'

Otto and Albert stared at each other.

'I am not going to leave you, Otto,' said Albert.

Under the grime on his face he had turned very pale.

Otto was about to speak. Then he decided not to after all.

'Not everyone can tell the story of their past,' whispered Albert. He paused. 'It can be like ripping the scabs off a wound. A wound that never heals inside.'

Otto shuddered.

'I understand, Mr Hush,' said Mab, very soft.

'I have a brother,' continued Albert. 'And his name is Arkady. It was very hard for both of us. Our father could be, well, could be . . . angry, he could be angry and we used to protect each other. We were very close. Mainly Arkady protected me. He was older, you see. *Is* older . . .'

Albert took a deep breath of the bitter, icy air.

'. . . When he was fifteen, and I was fourteen, he told me one night that he was going to run away. He wanted me to go too. Begged me. But I was born with the birthmark, you see. I knew I had a duty to our people and I couldn't follow the path he was going to take.'

Two people walked past carrying the front of a paper tram.

'I will never forget it,' Albert continued more quietly. 'Arkardy couldn't believe I said no. We had always stuck together. Always. Afterwards, years later, when I looked back, I realized that we both felt betrayed that night.'

There was a silence.

'We said goodbye. I've never seen him again. But I know that he did what he planned to do. He became apprenticed to a Bird Charmer. It takes years of study and it must be a lonely life. There are only a very few of them. And, as Mab will know, Bird Charmers live by theft . . .'

Mab nodded. She looked nauseatingly grown up.

'They use birds to steal jewellery,' Albert went on, speaking more quickly. 'To get in high windows. Unpick locks . . . I suppose he must want to shrink something that he has stolen, maybe it'll be easier to hide it that way. And no one knows the rooftops of the City better than a Bird Charmer. He would certainly have had a chance of seeing the Bargain Hunters at work. But it's very hard to imagine him threatening to tell the authorities where to find them . . .'

He seemed to have finished what he was saying. Then he suddenly added, in a different voice, 'And he was very good to me, you see, when we were young . . .' And there were tears in his eyes again.

Otto felt very scared, as if he was standing there on his own, surrounded only by the cold, and Mab and his father had disappeared.

A huge brown dog trotted slowly over to where they were standing. Its coat was matted and there were scars on its face. It came right up to Otto and sniffed his hand. Its eyes were clouded at the centre, where they should have been black.

'Can you see all right?' Otto asked in a whisper.

But the dog didn't care. It set off again, along the track near where they had landed, past the house which stood there alone, and then turned away into the town.

This house was wooden, like all the others crowded closer to the river. It was on stilts too, though not as high as some. Chopped tree trunks, ready for the stove, were piled underneath and on the veranda. There was a rowing boat there, slung between stilts. And whoever chopped the wood had left their axe propped up by the front door, the long handle darkened with use where they gripped it. The blade still bright.

Albert stared.

A light had come on downstairs.

'So does this Arkady look just like you, Dad?' Otto asked sharply.

'No,' said Albert. 'No. But he has an ability which runs in

our family. Something our family swore not to use . . . something I never thought he *would* use, ever . . . something that brought us nothing but shame . . .'

Mab stepped forward, her small face very serious.

'Mr Hush,' she said, 'the Karmidee know who your family are. They have always known. You are descended from the counterfeiters. They don't care. You are greatly respected.'

Unbelievable. Even now, in this mysterious and horrible situation, Mab knew more about something than Otto did. In this case something private and important about his family. About his own father.

'SO what *is* a counterfeiter, Dad?'

'Well, Arkardy has the ability to look like someone else. Exactly like them. To change his face. To counterfeit. It takes a lot of energy and it can only be held for a few minutes . . .'

'*To change his face!*'

'They used to pretend to be other people, Otto,' began Mab. 'Some of them did terrible things—'

'Shut up, Mab!' screamed Otto.

'Please, Otto,' said Albert.

Now someone was going from room to room in the mysterious house, drawing back the curtains.

'Honourable greetings,' whispered a voice.

They all turned round.

A man was standing behind them wearing the costume of

The Rainmaker. An especially beautiful costume which Otto had seen before. Under the stage at Marlene's concert.

The man took off his mask.

It was Albert.

No one moved.

Then the newcomer's face began to change. His yellow-brown hair grew paler. It became thicker and shorter, standing up on his head.

Now he had white hair. Like Otto.

His cheekbones, his nose, his jaw, all slightly realigned.

And now he held out his hand, arm straight. Smile like broken glass.

'Honourable greetings, Mr Hush,' he said.

Albert didn't move.

'How dare you, Arkardy,' he said softly. 'You will destroy us all.'

Arkardy smiled his strange, uncertain smile.

'I was just practising,' he said. 'Behind my mask.'

'I must also presume that the hooded crow who tried to break into my flat last night, injuring his wing, is in some way connected with you. And the disappearance of a number of small items recently, including a jewelled penknife—'

'I was just playing,' said Arkardy. 'I never stopped missing you, you see.'

At that moment the front door of the house burst open and

a man came stamping down the steps and along the track towards them.

'You should have come with me, Al,' whispered Arkardy, suddenly fierce.

'Is that you, Mr Librarian?' shouted the man on the path. 'Sneaking back to us after all these years? Too scared to knock on the door?'

Grizzle-faced. Broad-shouldered and short. A blast of hair.

'It's him, it's my Grandfather Cornelius,' whispered Otto to Mab. The two of them edged closer together.

Cornelius wore no coat. He didn't seem to feel the cold. His skin was like weathered rock. He put his big gnarled hand on Arkardy's shoulder.

'He's turning out to be a real son,' he said. 'He's taking his father's advice for a change.' He spoke harshly, deliberately, and unlike his sons he spoke in the clear accent of the stilt houses. '*He'll be a new kind of King for the Karmidee.*'

'*WHAT?*'

'He's going to take your place.'

'HE'S GOING TO TAKE MY PLACE?'

'You heard me,' said Cornelius.

Albert had clenched his fists. He shook his head slowly. A flash of colour filled the air around him.

'Getting angry, are you?' taunted Cornelius. 'Don't you want to know how we're going to do it?'

Albert turned away from him. Towards Arkardy. When he spoke his voice was shaking.

'He's talked you into something, hasn't he, Arko. You've come back to try again. To finally please him. To finally have the thing we never had. A father. But it won't happen. He's using you. He'll, he'll—' Very fast he seized the collar of Arkardy's extraordinary costume and dragged him close. 'He'll break your heart,' he whispered. 'Just like he always did.'

Arkardy was watching him without seeming to hear. Perhaps he heard other words, spoken at another time. For a moment he became very sad.

'You should have come with me, Al,' he said softly.

And then he looked away. Down at the unforgiving, frozen ground.

'Leave him alone,' hissed Cornelius. 'I'm proud of him. For the first time I'm proud of one of my spineless, clever-clever sons.'

'Save yourself, Arko,' said Albert.

But Arkardy's face was once more beginning to change. He was smiling. But it was becoming a different smile. Albert's smile. Gradually, inexorably, his face became Albert's face.

It was horrible.

Albert let him go.

Cornelius laughed.

'Enough of your sentimental bleating, Mr Librarian. I was going to visit you today. I've got some news for you. I used to think we should fight them. Die fighting. That's what I've always said. But Arkardy here made a little discovery and now I've got another plan. We aren't going to fight them, Mr Librarian. We're going to BECOME them.'

'WHAT? THE CURE?' Albert gasped.

'The very one. Arkardy has already had a private chat with that Bliss at the Town Hall. Known for his business interests. Prospecting. Mining. Bliss thought he was talking to you, of course. Not that he'd heard of the King. Didn't believe there was a King at first. Then you gave him the rights to that old mine on Rose Island where nobody goes. Very impressed he was, and that's just the beginning, he thinks you're a person of influence now—'

'Gave him the rights? That mine belongs to all our people. I don't *own* anything. It is a matter of honour—'

'You and your pathetic honour,' snarled Cornelius. 'Just like when you were a stupid, scrawny boy. You've got the mark. Use it! You could have been a fighter! Full of fire!—'

'Let the Karmidee *choose* their leaders,' shouted Albert. 'The King *advises*. I will not use my mark to, to seize power, to dictate, to exploit—'

'Well you will now!' snarled Cornelius. And Otto was

terrified to see that sparks of rage were flying around his grandfather as he spoke, sizzling and flaming in the snow.

'Things never change for our people. They are dreamers. Inferior. WE will CURE them. Then they will be Citizens. They can have everything that the Citizens have. They are going to take the Cure, Albert. And they are going to take it because *you* are the only one they trust and *you* – by which I mean Arko, counterfeiting you – *you* are going to go on television and *tell* them to take it. Tonight.'

'Never!' cried Albert. 'The Cure leaves us useless. No life. No energy. No imagination. Shadows. You've seen it for yourself. You think it's worth that just to make the Citizens accept us? You think the Citizens are better than we are? With their prisons and their uniforms and their endless possessions and their money, money, money? The Karmidee are different. Let them be different!'

Tiny flames danced in the air around Cornelius. He spat on the ground and the snow flared.

Mab screamed and jumped backwards into Otto. Smoke. There was a spark burning in her hair. Otto grabbed it out very fast, the palm of his glove scorched and smouldered into a hole, he clapped his hands to kill it.

They stayed where they were, very close together.

Cornelius was grinning up into Albert's face like a fighter in the ring.

'I cannot allow you to do this,' said Albert.

'He cannot allow us to do this,' mocked Cornelius, mimicking Albert's Citizen accent. 'Well, you'll have to allow us, Mr Hush. Arkardy found something very, very useful. On a roof. He worked out what it was all by himself. Couldn't resist creeping back here to tell me about it. And I had a brilliant idea. I don't think you want your precious people to die, do you? You have noticed there is a problem with the weather?'

He nodded. Still grinning. Watching Albert. 'You can save them, Albert, that's what you're good at, isn't it? Just stay quiet. Leave them to us. Go back to your books. Let Arkardy go on television. Let him counterfeit you and be King. Then the spring will come, very soon. That's all you have to do.'

There was a silence.

Then Arkardy reached into the air and flexed his fingers.

The red kite must have been waiting somewhere.

It dropped suddenly down on to his shoulder.

Slowly, lazily, Arkardy's face once more became his own.

'We own the secret of the weather,' said Cornelius. 'Arkardy was holding it only an hour or so ago, right here.'

And he snatched Arkardy's hand and held it out, palm upwards, dripping with an illusion of mist and rainbows.

Empty.

'Try and stop us,' Cornelius continued, very quietly. 'And the Karmidee will freeze to death.'

# Going Home

Albert turned and strode away into the Wasteland.

Otto and Mab followed him, staying at a distance.

On and on through tents and stalls and smouldering bonfires.

There were no clouds just then. The sun touched the snow-covered City and the Mountains with blue-white fire.

He stopped, put something to his lips for a moment and then set off again.

'He's whistling to FireBox,' said Otto, breathlessly, to Mab. Sure enough, a little further on, they saw the dragon waiting, surrounded by onlookers, squashed tents and melted snow.

'Greetings to the King,' called someone.

Albert raised his hand wearily in reply and then spoke to his son, without looking at him.

'I'm going to the flat, Otto, if you still consider it your home perhaps you'll join me.'

He turned towards them at last.

'And Mab, too,' he added. 'Mab is welcome, too.'

Mab tugged on Otto's arm but just then Otto couldn't move. He left a stretch of trampled snow and ice between himself and his father.

'There's this clock and we think it controls the weather. Mab worked it out. And Arkardy must have stolen it. That must be why he wanted the shrinking mixture,' he said at last.

'To make it small,' said Mab. 'Small enough to carry.'

'Make the clock small?'

'It's big,' said Mab. 'It's in a big tower. And it's got these wooden people that come out and dance. At least they *should* dance . . .' and here she pointed to Albert's cloak. 'The Ice King and Midsummer Night, when they dance together, that's like the meeting of the winter and the summer, you see. That's the spring.'

A harsh wind blew. Albert folded his blue and silver cloak more tightly around him.

'It's got lots of faces and dials and some wooden people and it's on the Town Hall roof,' said Otto miserably. 'But Arkardy's got it now.'

# The Weather Clock

'You couldn't get to it by climbing over the roof, you had to fly—'

'Yes, Mr Hush, we thought there must have been some sort of spell. People always say that this whole place is wound round with energies and things.'

Albert nodded thoughtfully.

'And you are certain it has something to do with the weather?'

'Mab worked it all out, Dad, it's to do with these wooden figures and they come out of these doors, except someone's tied something round the rail to stop them meeting.'

'Well, it certainly looks as if something has been taken away,' said Albert.

They were standing in the little sunken courtyard. The strange tower with all the dials and doors and the parapet was gone. There was a crater in the roof as if a tooth had been wrenched out. At the bottom the foundations of the tower glistened in the cold light. It had been built on a floor of obsidian. Blackglass from the volcanoes, used to hold magical energy.

A few bricks and a layer of dust lay on the snow. No footprints.

'He may have used a bird,' said Albert. 'Or perhaps he has some means of flight himself, that would probably have been safer. It would be hard for a bird to pick it up, even when it was, er, shrunk.'

'Someone fired arrows at me when I was flying,' said Mab. 'And I came down in the Pearly Oak. I thought they were after me because of the snow jinxer business. But maybe it was your brother, Mr Hush, the arrow had jewels on it and I lost my carpet. Maybe he went back and found it '

'You lost your carpet!' exclaimed Otto.

'Someone made me this one,' mumbled Mab. 'This really weird girl in a shop.'

'*Someone made it?*'

'We will not be defeated,' said Albert. 'We will find out where he has hidden it.' He paused. Surely this was a tremendous task. He put his hand on Otto's shoulder.

'We must find it and we must stop them tonight, on the television. Otherwise—'

And at that moment they were attacked.

'DON'T MOVE PUT YOUR HANDS UP NOT SO FAST!' yelled a wild and ferocious voice.

Three things, two woolly and bouncing and one small and fast came plunging towards them out of the sky.

The larger ones were whooping and shouting in a blood-curdling manner. Now, unbelievably, they seemed to halt in the air. Did halt, stop, float, just above Albert's head. They did this by each quickly undoing two of the saucer-sized buttons on the front of their extraordinary, bulky coats.

These coats were the same colour as flying carpets. They even had a pattern of butterflies on them.

'Feet firstly, remember,' said Roxie to Mattie.

Button by button they descended.

Meanwhile a speckled grey and brown bird glided down and landed in front of Otto. It looked up at him with its sharp eyes and then misted over, became indistinct. And then became a boy.

The instant Caractacus had changed, Roxie and Mattie swept their needles from inside their mysterious layers of clothing and held them up, pointing at Albert.

'Honourable greetings, Otto Hush,' said Caractacus coolly. 'Is this man bothering you?'

'No, no, no,' exclaimed Otto. 'No, no, put the needles *down*. This my *dad*. This is Mab, my *friend*.'

Albert, nevertheless, took a step away from Otto.

'Hello, Mab,' said Mattie, going a bit Strawberry Mousse.

'Do you like our flying jackets?' enquired Roxie proudly. 'Clever Mattie invented them. Same wool as your little rug things. She made young Proud Face a new one the other day. Only Proud Face was in a bit of a hurry and didn't have time for goodbying.'

Otto looked at Mab.

'I'm sorry,' she muttered. 'I was so worried about my gran.'

'Dad,' said Otto quickly, 'this is Caractacus and Mattie Mook and Roxie Lightning Needles Mook, the WoolBandits.'

The Bandits all bowed. Mattie raised her hat.

'And this is Albert Hush, King of the Karmidee,' continued Otto. He had not really seen Caractacus' expression change before. It changed now, however. Briefly. To a very satisfactory look of amazement.

'Greetings,' said Albert, calm and courteous. 'And I am indeed honoured to meet the legendary WoolBandits.'

'It's about the weather,' said Otto to the Bandits. 'You've got to help us.'

'Well, we was thinking of a short holiday in the Heights Hydro,' said Roxie dryly. 'But we might have time for the assistance of a friend in trouble.'

'It is the Karmidee who are in trouble, Ms Lightning Needles,' said Albert. 'And we have almost no time at all in which to save them.'

He turned to Caractacus. 'I understand that you may be very well acquainted with a certain Bird Charmer. He has the same colour hair as my son, here. He—'

Albert stopped. Roxie had leapt forwards and was pointing her needles into Albert's face. Mattie had also leapt forward – to hold her back.

'Where is he?' cried Roxie. 'I'll have his gizzard, I'll rip out—'

'Let him tell us,' said Caractacus, who hadn't moved.

No one spoke.

'Put down the needles,' said Caractacus, quietly. 'You are a Citizen, you don't understand. Otto's father is the King of the Karmidee.'

Roxie slowly lowered her needles and Otto frowned with pride.

'The Charmer has stolen a special clock from here. It controls the weather and that is why the spring hasn't come,' explained Otto's father, the King of the Karmidee. 'He has shrunk it using the Small—'

A groan from Roxie.

'He will not allow the spring to come. He's using it to force me to let him persuade the Karmidee to take the Cure.

There is a way he can persuade them. It would take a long time to explain now. But he will do it, on television, at six o'clock tonight, and I must find the clock before then.'

Everyone looked at Caractacus.

'There are many places where it could be hidden,' he said after a moment. 'Charmers have secrets all over the rooftops of the City.'

Albert nodded.

'I will make a list,' said Caractacus. 'With the places he used most often first. I will help you to search.'

'And I will too,' said Mab. 'On my carpet.'

'And so will I,' said Otto.

'But we must all search separately,' said Caractacus. 'Because there are many hiding places and some of them are very far away.'

'We can help, I should hope,' growled Roxie. 'Now we have our jackets to ascend in. Unless there is some other service we can render. Me and Mattie do Combat Knitting, your Highness, and Mattie has a scientific brain.'

Mattie raised her hat again and Albert raised his hat in polite reply.

And then, despite the terrible cold, he wiped a sheen of sweat off his forehead.

# The Roof Garden

The sky sparkled with ice and evening stars.

Dusk was coming to the frozen City of Trees.

Soon, very, very soon, Arkardy would go on television with Councillor Bliss and betray his people forever.

Otto was alone. He steered his mat low over the place known as The Watchers. He had with him a small bottle of the Big and a map drawn by Caractacus, showing secret places where Arkardy might have hidden the weather clock. Now Otto had come to the last and furthest one of all.

Caractacus had been there just once, in the dark, some years before, and all he could remember was an abandoned roof garden, high up on a warehouse. He didn't know who it belonged to, or why the Charmer had taken him there. It had been deserted. They had hidden a parcel and left. That was all.

Well there it was, below Otto now.

He landed between the leafless trees, rolled up his mat and crept past ruined flowerbeds and ancient, shattered pots. No snow. Had someone been sweeping here? Something crunched under his foot and he looked down and saw that he was walking on broken bones. He turned through an archway of twisted branches and stopped.

A man was sitting there on a stone chair and he was holding the weather clock on his knee.

He uncovered a worm lantern and smiled at Otto. His hair was red-brown, flecked with white, his skin like milk. His eyes were bright and full of scorn.

'Good evening,' he said. 'Can I help you?'

'Who are you?' blurted Otto.

The man said nothing. He just continued to smile. His hands were closed around the little stone tower. He wore a number of gold rings. His coat was made from that popular mixture, Wanderer's Return.

Suddenly Otto didn't need an answer. He didn't understand, but he recognized him.

'You're looking at the next Deputy Mayor,' said the man. 'Mayor Bliss will be announcing it tonight.'

'So you've finally almost got what you wanted,' said Otto. 'Not actually Mayor, the next best thing. Sixty years later.'

Madness. Danger. Don't say any more.

The man's confident gaze wavered just a little. He stood up.

Otto backed a couple of steps.

'What do you mean, boy?'

'Your ambition to be Mayor. And what did you do with Caractacus' parents? Did you kill them?'

The man put down the weather clock.

He walked towards Otto and his face emptied of feeling. Only his eyes were alive, watching whatever he was going to do next.

'Did you kill them?' screamed Otto. 'Are they dead?'

'No one is going to stop me this time,' snarled the man. He made a grab at Otto who dived sideways and past him.

Otto had the clock.

'What did you do to them?' he screamed, because he had to know. 'Where are they, *Bagsey*?'

Roland Carmichael stared at him.

'What are you?' he whispered.

'I saw you. I was there. You gave my friend to a Bird Charmer. In his fancy carriage. It was raining.'

Carmichael seemed too shocked to move. Silenced for a moment.

'You gave my friend to a skinking, rooftop thief.'

'You are speaking of Daedalus WellBeloved, the greatest

Charmer who has ever lived. And you are some sort of ghost. Or cheap time traveller. Or worse . . .'

Carmichael kept staring at Otto, a fixed and terrible stare.

'Give me that clock, boy. You don't know what it is. It's no use to you.'

'Be careful,' said Otto, holding it up. 'Don't come any nearer. I might drop it.'

'Your so-called friend the merlin is probably dead by now. Sold to another Charmer long ago. They especially like merlins. Clever. Strong. Small. And his parents,' Carmichael managed another smile, holding out his hand for the clock, creeping nearer, 'well, let's just say Daedalus had unequalled abilities.'

Otto, backing away, felt something against his legs. The parapet. He had reached the edge of the roof.

'Daedalus could draw any bird. Any bird at all. When he called it was like Mother Earth herself, calling them home.' Carmichael, just for a moment, seemed overtaken by a memory, his eyes were bitter, rueful.

'But that's not the end of it. He could go on calling, you see. Catch the threads of their very selves. Drag the beat right out of their hearts. Turn them to stone.'

He snatched at Otto's arm and caught him just above the elbow.

'And if you're wondering if anyone could put that energy

back, well, *he* could have done it, I've no doubt. But there's been no Charmer since his time with even half his powers.'

Otto struggled.

They hit the parapet. Otto fell backwards over it.

Felt Carmichael let go of him.

Felt the mat slip from under his arm.

Writhing. No breath to scream. Freezing air rushing past.

Felt himself land on something with a thud. Bounce. Not the ground.

The mat. It had caught him. And he still had the clock.

He grabbed at the fringe. Then he looked down.

There was Carmichael below, still falling, tumbling, hurtling towards the ground. And then, in the air, spinning, becoming something else.

Roland Carmichael became a bird.

The red kite.

# The Chase

He saw the kite spread its great wings. Catch itself in its fall.

For a moment they both seemed suspended in cold space.

Then it began to climb towards him.

Nothing was over. It was beginning now.

He dragged on the fringe of the mat and went higher, steeper, higher still. The kite below, relentless and gaining.

Otto aimed wildly back towards the Boulevard, lunging through the sky and the kite wheeled and followed like a shadow.

Otto sped on, hunched over the clock. Expecting the attack at any moment.

Mind screaming.

Over the southern end of the Boulevard now. Spine of

lights to follow. The clock against his chest. Ticking like a heart.

I might die.

The kite, tireless.

It didn't need to risk attacking in the air. It just had to wait for him to land.

Or try to land.

The Town Hall loomed ahead. One of the tallest buildings on the Boulevard. Otto risked dropping height.

The kite dropped too.

You aren't going to try it in the air. You're too scared that the clock might smash into the ground. He dropped a little further. Forcing the kite down between the buildings, down as low as the tops of the frozen trees.

Then, his only chance, he banked steeply up over the roof, leaving the bird a second behind.

A vital second.

Eyes almost shut. Almost hitting everything.

In the sudden quiet he could hear the sound of wings rushing up behind him.

Now!

He crashed into the hidden courtyard on the roof, skidded off the mat, slammed the tower down on to its base, held it there with one hand, pulled out the bottle with the other. Felt the clawed feet of the kite sink into his coat. Something tearing at his hair, trying to lift him, now piercing his gloves, heard himself screaming, blood between his fingers.

He bit the cork out of the top of the bottle and threw the mixture over the tower.

There was a huge gust of something. A surging of air. A creaking like a great forest in the wind.

He couldn't hold on any longer. He was dragged backwards. He rolled and covered his face, kicking. Trying to save his eyes.

Then he heard a terrible sound. A scream of rage and hate and grief. Rising up into the night. Higher and higher, spiralling away, lost in the infinite sky.

# Mayor Crumb is Surprised

'I fully understand that you may wish to examine it,' continued the smooth, confident voice outside the front door. 'You will find it is just a winter coat. We thought the Mayor might be chilly, in this unusual weather.'

'Funny-looking coat,' said Mr Six. Or was it Mr Eight? They were both out there, of course. On guard.

Mayor Crumb crept along his hall, reassembling his dressing gown over his pyjamas. Slippers quiet on the carpet.

He reached the front door and listened.

'He'll need it where he's going,' said Mr Eight, or possibly Mr Six. 'Bliss is sending him for an arrest cure in the hospital. That big old place near the prison. Got an entrance and no exit, if you know what I mean.'

'Really,' murmured Max Softly, Theatrical Agent, his voice now easily recognized by Mayor Crumb. 'Well, if you would just allow my children to go in and give it to him.'

'No one is allowed in, orders of the Town Hall.'

'Of course they aren't.'

'And you'll notice that I've checked the pockets. No messages allowed either.'

'Of course not. Perhaps you are having difficulty recognizing me. My name is Max Softly. I have recently had a haircut. I used to have rather distinctive plaits, like my son here, Sween the Child Prodigy. And this is Mab. I can't really believe that you would be afraid of two such young, Respectable people. And after all, this is probably the last chance they will have to see their Uncle Cedric, before he is taken away.'

Murmuring from Six and Eight.

'I can assure you, we are highly trained to detect Suspicious non-Respectables and persons of that nature, Mr Softly,' said one of them importantly. 'In view of your extreme Respectability and reputation we will allow one visitor, your little girl, as long as she's quick.'

There was a crunching of keys in the lock.

Mayor Crumb stood back and the door opened.

There was a girl standing between Mr Six and Mr Eight. Her long hair was decorated with plaits and ribbons and she wore a blue and brown dress with necklaces of flowers made from some soft material.

She kept her eyes cast down demurely. Her face looked tired, pale and delicate, like the forest spirit in the stained-glass window behind his desk at the Town Hall. She was holding a disintegrating parcel, dangling with string.

'Be quick now,' said Mr Six. Handsome Max and his son smiled encouragingly at Mayor Crumb.

The Mayor took the parcel and he and the little girl took a few steps along the corridor.

Slowly, he shook out the strange coat. It was very bulky and covered in a pattern of dark butterflies and there were five enormous saucer-sized buttons down the front.

The girl had her back to the door. She suddenly came to life.

'Honourable greetings,' she whispered, very intense. 'Go to the window. Open it, put on the coat.'

Mayor Crumb was good at recognizing accents. This one, mysteriously, was from TigerHouse.

'All right, dear, come along out now,' called Mr Six.

The girl winked at Mayor Crumb. A moment later the front door thumped shut behind her.

Mayor Crumb's flat was on the sixth floor. Nevertheless, with the measured tread of the prisoner, he walked back into his living room and over to the window. And on his way, smiling vaguely to himself, he slipped on the massive coat over his dressing gown. Someone had guessed his size. Even he wasn't that big.

He reached the window, drew back the curtains and opened it. Perhaps Mr Softly was on the pavement down below and wanted to see if the coat fitted.

No.

A wild and wrinkled woman and a round-faced girl shot down from somewhere.

They bobbed about in the air.

Then they saluted him with what appeared to be knitting needles.

The woman gave him a moonlit grin of teeth.

'Button up the buttonings, your Mayorfulness,' she said hoarsely.

Blinking in amazement, Mayor Crumb fumbled with the saucer things.

Then Roxie and Mattie grabbed his arms and pulled him out into the void.

# Communicator

Otto was still on the Town Hall roof, crouched behind a great bank of chimneys, clutching his communicator, trying to speak to his father. His breath kept covering the communicator with steam. The backs of both his hands were bleeding. He was shaking with cold and shock.

The communicator flickered. It filled with silvery-blue light.

'Dad!' yelled Otto hoarsely. 'Dad! Can you hear me?'

Albert's face appeared. Where on earth?

'Is that you, Otto?'

'Dad, I found it, I put it back—'

There was a sound like a cheer from inside the communicator. Otto could just make out someone who seemed to be Mayor Crumb. What was that beside him? A giant letter?

'You found it and you put it back? Are you all right? Where are you now?'

'I'm still on the Town Hall roof. There's no moon any more. It's really hard to see and I haven't got a worm torch. I still haven't got the twine off the rail—'

'Can't hear you,' yelled Albert. It was a letter T. Lit up. Huge.

'Are you sure it's the right thing? And you've put it back in the right place?'

'Yes!' shouted Otto, wiping the communicator with the end of one of his scarves.

'What?'

'YES!' screamed Otto, hurting his throat. 'But I still haven't cut—'

'I'll communicate to Mab and Caractacus to stop them looking then. They're both miles away. We're on top of the Television Studios. I need you here, Otto. Get here as quickly as you can.'

# The Face Behind the Face

Giant letters, CTBC, illuminated in red, lit the snow on the roof of the City of Trees Broadcasting Co-operative.

Otto crash-landed next to a transmitter, looming and sinister in the dark.

Albert was still in his carnival costume, now more ragged than ever. Mayor Crumb stood beside him in his flying jacket. Roxie and Mattie bobbed in the air.

'Good evening, sir,' said Otto, still breathless.

'I understand that you and your friends have acted with intelligence and fortitude and we are much in your debt,' said Mayor Crumb.

'They have, we are, and it's not over yet,' said Albert briskly, checking his watch. 'You should know, Otto, that someone, probably my father, must have warned Councillor Bliss that we may create a problem with this broadcast. I am told that our flat and the library have both been raided this afternoon. Obviously they didn't find me. Now there are Normal Police guarding the doors downstairs. Mayor Crumb knows another way in, from here.'

'Your father insists that I can only prove that I have been imprisoned, and that I am not ill, if I appear before the City in person on the television,' said Mayor Crumb. 'I'm looking forward to seeing that cursed Blister's face when I walk in.'

'Thank you, Ms Lightning Needles,' he added, as Roxie deftly knocked a lump of melting snow off the top of his head with a knitting needle.

Mattie disappeared into a cloud of smoke for a moment and then handed Otto a new pair of gloves with his initials, in gold thread, on the inside. She looked very solemn.

'Do something for me, Otto,' said Albert. 'Keep to the back. See everything that happens. You are the witness for our people. If it goes wrong and the Police take me, run. Roxie and Mattie can look after themselves. Do you understand?'

'Yes,' said Otto.

'You are my son. If you tell the people that there has been counterfeiting, that you saw it for yourself, they might believe you. More than anyone else. Do you understand?'

'Yes.'

'Do that for me. For the Karmidee. And then, whatever happens, if Mum doesn't come back, contact Max Softly. I'm sure he will help you after what you've done for him. And remember, your energy manifests as heartsight, people don't need to know about that. It doesn't show. If it comes to it you can pass as a Citizen. Do *not* take the Cure. *Even if everyone else does*. Do you understand?'

Otto nodded. Unable to speak.

A clock somewhere nearby struck six.

It was time.

Mayor Crumb led the way to a trap door in the roof.

They crept down a narrow staircase, along a dim corridor and reached a door marked Studio A. Even here, indoors, a lace of frost lined the walls.

There was no problem about deciding if this was the right studio or not. Mr Six and Mr Eight were standing outside.

Not for long.

Otto followed the Mayor and Albert, stepping over the two writhing sacks on the floor, coughing as quietly as he could in the cloud of smoke from the knitting. Roxie and Mattie stayed in the corridor to guard the prisoners and the door.

Otto found himself in a darkened anteroom. They could see into the studio itself through a glass wall. Everything could be heard through a speaker.

At that moment the presenter was introducing Councillor Bliss, Acting Mayor and leader of the Guardians of the Normal. Unlike Albert, the good Councillor was no longer wearing his carnival costume. Nor was his companion, soberly dressed in grey and sitting rigidly beside him. A man with Albert's face.

'And we would also like to welcome Mr, er . . .'

'Hush,' said Councillor Bliss. 'Mr Hush is known as the King of the Karmidee,' he continued, like a smug ringmaster introducing a new exotic animal. 'He is very important to them. A person of influence. He would like to speak to the Karmidee now.'

'Let's hear him,' whispered Albert. 'My brother.'

'Good people,' said the man with Albert's face. 'You have trusted me through dangerous times and I have not failed you. I want to help you again now. I want to set you free. To unlock the cage that destroys you. The cage that prevents you from living the lives you could lead.'

He breathed deeply, he seemed to be choosing and pronouncing every word with care.

'Brothers and sisters, fellow Karmidee. Our magical, Impossible energy is ancient and primitive. It is nothing but a weakness. We could be just like the Citizens, and live among them and have what they have. I am asking you to give up your energy. Rid yourselves of it now. And forever. Take the

Cure Mayor Bliss and the Guardians of the Normal are offering. Take your rightful place among the Citizens.'

'Well, this is extraordinary—' exclaimed the presenter.

'I have his word,' interrupted Councillor Bliss. 'He is acting on my instructions, of course, and he has given me his assurance that there will be no more snow jinxers and the weather will—'

But he didn't finish.

The door of the studio burst open and Mayor Crumb strode in like a bear.

His eyes were bloodshot. His eyebrows were covered in frost. His usually pasty face was rosy and blue. His monstrous flying jacket flapped open, revealing his purple dressing gown and striped pyjamas.

He was magnificent.

And Albert followed him. The real Albert.

Otto, at the back, was in the doorway. The witness for his people.

Mayor Crumb barged in front of the cameras.

'What are you doing here, you idiot?' snarled Councillor Bliss, clearly forgetting that everything he said could be heard by millions of people. 'How did you get out?'

'This,' boomed Mayor Crumb, indicating Albert, 'is the true King of the Karmidee.'

'Are you recovered, Mayor Crumb?' asked the presenter,

eyes darting about, shuffling papers. 'We were told—'

'I WAS NEVER ILL,' thundered Mayor Crumb. 'I HAVE BEEN A PRISONER IN MY OWN HOME. HIS PRISONER.' And he pointed a sturdy finger at Councillor Bliss.

'I thought something like this might happen. Our ex-Mayor is suffering from stress,' said Councillor Bliss, quickly. 'He is unbalanced in his mental capacities. And I can assure you that the other gentleman is an impostor. He is certainly not dressed like a King. Please call the Police. There are some outside.'

'That won't be necessary,' said Albert. 'We just need a few more minutes. If we all sit here for a few more minutes then everyone will know who is the impostor.'

The counterfeit King stood up. Mayor Crumb pushed him back into his seat.

'Are you going to allow a mentally unstable person and a criminal to take over your studio?' hissed the Councillor. He was no longer a man of peace and brotherhood. He stood up himself and swept a short wooden club from under his cloak. It was studded with nails.

'Nobody move!' he shouted. 'Mr Six! Mr Eight!'

Otto ducked as something rushed past his head in the air.

Councillor Bliss screamed as Caractacus dived at him with a piercing and horrible cry, landing in his hair, digging his claws in, scratching ruthlessly at his face—

'Enough!' shouted Albert.

The merlin was holding open its wings to balance. It leant forward until its savage beak was reflected in the Councillor's terrified eyes.

Millimetres away. Then it became still. And Councillor Bliss became still also.

Silence.

Except for the ticking of the studio clock.

Minute after minute ticked past.

The programme would have been over by now.

And then suddenly everyone was looking at the man beside Councillor Bliss. The one he had introduced as Mr Hush.

This man's face seemed to be melting.

Very slowly, fighting it, another face was becoming visible. Arkardy's face.

The presenter's eyes and mouth opened wider and wider.

'I am Albert Hush, known as Albert the Quiet, the true King of the Karmidee,' said Albert, dignified in his rags and dirt. 'The people know me. They know I would never tell them to take the poisonous Cure. It is not my task to lead them. But I can tell them that they are of greater value if they do not sacrifice the qualities which make them different. To be different is not a crime. There are many ways to be.'

'I would like to detain Brother Bliss,' said Mayor Crumb. 'He has a number of matters to explain.' He took the club out of Councillor Bliss' trembling hand. Caractacus didn't move. Neither did the Councillor.

'And I will now address the people,' added the Mayor, removing the microphone from in front of the grey-faced presenter.

Then, suddenly, Arkardy made a run for the door. Chased by Albert.

They reached the anteroom.

Right next to Otto.

'Not so fast,' whispered Albert, blocking his brother's path. 'You have betrayed me. You have betrayed our family. You have tried to destroy our people. Despite everything, our different lives, the years that have passed, I never believed—'

'Let me through,' hissed Arkardy. Trying to shove his way past. His voice strangled. Sweat beading on his face.

They stared at each other.

'I can't believe he persuaded you, Arko,' said Albert.

'Let me through, you weakling,' snarled Arkardy. He clenched a square, savage fist, strangely scarred and old, and he pushed it into Albert's face. 'You were always full of words. What use are they? The butterfly should have been on *my* skin, I would have, I would have—'

Otto, terrified, started forwards yelling something—

'Get back!' shouted Albert.

Arkardy seemed to be choking. Tiny points of flame began to burn and dance in the air around him.

His face was contorted with rage . . . more than rage . . . it was beginning to lose its shape. His skin was sinking into folds and tiny scars, his hair was growing shorter, his grey eyes became bluer, smaller, harsher . . .

It wasn't Arkardy. Arkardy had never been in the studio at all.

It had been Cornelius all the time. Hiding behind the face behind the face.

'Your Charmer brother ran scared after all,' he said, quieter for a moment, full of bitterness. 'Changed his mind. Made some speech about honour, would you believe. Just before we were going to leave. Your bleating got into his stupid head.'

Albert's eyes softened.

'But don't get too pleased with yourself,' Cornelius went on. 'I was always stronger than you, Scrawny, wasn't I? And I'm still stronger now. You will tell our people to take the Cure. You will tell them personally. Because I still control the weather.'

'My son has put the weather clock back where it belongs,' said Albert.

Cornelius' eyes narrowed, just for a second. Then he smiled his fighter's smile.

'Then fix it,' he said quietly. 'Fix it if you can. I haven't noticed anything melting so far.'

Albert's costume was decorated with fragments of broken glass, lightly polished, almost sharp. They glittered, blue-white.

'Good costume for you, isn't it, the Ice King?' whispered Cornelius. And he twisted his hand into the web on Albert's shoulder and tore it away.

'Leave him alone!' screamed Otto.

He flung himself at Cornelius, seized his wrist with both hands and bit into it. He held on, sinking his teeth deeper, his jaw immediately starting to throb, salt on his tongue. He heard Cornelius cursing, his father shouting, he felt his feet lift clean off the ground, tasted blood now, hot. Then he was slammed against a wall, his head jolted backwards, and he slid down to the floor, shaken off with one great swing of his grandfather's arm.

Otto could see nothing, no one. Except Cornelius standing over him, his heavy fist raised like a mallet.

'NO!' shouted a voice. Albert's voice. Bigger, fiercer than Otto had ever heard it before.

'You will NOT lay ONE FINGER on HIM!'

Otto was trying to stand. His legs buckled.

Albert's hands were around Cornelius' neck. Flashes of colour and stabs of fire were exploding in the air around them.

'The King of the Karmidee should have a burning heart,' snarled Cornelius, every word heavy with terrible contempt. 'A living, burning heart, full of fire. Not a heart full of honour and duty and ICE!'

He threw the handful of broken glass upwards hard and it crashed and ricocheted from the ceiling and the walls and showered Albert and Cornelius and Otto with pieces of frozen light.

He arched his body and spat in Albert's face.

Still Albert didn't let go.

'*No more*,' whispered Albert. The Quiet.

Then, at last, he pushed his father away.

They did not speak again.

Cornelius crossed the room, sending Otto skidding out of his way, and slammed the door behind him.

'Everything all right in here?' asked Mayor Crumb, coming through from the studio.

Silence.

'We can fix the clock, Dad,' cried Otto. 'Me and Mab. We know what to do.'

# Mattie's Present

Otto woke up early. The flat was full of breathing. Everyone had stayed except Albert, who had been out all night, looking for Dolores.

Otto crept around, stepping over people.

Only one person was already up, Mattie Mook.

She was standing by the front door. Ready to go out, it seemed, but not actually going.

'Good morning, Otto,' she said.

'Good morning,' said Otto.

'I've got to go and open the shop,' she added, frowning. 'People need wool in this weather. It's even more important than usual.'

'Of course,' replied Otto.

He unbolted the door and opened it. Now their breath was making white clouds in the air of the passageway.

It seemed like a very good idea to close the door again at once but he couldn't because Mattie continued standing there. She was looking at the floor.

'I could knit your family a new doormat,' she said.

'Thanks,' he said. His teeth were beginning to chatter.

She continued to look at the floor, still frowning. Then she dug her hand into a pocket in her flying jacket and pulled out a crumpled, bulging paper bag with the Wool Shop symbol, the crossed needles, on the side.

'This is for Sween Softly,' she said in a rush. 'From me. I want you to give it to him.'

'He'll be awake in a minute,' said Otto. He could hear someone moving about in the kitchen now. 'You could give it to him yourself—'

'No, no. You give it to him. It's musical. Musical wool. Very, very old and Impossible.'

'Musical?' He jiggled from foot to foot, rubbing his hands together. 'Does it make a noise?'

'Not exactly. I want him to have it, you see,' she continued, rather sternly. 'He should have it. He's sure to need it one day.'

'But why can't you—'

'He's my brother,' said Mattie.

*   *   *

And she turned and marched off towards the stairs, raising her hat to the new concierge, who was sweeping snowy footprints into a bucket.

# The Dancing Day

Otto found Mab in the twins' room, curled up on the floor.

'Wake up,' he whispered. 'We've got to go and mend the clock.'

She was rubbing her eyes. Peered at him sleepily. Cloud River Blue.

'Is your dad still wearing his Ice King costume?'

'What?'

'Is your dad still wearing his costume?'

'I expect so, why?'

She yawned like a cat and didn't reply.

'I heard something about what happened,' she said, peering again. 'Are you OK?'

Otto shrugged.

'Want any breakfast?'

He shook his head. Saw Dolores in his imagination, a towel wrapped around her hair, pouring batter like sunshine into the frying pan.

'The Mayor said that your dad said that it turned out to be your grandfather and there was a bit of a scene—'

'There was,' replied Otto, curtly.

'You were asleep when I got here. You went straight to sleep, as soon as you all got home, they said. After you'd been sick—'

She had seen his face.

She stopped talking.

Shortly afterwards they flew to the Town Hall roof.

It was a pale blue morning, burning with cold.

Otto crouched over the rail on the parapet of the weather clock, sawing at the twine with a kitchen knife.

Mab, who knew about the red kite, traced the scars and bloodstains on the snow. She found a tail feather and came back to him, just as he finished unravelling the last of the twine. She stood and waited, watching him. Then spoke.

'That was a big bird to fight on your own in the dark, Mr Hush.'

He looked at her, surprised by the tone of her voice,

and she held up the feather and raised her eyebrows.

'Not really,' he mumbled, dropping the knife.

All the time they had heard ticking and whirring sounds coming from inside the tower, cogs turning, creaks and rattles, but no music.

'Do you think they'll come out soon? And dance?' whispered Otto. 'Should we wait?'

Mab looked thoughtfully at the two doors at the bottom, now so firmly shut, so smooth in the stone, it was hard to believe they had ever opened at all. Then she shook her head and unrolled her mat.

'Where are we going now?'

'To see if your dad is back.'

More hero-worship presumably. So tedious.


Parry Street was always decorated for carnival times. Even this year there were lanterns in the skeletons of the trees. People had been dancing the night before, the pavements were swept clear of snow, and embers still glowed in abandoned bonfires.

Max and Sween Softly had revived a fire. They were sitting beside it. Both wore very beautiful and Impossible costumes. Max was the Blue Hare and Sween, tuning his guitar, was a tiger. Rosie was dozing on his head. The Wool Shop bag was on the ground beside him.

Roxie and Caractacus, apparently, had insisted on escorting Mayor Crumb back to his flat.

'There's someone here to see your father,' said Sween, as soon as Otto had finished skidding about, trying to land his mat. 'Over there.'

Otto straightened his hat and turned to see a wolf sitting on the steps of a building opposite.

The wolf had a new and silvery winter coat but Otto still recognized him by the dark markings around his eyes.

It was SkullFace, known as Skull. One of the creatures whom Albert counted as a friend and who had, in the past, led Otto to where his father was hiding from the Normal Police.

And he was not alone. Two small children with dark red hair were clinging to his back.

A woman stood close by, stamping from foot to foot, her breath clouding her face. She wore heavy boots and at least one scarf but the tattered green and gold of her Midsummer costume showed beneath the hem of her coat.

It was her. She had come back.

Otto didn't move.

He just looked.

The twins waved and he waved back. Even his arm felt heavy.

Sween had started to play his guitar. Some people had seen

the bonfire from further down the street and came towards them. They started to dance.

And then there was a familiar blasting and thundering in the air and everyone grabbed hold of someone else and there was FireBox, crashing through part of a tree, out of control, dropping with terrifying speed and landing on his four great clawed feet, one in the middle of the bonfire.

Albert Hush, grey and worn and desperate, climbed slowly down on to the pavement.

FireBox, obligingly, relit the fire, having first removed his foot.

Albert crossed the street to Dolores.

'Your friend here found me,' she said dryly. 'I have been in TigerHouse.'

'We didn't know where you were,' said Albert.

'That's why I am wearing my carnival costume. I left the flat wearing it, if you remember.'

'I see.'

'I took the twins to the Karmidee hospital, Al.'

He stared at her, cold. The Ice King.

'They tested the vitamin and mineral syrup I had given them. They said it was vitamin and mineral syrup.'

Albert glanced over at the twins. Skull was sitting down on the step and they had curled up against him, half hidden in his fur.

'I gave them vitamin and mineral syrup, Al, because they seemed to be lacking in energy. The Karmidee doctors had a look at them too.'

Albert still said nothing.

'They think the twins have stopped flying because they are unhappy. Flying is a joyful thing, like dancing, they don't feel joyful any more. Their home isn't joyful, you see.'

'But the parcel, the bottle—'

'I got the syrup from an advertisement in the newspaper. It's very good. The cavers supply all the minerals, apparently.'

A lot of people were dancing now. Sween finished one tune and started another. Otto recognized it straight away this time. It was the tune from the weather clock.

Mab had been huddled by the bonfire. She stood up and came over to Otto. 'This is it,' she whispered, grabbing his wrist and squeezing it hard.

He nodded, half listening, thinking she meant the tune.

His eyes were fixed on his mother's face. The warm bright centre of the frozen world.

'It would seem that I have wronged you, Dolores,' said Albert. Very formal.

A strange breeze moved through the trees above them.

Impossibly, inexplicably, they began to uncurl their frozen buds.

There was a rustling, hard to hear through the music. The

sound of leaves unfolding. Of blossom flowering.

Dolores did not reply in words. Nor did she smile.

But she did raise her hands and hold her palms towards Albert. Dirty and graceful.

They stood still among the flow and ebb of the dancers.

'Go on,' whispered Mab, full of mysterious tension, fingers crushing Otto's wrist.

Albert, at last, raised his hands too.

They touched their palms together and circled. Joined in the dance. The Ice King and Midsummer Night.

'Daddy funny!' shouted Hepzie.

And now, at last, a warm wind swirled all around them. It grew stronger. It rushed through the reaching trees. It sent clouds of blossom spinning and falling, filling the street.

'Look, Mab,' whispered Otto. 'Look, everything's coming to life, it's the weather clock, it must have started working again.'

# Arkardy in BirdTown

There was only one more thing left for Otto to do.

It was the next day.

He was alone in BirdTown Square.

No one danced here.

The carnival swept around it. An island of quiet.

He sat on a bench in the sun.

He had asked Mab to take a message to someone at an address suggested by Caractacus. Now he was waiting to see if that person would arrive.

Stone birds surrounded him. Several on the ground close to the bench. Others on the rooftops nearby. But most of them in the trees.

Dammerung especially trust the trees and will flee to them

if they are in danger. And Otto was sure now that some, at least, of the stricken birds were dammerung.

'*He could go on calling, you see. Catch the threads of their very selves. Drag the beat right out of their hearts. Turn them to stone . . . Daedalus WellBeloved had unequalled abilities. The greatest Charmer who has ever lived . . .*'

Maybe Carmichael was right. Or maybe there was another Charmer now, as powerful as Daedalus.

Otto pushed his hat back even further on his head. He was hot.

All over the City icicles were melting into tears.

Footsteps, clear in the strange silence, were coming across the square towards him.

'I got your note,' said Arkardy. His voice was cold and wary. He looked as if he suspected a trick.

Otto, staring at him, recognized the pattern of his own freckles across his uncle's face.

It had been stupid to try and do this. Arkardy was a stranger. Too late to back out now.

'I understand it is a matter of life and death,' said Arkardy.

'The merlin you lost is a dammerung,' said Otto.

Arkardy's eyes widened. He said nothing.

'Did you know?' asked Otto.

'No,' said Arkardy. 'I would not have kept it. I would have let it go.'

'But you must know how Charmers poison dammerung birds, make them forget their names, so they are trapped and can't change back?'

'Yes,' said Arkardy evenly. 'I know about that but I chose never to do it. It is cruel and it disgusts me. If you think I am capable of something like that then you misjudge me.'

'But you knew about Carmichael?'

'He could change back whenever he wanted. Very convenient. He introduced himself to me a few years ago. I didn't know until last night that he had his own plans, arrangements he'd made with Bliss. That's when he told me who he used to be. He worked for the Excise way back before I was born. He was the one who captured the WoolBandits. Everyone's heard of them. The children who saved so many people from dying of cold.' He paused. 'They were just kids. Two kids. He wouldn't tell me what he did with them. But he's still proud of it.'

He sat down at the end of the bench and Otto saw how like Albert he looked. Especially now as he stared, unseeing, across the square.

'I finished with him then,' he said. 'He won't come near me again.'

And then suddenly, without warning, Otto's mind tumbled into a heartsight. For an instant he thought he was just remembering the night before at the television studio because he immediately felt the same sickening feeling of fear and danger. But then he realized that he was outside the house at the end of the track in TigerHouse. It was dark.

Just as it had done only the day before, the door flew open. But this was different. This was a long time ago.

A skinny yellow-haired boy stumbled out on to the veranda. He looked about the same age as Otto. He fell.

'Out of my sight!' shouted a voice. A familiar voice. 'And you, you too, out!'

A second boy, taller, white-haired, came crashing after the first. He landed on his knees and turned round quickly, pulling himself up and pushing the younger boy behind him.

Cornelius appeared in the doorway. Filled it. Otto had seen him as an old man. Here he was at the height of his strength. He towered over his skinny sons. In the prime of his trapped and wasted life. The lion in the cage.

He pushed the white-haired boy in the chest and the boy fell against the veranda railing.

'You, the *firstborn*, the scarecrow, trying to hide him with your pathetic arms like sticks. And *you*, with the priceless mark. Daring to sit there and tell *me* how it should be used!

Burying your head in history books. Talking to *me* about your *duty*—'

He pushed the white-haired boy again, harder, and the two children fell together.

'I wanted SONS, not *whimpering rags and bones*, I wanted SONS!'

Otto watched in horror as the boys scrabbled to their feet once more, slipping on the wood, holding on to each other, starting to back down the steps . . .

The door slammed. The whole house seemed to shake.

And now Otto could see BirdTown Square. Although he didn't recognize it at first. And Arkardy, leaning towards him . . .

'Are you all right?'

'Yes,' he said, his heart thumping, still half seeing the boys running down the track, into the night and the Wasteland, faces white in the dark. 'Are you?'

'Me?' said Arkardy, sounding surprised.

Otto stared around him.

The sunlight hurt his eyes.

Moments passed.

'Any more questions, kinsman?' Arkardy asked quietly.

Otto looked at the stone birds. Remembered why he was there.

'There are some dammerung here.' He pointed around

him. 'And lots of other birds. Daedalus WellBeloved did this to them. It's a long story.'

'I know about Daedalus WellBeloved,' said Arkardy. 'The greatest—'

'No,' said Otto quickly. 'He was cruel. You aren't. And you are just as, as great a Charmer as he was—'

'Me?' Arkardy laughed. 'There's nothing great about me—'

'You were brave!' yelled Otto. 'You tried to protect my dad. You did protect him. And in the end you didn't do that thing with your face and, and betray us, even though you knew that my, my—' he could hardly say the word, '. . . my *grandfather* might *finally have been proud . . .*'

'ALL RIGHT,' said Arkardy. As pale as the boy running in the night.

'You call birds,' continued Otto, more calmly. 'You call them, you pull at the sinews of the, of the sky thing. You can add energy to the bands of whatever it is. That's what you do. Daedalus stole it away from them. From right inside them. He was a real thief. You can give it back.'

Arkardy stared at the stone birds on the ground and in the trees all over the square.

Otto waited.

'I understand,' said Arkardy softly.

He took a cloth from his pocket and wiped one finger after another. Meticulous.

Then, as Otto watched and time seemed to slow, he reached up into the air.

He flexed his fingers.

The silence deepened.

Otto was afraid to breathe.

Arkardy, pale with effort, electric with concentration, now raised his other hand. The leaves in the trees above him were trembling. The air came to life. Swirled around Otto, spiralled upwards.

And still Arkardy did not stop.

And now there was a cracking sound. Single sharp reports as if rocks were falling on to the paving stones beneath the trees.

Except there were no rocks. And nothing was falling.

Instead, in a great surge of wings, birds rose into the air all over the square. They flew unsteadily at first, stiffly, as if they had almost forgotten how.

Then they soared up. Too many to count.

Daedalus WellBeloved had only sought to trap two of them. They had fled to this place, far from home, and taken refuge, believing their bandit son was safely hidden in his cellar underground.

But Caractacus had gone to try and find Roxie and he had not been safe at all.

Now these two birds flew up in the sunshine.

They saw the great City beneath them.

Together they climbed the sky, wheeling in the golden light.

And then they turned towards Beginners Luck and BlueRemembered Mountain.

Home to the HighNoon Hotel.

# Author's note

A bit thank you to LB for the names of the Sunday Meadows and the Amaze.

The word doobco is not heard on the Outside. It means someone who cannot be trusted. A person of dubious character. A dodgy geezer.

I am grateful to Mr Frank Wheeler of London Zoo for information about Normal armadillos and to Mr Charles Hole for photographs of red kites. Normal red kites are not dangerous to humans.

Obsidian can be found on the Outside. It is a black glass formed from rapidly cooled lava.

I would like to thank my father Joe, my mum Sheila, Peggy, the writer Sandra Horn, Fionnuala, the Magnificent Whitbreads and Bettina for their unstinting support in connection with this book. Sandra Horn has provided a wise listening ear throughout. Sheila has never failed to respond to any request with imagination and zeal, and it is because of Joe's generosity that the enterprise has been possible.

I am indebted to Ms Fringe of the City Central Library for providing the correct spelling of street and district names, etc., and answering other questions about the history and geography, the harmony and the counterpoint of the City of Trees.

I would like to extend honorable greetings to the Finoo of Hampe.

Finally, many thanks to Beverley Birch and Rachel Wade at Hodder Children's Books for their hard work and patience. These people deserve better air conditioning.

Charlotte Haptie
April 2004